Also by Paul Melko

Singularity's Ring
The Walls of the Universe (forthcoming)

TEN SIGMAS
& OTHER UNLIKELIHOODS

TEN SIGMAS

& OTHER UNLIKELIHOODS

PAUL
MELKO

FAIRWOOD PRESS
Bonney Lake • Seattle

TEN SIGMAS
A Fairwood Press Book
March 2008
Copyright © 2008 by Paul Melko

Fairwood Press
21528 104th Street Court East
Bonney Lake, WA 98391
www.fairwoodpress.com

Cover illustration by Adam Hunter Peck
www.adamhunterpeck.com
Book Design by Patrick Swenson

ISBN: 0-9789078-6-8
ISBN13: 978-0-9789078-6-0
First Fairwood Press Edition: March 2008
Printed in the United States of America

Dedication

As if there could be any doubt,
to my dearest friend and love.

Copyrights

CONTENTS

TEN
SIGMAS

A t first we do not recognize the face as such.
One eye is swollen shut, the flesh around it livid. The nose is crusted with blood, the lip flecked with black-red, and the mouth taped with duct tape that does not contrast enough with her pale skin.

It does not register at first as a human face. No face should be peeking from behind the driver's seat. No face should look like that.

So at first we do not recognize it, until one of us realizes, and we all look.

For some the truck isn't even there, and we stand frozen at the sight we have seen. The street outside the bookstore is empty of anything but a pedestrian or two. There is no tractor trailer rumbling down Sandusky Street, no diesel gas engine to disturb the languid Spring day.

In some worlds, the truck is there, past us, or there, coming down the road. In some it is red, in some it is blue, and in others it is black. In the one where the girl is looking out the window at us, it is metallic maroon with white script on the door that says, "Earl."

There is just one world where the girl lifts her broken, gagged face and locks her one good eye on me. There is just one where Earl reaches behind him and pulls the girl from sight. In that world, Earl looks at me, his thick face and brown eyes expressionless.

The truck begins to slow, and that me disappears from our consciousness, sundered by circumstance.

No, I did not use my tremendous power for the good of mankind. I used it to steal the intellectual property of a person who exists in one world and pass it off as my own in another. I used my

incredible ability to steal songs and stories and publish them as
my own in a million different worlds. I did not warn police about
terrorist attacks or fires or earthquakes. I don't even read the
papers.

I lived in a house in a town that is sometimes called Delaware,
sometimes Follett, sometimes Mingo, always in a house on the corner of Williams and Ripley. I lived there modestly, in my two bedroom house, sometimes with a pine in front, sometimes with a dog-
wood, writing down songs that I hear on the radio in other worlds,
telling stories that I've read somewhere else.

In the worlds where the truck has passed us, we look at the
license plate on the truck, framed in silver, naked women, and wonder what to do. There is a pay phone nearby, perhaps on this corner,
perhaps on that. We can call the police and say . . .

We saw the girl once, and that self is already gone to us. How
do we know that there is a girl gagged and bound in any of these
trucks? We just saw the one.

A part of us recognizes this rationalization for the cowardice it
is. We have played this game before. We know that an infinite
number of possibilities exist, but that our combined existence hov-
ers around a huge multi-dimensional probability distribution. If we
saw the girl in one universe, then probably she was there in an
infinite number of other universes.

And safe in as many other worlds, I think.

For those of us where the truck has passed us, the majority of
us step into the street to go to the bagel shop across the way. Some
fraction of us turn to look for a phone, and they are broken from us,
their choice shaking them loose from our collective.

I am — we are — omniscient, at least a bit. I can do a parlor
trick for any friend, let another of me open the envelope and see
what's inside, so we can amaze those around us. Usually we will be
right. One of me can flip over the first card and the rest of me will
pronounce it for what it is. Ace of Hearts, Four of Clubs, Ten of
Clubs. Probably we are right for all fifty-two, at least fifty of them.

We can avoid accidents, angry people, cars, or at least most of
us can. Perhaps one of us takes the hit for the rest. One of us is hit

first, or sees the punch being thrown, so that the rest of us can ride the probability wave.

For some of us, the truck shifts gears, shuddering as it passes us. Earl, Bill, Tony, Irma look down at us or not, and the cab is past us. The trailer is metallic aluminum. Always.

I feel our apprehension. More of us have fallen away today than ever before. The choice to make a phone call has reduced us by a sixth. The rest of us wonder what we should do.

More of us memorize the license plate of Earl's truck, turn to find a phone, and disappear.

When we were a child, we had a kitten named "Cocoa." In every universe it had the same name. It liked to climb trees, and sometimes it couldn't get back down again. Once it crawled to the very top of the maple tree out front, and we only knew it was up there by its hysterical mewing.

Dad wouldn't climb up. "He'll figure it out, or . . ."

We waited down there until dusk. We knew that if we climbed the tree we would be hurt. Some of us had tried it and failed, disappearing after breaking arms, legs, wrists, even necks.

We waited, not even going in to dinner. We waited with some neighborhood kids, some there because they liked Cocoa and some there because they wanted to see a spectacle. Finally the wind picked up.

We saw one Cocoa fall through the dark green leaves, a few feet away, breaking its neck on the sidewalk. We felt a shock of sorrow, but the rest of us were dodging, our arms outstretched, and we caught the kitten as it plummeted, cushioning.

"How'd you do that?" someone asked in a million universes.

I realized then that I was different.

We step back on the sidewalk, waiting for the truck to pass, waiting to get the license plate so we can call the police anonymously. The police might be able to stop Earl with a road block. They could stop him up U.S. 23 a few miles. If they believed us.

If Earl didn't kill the girl first. If she wasn't already dead.

My stomach lurched. We couldn't help thinking of the horror that the girl must have faced, must be facing.

Giving the license plate to the police wouldn't be enough.

We step into the street and wave our hands, flagging Earl down.

We once dated a woman, a beautiful woman with chestnut hair that fell to the middle of her back. We dated for several years, and finally became engaged. In one of the worlds, just one, she started to change, grew angry, then elated, then just empty. The rest of us watched in horror as she took a knife to us, just once, in one universe, while in a million others, she compassionately helped our retching self to the kitchen sink.

She didn't understand why I broke off the engagement. But then she didn't know the things I did.

Earl's cab shudders as he slams on the brakes. His CB mic slips loose and knocks the windshield. He grabs his steering wheel, his shoulders massive with exertion.

We stand there, our shopping bag dropped by the side of road, slowly waving our hands back and forth.

In a handful of worlds, the tractor trailer slams through us, and we are rattled by my death. But we know he will be caught there. For vehicular manslaughter, perhaps, and then they will find the girl. In almost all the worlds, though, Earl's semi comes to a halt a few inches from us, a few feet.

We look up over the chrome grill, past the hood ornament, a woman's head, like on a sea-going vessel of old, and into Earl's eyes.

He reaches up and lets loose with his horn. We clap our hands over our ears and, in some universes, we stumble to the sidewalk, allowing Earl to grind his truck into first and rumble away. But mostly, we stand there, not moving.

It didn't matter who was president, or who won the World Series. In sum, it was the same world for each of us, and so we existed together, on top of each other, like a stack of us, all living together within a deck of cards.

Each decision that created a subtly different universe, created another of us, another of a nearly infinite number of mes, who added just a fraction more to our intellect and understanding.

We were not a god. One of us once thought he was, and soon he was no longer with us. He couldn't have shared our secret. We weren't scared of that. Who would have believed him? And now that he was alone — for there could only be a handful of us who might have such delusions — there could be no harm to the rest of us.

We were worlds away.

Finally the horn stops and we look up, our ears benumbed, to see Earl yelling at us. We can't hear what he says, but we recognize on his lips "Mother Fucker" and "Son of a Bitch." That's fine. We need him angry. To incite him, we give him the bird.

He bends down, reaching under his seat. He slaps a metal wrench against his open palm. His door opens and he steps down. We wait where we are.

Earl is a large man, six-four, and weighing at least three hundred pounds. He has a belly, but his chest and neck are massive. Black sideburns adorn his face, or it is clearly shaven, or he has a mustache. In all worlds, his dead eyes watch us as if we are a cow and he is the butcher.

I am slight, just five-nine, one hundred and sixty pounds, but as he swings the wrench we dodge inside it as if we know where it is going to be. We do, of course, for it has shattered our skull in a hundred worlds, enough for the rest of us to anticipate the move.

He swings and we dodge again, twice more, and each time a few of us are sacrificed. We are suddenly uncomfortable at the losses. We are the consciousness of millions of mes. But every one of us that dies is a real instance, gone forever. Every death diminishes us.

We can not wait for the police now. We must save as much of ourself as we can.

We dodge again, spinning past him, sacrificing selves to dance around him as if he is a dance partner we have worked with for a thousand years. We climb the steps to the cab, slide inside, slam the door, and lock it.

*

I am a composite of all versions of myself. I can think in a millions ways at once. Problems become picking the best choice of all choices I could ever have picked. I can not see the future or the past, but I can see the present with a billion eyes and decide the safest course, the one that keeps the most of me together.

I am a massively parallel human.

In the worlds where the sleeper is empty, we sit quietly for the police to arrive, weaving a story that they might believe while Earl glares at us from the street. These selves fade away from those where the girl is trussed in the back, tied with wire that cuts her wrists, and gagged with duct tape.

She is dead in some, her face livid with bruises and burns. In others she is alive and conscious and watches us with blue, blood-shot eyes. The cab smells of people living there too long, of sex, of blood.

In the universes where Earl has abducted and raped this young woman, he does not stand idly on the sidewalk, but rather smashes his window open with the wrench.

The second blow catches my forehead, as I have no place to dodge, and I think as my mind shudders that I am one of the sacrificed ones, one of those who has failed so that the rest of us might survive. But then I realize that it is most of us who have been hit. Only a small percentage have managed to dodge the blow. The rest of us roll to our back and kick at Earl's hand as it reaches in to unlock the cab door. His wrist rakes the broken safety glass, and he cries out, though still manages to pop the lock.

I crab backwards across the seat, flailing my legs at him. There are no options here. All of my selves are fighting for our lives or dying.

A single blow takes half of us. Another takes a third of those that are left. Soon my mind is a cloud. I am perhaps ten thousand, slow-witted. No longer omniscient.

A blow lands and I collapse against the door of the cab. I am just me. There is just one. Empty.

My body refuses to move as Earl loops a wire around my wrists and ankles. He does it perfunctorily — he wants to move, to get out of the middle of Sandusky Street — but it is enough to leave me helpless on the passenger side floor. I can see a half-eaten Big Mac and a can of Diet Coke. My face grinds against small stones and dirt.

I am alone. There is just me, and I am befuddled. My mind works like cold honey. I've failed. We all did, and now we will die like the poor girl in the back. Alone.

My vision shifts, and I see the cab from behind Earl's head, from the sleeping cab. I realize that I am seeing it from a self who has been beaten and tossed into the back. This self is dying, but I can see through his eyes, as the blood seeps out of him. For a moment our worlds are in sync.

His eyes lower and I spot the knife, a hunting knife with a serrated edge, brown with blood. It has fallen under the passenger's chair in his universe, under the chair I have my back against.

My hands are bound behind me, but I reach as far as I can under the seat. It's not far enough in my awkward position. My self's eyes lock on the knife, not far from where my fingers should be. But I have no guarantee that it's even in my own universe at all. We are no longer at the center of the curve. My choices have brought me far away from the selves now drinking coffee and eating bagels across the street from the bookstore.

Earl looks down at me, curses. He kicks me, and pushes me farther against the passenger seat. Something nicks my finger.

I reach gently around it. It is the knife.

I take moments to maneuver it so that I hold it in my palm, outstretched like the spine of a stegosaurus. I cut myself, and I feel the hilt get slippery. I palm my hand against the gritty carpet and position the knife again.

I wait for Earl to begin a right turn, then I pull my knees in, roll onto my chest, and launch myself, back first with knife extended, at Earl.

In the only universe that I exist in, the knife enters his thigh.

The truck caroms off something in the street, and I am jerked harder against Earl. He is screaming, yelling, pawing at his thigh.

His fist slams against me and I fall to the floor.

As he turns his anger on me, the truck slams hard into something, and Earl is flung against the steering wheel. He remains that way, unconscious, until the woman in the back struggles forward and leans heavily on the knife hilt in his leg, and slices until she finds a vein or artery.

I lie in Earl's blood until the police arrive. I am alone again, the self who had spotted the knife, gone.

The young woman came to see me while I mended in a hospital bed. There was an air of notoriety about me, and nurses and doctors were extremely pleasant. It was not just the events which had unfolded on the streets of their small town, but that I was the noted author of such famous songs as "Love as a Star" and "Romance Ho" and "Muskrat Love." The uncovering of Earl's exploits, including a grim laboratory in his home town of Pittsburgh, added fuel to the fire.

She seemed to have mended a bit better than I, her face now a face, her body and spirit whole again. She was stronger than I, I felt when I saw her smile. My body was healing, the cuts around my wrist and ankle, the shattered bone in my arm. But the sundering of my consciousness had left me dull, broken.

I listened to songs on the radio, other people's songs, and could not help wondering in how many worlds there had been no knife, there had been no escape. Perhaps I was the only one of us who reached the cab to survive. Perhaps I was the only one who had saved the woman.

"Thanks," she said. "Thanks for what you did."

I reached for something to say, something witty, urbane, nonchalant from my mind, but there was nothing there but me.

"Uh . . . you're welcome."

She smiled. "You could have been killed," she said.

I looked away. She didn't realize that I had been.

"Well, sorry for bothering you," she said quickly.

"Listen," I said, drawing her back. "I'm sorry I didn't . . ." I wanted to apologize for not saving more of her. For not ending the lives of more Earls. "I'm sorry I didn't save you sooner." It didn't make any sense, and I felt myself flush.

She smiled and said, "It was enough." She leaned in to kiss me.

I am disoriented as I feel her lips brush my right cheek, and also my left, and a third kiss lightly on my lips. I am looking at her in three views, a triptych slightly askew, and I manage a smile then, three smiles. And then a laugh, three laughs.

We have saved her at least once. That is enough. In one of the three universes we inhabit, a woman is singing a catchy tune on the radio. I start to write the lyrics down with my good hand, then stop. Enough of that, we three decide. There are other things to do now, other choices.

THE TEOSINTHE WAR

The cluster of poodle-skirted sorority girls gave me a vague smile when I sat down beside them. I liked the way the skirts' material kept rising up on the poofy slips beneath them, exposing bobby-socked calves and saddle shoes. The girl I had my eye on was tall, blond, and curvy. She met my glaze and my daemon pinged to tell me she'd accessed my site. Then the smile turned cold. Apparently minority grad students didn't meet her standard. At least I got her name — Beth Ringslaught — when she pinged me. But that was all I was going to get. The rest of the girls turned away; they were probably hooked into a local IRC, and Beth had shared my CV with the rest of them. I leaned back in my chair and sighed.

Dr. Elk strode in, a wild pile of paper under one arm and a teacher's stick in his hand. He tapped the teaching computer with his stick and the lights dimmed.

"Class! Welcome to your senior thesis! I'm Dr. Elk, and I'm as excited about Thesis as all of you are. Our topic this year is 'Factors of Old World Imperialism.'" Elk was a tall, thin man, his dark hair starting to fade to gray. He had been my advisor — no doubt we were teamed up by some politically correct wonk because of our similar genetic heritage — when I was in the history department, but I'd not talked with him for a year, not since I'd moved to engineering my junior year.

"Why did European culture eradicate every New World culture it came into contact? Were Europeans intrinsically smarter? No! Did they have God on their side? I doubt it!" He slammed his notes on the word 'God,' and the poodle girls jumped. I'd known it was coming; his lectures went back to the aughts.

My mind began to drift, watching the clock tick. I'd heard this lecture a half-dozen times since my freshman year. Professor Elk had asked me to audit, and possibly TA, the senior thesis class, so I signed up for it, but never with any more intention than to check out the women in the class. I glanced around. Slim pickings among the rest of the history seniors. I looked over at Beth; the fabric poodle on her skirt was watching me, panting. Nice effect. Maybe one more try, I decided.

"Were they just better?" Dr. Elk picked up a piece of chalk and wrote a word on the board, punctuated by dull clicks. "No, of course not."

"They had germs," I whispered to Beth. She glared at me.

"What they had that was better was G-E-R-M-S. Germs. Centuries of city-life had turned their cesspool cities into disease incubators. Those city-dwellers that survived to breed were slightly more resistant than the ones who clogged their cemeteries. The New World had nothing like it. Pizarro was no better than Atahuallpa. His forefathers had just been lucky enough to have a slightly higher than average immunity to small pox!"

"How about some dinner?" I whispered to Beth.

My daemon beeped that a class one harassment complaint had been lodged against me. The poodle bared its teeth.

"By the end of this year, we will have expanded this idea of Old World disease conquering the new world. We will have built a hypothesis and tested it. And we will prove once and for all, that the exploitation of the New World by the Old was a fluke, a whim, a side-effect of barbaric living conditions and chance."

I yawned. Elk would have to find himself another TA. There were too many other classes I needed to take, and I wasn't interested in his hypothetical world — probably some world simulator his grad students wrote — in which the New World tribes beat the imperialist dogs of the Old World. That's why I dropped history in favor of engineering; I wanted to play with real things in the present, not guesses from the past. I slipped out of class, avoiding eye contact with Elk, and headed to the administration building for a quick add-drop.

The doorbell wouldn't shut the hell up, no matter how many times I folded my pillow through four dimensional space. I tossed it aside and stumbled to the door. I kicked aside a pizza box, sending it sailing into my CD collection. The thermo text didn't budge, and I hopped the rest of the way, holding my throbbing toe.

"What the fuck?" I said, opening the door.

"Ryan Greene?"

About the same time my reptilian brain had determined that a reproduction-aged female was standing in my doorway, my daemon had informed me it was Beth Ringslaught, the poodle-skirted cutie from Elk's senior thesis class, who'd dropped a class one harassment memo on my ass. My boner flagged.

"Oh, it's you."

She didn't have a poodle skirt on today. She was wearing tight-fitting riding pants that hugged her calves, making her look like she had marathon runner legs. My reptilian brain stirred, then went back to sleep.

"What do you want?" I asked, leaning on the door, scratching my nuts.

It didn't faze her. "Professor Elk asked me to come see you. He wants you to re-add his class." Too much sun was beaming down on the apartment courtyard and its leaf-filled pool. I leaned my head against the door frame.

"Why?"

"He needs your help, he said."

"Listen, I'm not interested in being his Native American poster boy. You seniors just blithely run your sims and make the world a pretend happy place. I'm not interested."

She shrugged. "Don't take it out on —"

"Just like you aren't interested in a guy like me, a poor minority grad student."

She blinked, her eyebrows slowly rising, her cheeks flushing. "What are you talking about?"

"The way you and your poodle-friends shut me down in class the other day. It's clear you think talking with me is slumming."

Her mouth crooked into a half-smile. "Your site says you're dating a Miss Janice Huckabee."

"Your daddy — What?"

"Your site says you're in a monogamous relationship."

"Oh," I said, feeling the heat on my face. "That's out of date, I guess." Janice had dumped me at the end of senior year, when I took the grad school gig instead of the Buckell Chemical job on St. Thomas. She hadn't wanted to date a poor grad student either, though the reception her parents had given me when we drove up from Columbus to Lansing for Christmas break might have had something to do with it.

"As attractive as you may have *seemed* last week, the fact that most of us poodle-girls would like a monogamous, dedicated boyfriend eliminated you as a candidate quickly." She turned and added over her shoulder, "I'll let Dr. Elk know your answer."

I watched her go, noted the lack of panty lines, and made a note to change my site.

I was deep in next week's Plasma notes, Chen's *Plasma Physics Fundamentals* open on my lap, trying to stay one lecture ahead of the students I was TAing for, when someone knocked on my cube door. I figured it was one of my students coming by for a freebie on the homework set.

"Remember that the magnetic moment is invariant!" I called over the cube wall.

Someone cleared his throat, then said, "I'll keep that in mind, Mr. Greene."

"Dr. Elk, I thought you were a student." I sat up, brushing the pork rind crumbs off my chest.

"Aren't we all?"

"Um, yeah."

"I know you rebuffed Beth, but I wanted to take one more go at you."

"Beth?" My daemon supplied the relevant image. "Oh, your senior thesis class. Really, Dr. Elk, my load is tough this term. Grading, teaching —"

"I have funding and permits for use of the MWD," Dr. Elk said. His bushy eyebrows rose. Then he winked. Then he left.

I sat there, my jaw aching from where it had kerchunked onto the floor. The bastard. He'd tricked or greased some government cog into letting him use the MWD. Casino money, probably. Or some oil-Indian from Texas. Son of a bitch. He was going to use the Multi-Worlds Device to build a new universe. And he'd just pulled me in too.

I slammed Chen shut and ran after him.

"Hold on, Dr. Elk!"

*

See, the MWD is really about time travel. Only time travel in our own universe is impossible, since it never happened. No time travellers ever showed up in our universe to save Kennedy or patch the O-ring, so there's no way it'll work here. If you go back in time and make a change, you build a whole new universe, a malleable one, flexible from the point you make your first change.

Sounds wacky, I know. Where does all the energy come to make a whole universe? Or was the universe already there and we were just tapping into it? And how many universes can the multiverse contain? Are we filling it up to some limit? Is it all going to collapse in on itself? What were the cosmic implications, man? Think!

Back then I didn't care. I wasn't a physics wonk, or a morality dweebie. I was just an engineer, but — god damn! — I thought the MWD was cool shit. And the only way I figured I'd ever get involved was from the fusion side of it. It took a lot power to push things to another universe.

That's why Dr. Elk wanted me. He needed a techie on his side.

Beth Ringslaught gave me a wry look when I sat down next to her the next day in class.

"It's a little late to add-drop, isn't it?" Her poodle posse giggled.

"You're not going to file another harassment memo if I sit next to you are you?"

"Maybe. I see you updated your site."

"You didn't tell me he was going to use the MWD."

"The what?"

"The Multi-Worlds Device!"

"Oh, that. That's just engineering details. I figured working with Dr. Elk would motivate you enough."

I shook my head. "Can I borrow your notes?"

"I guess."

Dr. Elk walked in, beamed at me, then began lecturing on the Incas, discharging large expository lumps on the desecration by Pizarro, the effect of European disease, and the exploitation of native culture in the name of god and king. I'd heard it before, so I flipped through Beth's notes to see what the project was.

Beth kept good notes. Not a single doodle. So I started to add one. Beth grabbed my pen.

"Don't do that," she whispered. Her hand shook as she held the end of my pen. Apparently she took her notes seriously.

"Fine."

Dr. Elk's thesis was this: European crowd diseases decimated ninety-five percent of the American native populations. Crowd diseases were prevalent in Europe due to high population densities, which were unobtainable in the Americas. High crowd densities were possible in Europe due to the wide range of large-seeded grains, pulses, and domesticated animals that seeped up from the Indus Valley. North America had sunflowers and sumpweed, and the only domesticated animal was the dog. Try pulling a plow with a dog.

The best grain the Americas had was maize. Only it had taken thousands of years to go from corn's natural ancestor teosinte to the foot-long ears of the modern world. Worse, teosinte had been domesticated in lower Central America, in a climate that was so unlike the rest of the Americas that its propagation was extremely slow. All this added up to the fact that the Americas lagged Europe in food production by about 6000 years.

"Holy shit!" I said. "You're going to introduce modern maize into ancient America!"

Dr. Elk stopped in the middle of his harangue on smallpox. "I see my faith in you is well-founded, Mr. Greene. It only took you fifteen minutes to catch up with the rest of us."

"Uh, sorry," I said, handing the notes back to Beth. She rolled her eyes at me.

"So what does that do?"

Kyle looked at me out of the corner of his eye. He sighed. "I'm trying to calibrate the spatial locator." We were sitting in the control room of the MWD lab in the Barzak Building, overlooking the clean room where the cross-dimensional hole would be opened up.

"Spatial locator of what?"

"A hole."

"To where?"

"Ancient Mesoamerica! Don't you have a screen you need to be watching?"

I did, but the power system was running flawlessly. Watching Kyle run the MWD was much more fun. It had been too much to hope for him to actually let me run the machine myself. Only a licensed MWD engineer could do that, someone with a PhD in Macro Quantum Physics, which Kyle had. To him I was just some engineer.

I'd been watching Kyle all day, and I pretty much could see what he was doing. Find the anchor, locate your temporal zone in relation to the anchor, get within a few thousand years, calibrate, recalibrate, repeat until you find the right time. Then do the same with the X-Y-Z coordinates. I couldn't see why you needed a PhD to do it.

"So how do we know our universe isn't one that someone else made?" I asked.

Kyle shook his head. "Dr. Skillingstead proved that we're the primary universe using a Copenhagen variant —"

My phone beeped and he frowned as I ignored his explanation and answered it.

"Hello?"

"It's Beth. Is the 7500 BC probe ready yet?"

"Kyle's taking his sweet old time calibrating the spatial locator."

He glared at me. "Do you want it over Panama or Greece?" he growled.

"I'll call you when he's done."

"Thanks."

"How about dinner?"

"No." She hung up. At least she didn't file a memo.

Kyle smirked. I don't know why; I'd seen his Frankenstein's girlfriend. I didn't know if he'd picked her up in a bar or built her in the lab. Better for Beth to reject me than to date the greasy-haired grad student from Hell.

"Why can't this be done robotically?" I asked. "I mean, do we really need a PhD to run this thing?" Yes, I was baiting him.

"Maybe one day, this can all be done automatically. But if we blow a calibration, we black out a whole time zone. I don't think Dr. Elk would be happy with that."

That was for sure. His schedule was exacting. And once you closed a hole in a time zone, there was no going back. The future in a new universe was like Schroedinger's cat, alive or dead until you opened the box. But once you closed a hole and moved forward, you couldn't go back, since it never happened. Only the unknown future was open.

7500 BC was where we were going to drop the modern maize. Then every one hundred years we'd drop in spyeyes to track the propagation. By 1500 CE, the Americas should be as much a power house as the Europeans. Perhaps the Aztecs would discover the Old World.

They just needed a little help.

The next call was Dr. Elk.

"Are we ready to sow yet?"

"We haven't even pushed the spyeyes through."

"What's the hold up?"

"Calibration. What's the hurry? We have as long as we want."

"I'd rather have results sooner than later, Mr. Greene. Dr. Skillingstead at the University of Michigan is attempting similar studies in the area of history as a testable science."

"I'll let you know when the spyeyes are in."

"Good. Make sure you understand everything that's going on with the MWD. Understand?"

"Yeah, I guess."

He hung up.

"I'm glad you're here to buffer me from him," Kyle said. "He's one driven son of a bitch."

"Now you're glad I'm here."

"I wouldn't go that far."

We opened three holes over the Americas in 7500 BC: North, Meso-, and South America. With spyeyes, we surveyed the locale and found indigenous bands of hunter-gathers. Beth built a huge database of video, and we watched highlights in class. She could have been a fine anthropologist.

"Here we see a group of hunter-gathers — we call them the Snake People because of the tattoo on their chests — gathering the wild teosinte. It grows naturally near their tents." Small brown men were grabbing handfuls of what looked like grass. None of them used tools. A couple of the students giggled at the nearly naked men.

"Here is a close up of the teosinte. Note the size of the cobs. Three to four centimeters long. Now watch Bob."

"Bob?"

One of Beth's friends leaned over. "We've named them all," she whispered.

On the video, Bob took a stalk of teosinte, peeled off the husk and looked closely at it. Then he shook the seeds loose. They fluttered to the ground.

"Some sort of artificial selection," I said.

Beth smiled at me.

"Yes! Perhaps he was propagating a larger seed case; perhaps it had more rows than the typical two-rowed teosinte; perhaps it had a more perpendicular spikelets. Whatever he saw, he decided to make sure more came back next year. I think this is evidence of human selection of maize-like traits."

Dr. Elk clapped his hands. "Excellent work. I think we've found our Mesoamerican drop site." On the screen Bob took another stalk of teosinte, ripped off the cob, and dumped it into a fur sack. "Mr. Greene, I'd like you to schedule a drop of the modern maize kernels."

The sowers were modified spyeyes that could carry a dozen kernels at a time. The idea was to push it through the hole, fly it near the ground, and drop the kernels in a likely place. Come summer, we'd have a cluster of modern maize. The next step was beyond our control. Bob and his cohorts would have to discover the corn, figure out that it was a useful grain, and propagate it.

That was the problem with modern maize. The grain didn't do a good job self-propagating; it was dependent on human interaction to keep its genotype going. If our little brown people didn't drop seeds from the cobs onto the ground, there wouldn't be a second season of maize.

"There, I want it there on that plain," Dr. Elk said. I was flying the spyeye across the terrain from Beth's video. I dropped it to hover a few meters above the grass.

"Here?"

"No, a little to the left. See that open area there?" His hand was practically guiding the joystick. I bounced the spyeye a bit to the left.

"Here?"

"Yes."

I toggled the payload button.

"Corn away!" I shouted. I jiggled the spyeye to shake free any clinging kernels. Each one of those kernels cost us ten megawatt-hours of power.

I spun the eye around and came in low. There were the kernels sitting on the ground, waiting for rain and spring.

"Now move us ahead six months," Dr. Elk said to Kyle. "I want to see what happens."

Kyle nodded. "That will close out this time zone."

"I know. Do it."

The spyeye went dead as Kyle deactivated the 7500 BC holes; there was no bringing the eye back across. The power costs dwarfed the cost of the spyeye. Plus there was the concern of disease coming from the other universe.

A few minutes later a new hole appeared, 180 days later. I watched the power level surge as another spyeye pushed through. No human from our universe would ever walk this parallel universe. The spyeyes weighed about a kilogram. The power needed to do an insertion varied with the mass of the object to the third power.

"You guys won't need me for a while, right?" Kyle asked.

Dr. Elk nodded absently, intent on the image from the spyeye.

"You all have fun, playing god," he said, leaving.

The sky of the other world was bright, late summer in prehistoric Mesoamerica. I zoomed through the air, looking for the rock that marked our band's location.

"There it is," Beth said.

"Let's see if they figured out how to use corn."

I sent the spyeye in a barrel roll over the village, then swung down Main Street. All right, it was the only street.

"Nobody home," I said.

The village was empty. I pulled back, circling around, higher and higher. The fields where they picked teosinte, where we had sowed the maize were overgrown. The stream where they pulled water was empty. Nothing. The village looked abandoned.

"Can you enter one of the tents?"

"Sure." The tents were tepee style, with off-centered ceiling holes for smoke. I slid down one of the chimneys and switched to IR.

Empty, except for a pile of skins.

"They're gone."

"All their tools are still there."

"Look! There's a body in the skins."

I spun the spyeye around the tent to the skins and hovered there. A shrunken face stared up at us, and my hand shook on the control.

I barely got the spyeye up and out without bouncing it off the walls of the tent.

I hovered the spyeye until my hands didn't shake, then I tried a second tent.

Inside were a family of four, a mother, father, and two children. All dead.

"What did we do?" I asked.

"Nothing!" spat Dr. Elk. "This happens all the time in prehistoric societies. We were just unlucky."

"*We* were unlucky? Those people are dead."

"This had nothing to do with us," he said. "Move us ahead one hundred years. We'll find a new tribe."

"I can't do that."

"Of course you can. It's easy."

"I mean, I can do it. But I'm not allowed."

"Mr. Greene, we need to keep this project moving forward. This time zone and this tribe is useless to us. Now move the hole forward one century." Dr. Elk held my gaze, his face red and sharp.

Beth touched my arm. "It's okay, Ryan. No one cares if we move ahead a hundred years. Kyle won't even notice."

Okay, I'm not stupid. I know when I'm being manipulated. But I suddenly wanted to be as far away from Bob as I could be. Nothing like a century to turn your friends to dust.

"Okay."

I turned on the MWD and pushed the hole uptime, just as I had watched Kyle do.

That night as I walked back to my apartment, I found Beth walking beside me. We passed the student bars, ringing with techno hip-hop, stepping out into the street to avoid the crush of undergrads waiting to test their fake IDs. In the lab, we'd dropped another load of maize in the new century, near a tribe that had settled in the same place as our old tribe. We'd ask Kyle to move us forward a year in the morning, pretending we hadn't closed the hole one hundred years before. I hadn't looked closely at the new tribe. I didn't want to recognize any faces or name them if they were all dead in the morning.

"Going home to see your folks for Thanksgiving?" Beth asked.

I'd forgotten she was with me.

"Um, no. My family is in Oklahoma, and it's not our favorite holiday."

"Oh, right. My family's local." She looked tired and stumbled once on the curb. I reached out to steady her.

"Careful."

"Sorry, I'm just tired." Under my hand her arm was shaking.

"Cold?"

She shrugged.

I stopped in front of my apartment building. "Good night," I said, without looking at her. A part of my brain was telling me I should have been hitting on her. Maybe it was the pre-bellum hoop skirt that was putting me off. But probably it was the stench of death that seemed to hover over everyone associated with the senior project.

"Listen, Ryan. It wasn't our fault about those people."

"Yeah, I know. Death is common in the ancient world."

"It was just a fluke that they died. It had nothing to do with us."

"Did Dr. Elk ask you to discuss this with me? Are you here to spin this for me?"

"Hey, I saw dead people today too! It's not just you who's feeling like shit."

"Yeah, sorry." I turned and opened the door to my building. I paused, then pulled it wide enough for both of us.

"Coming up?"

She looked at me, her face pinched. Then she swooshed past me.

It's not what you think. We didn't do it. We just . . . talked and hugged. And maybe we kissed once. Yeah, weird.

Kyle didn't even mention the extra century. If he noticed anything, he probably blamed his own calibration skills. When we punched a new hole the next day, we found a vibrant village. Better yet, we found evidence of the maize being harvested. It wouldn't be long before the tribe found uses for it, we hoped.

We moved forward in jumps of one year three times, and each time, the maize crop was larger. The tribe was sowing the seeds wider and wider.

"We've done it!" cried Dr. Elk. "We've successfully introduced modern maize to ancient Mesoamerica. Now we need to do the same in North and South America!"

By the end of the week, or rather by the end of the century, we had three successful tribes across the two continents sowing and harvesting maize. We watched them for a few decades, modeling the dispersal of the maize between other tribes. It caught on quickly, it was so much better than the native teosinte, with more yield and with bigger grain size. Then we moved ahead a century.

The first thing we saw was that our Mesoamerican site, dubbed Columbus, had grown to the size of a small town.

"They've set aside hunting and gathering in favor of maize farming," Dr. Elk explained in class. "With the higher yields of modern maize, they can afford to stay in one spot. They can start to accumulate the immovable technologies that only a city-based culture can."

Cleveland, the tribe in North America, was also growing. Cincinnati, however, had disappeared, the tribe moving on, uninterested in domestication. The maize was gone.

"Our next step is to watch as the population density increases. Watch as the maize spreads through the continents. Watch as it supplants the native and less domesticated plants. We can expect larger cities, larger populations. All of these starting at the same time as they are in the Indus Valley. Success, ladies and gentlemen. Success!"

Beth and I never said we were dating. She just spent a lot of time at my place. Mostly we talked about the project.

"This would make a great PhD dissertation," she said one day.

"Thinking of doing grad work, are you?"

"For you, I was thinking."

"I'm in engineering, remember. I don't do the history stuff anymore."

"Except when it's a cool project."

She was right. I was spending more of my time on the senior project than I was on my grad studies.

"It's a cool project."

We'd been moving ahead centuries at a time, watching the progression of civilization through the New World. Columbus was spreading out into a megalopolis, an Aztec empire eight millennia early. Cleveland had fragmented into a dozen city-states up and down the Mississippi River. But Vicksburg had shown signs of bronze-working. And Cairo had the wheel.

"If only we could give them a decent domesticated animal," Beth said.

"We barely got the spyeyes through with the maize. It would take a terawatt-hour to push through a breeding pair of horses," I said. We were eating up Dr. Elk's funding at a horrendous rate as it was.

"There will be more money if this works," she said. She looked fetching in Amerind faux cow-skin slacks and vest. A lot of the sorority girls were wearing them, since the article came out in the school paper.

"Why? Once we prove the theory on the impact of domesticated grain, what more do we need money for?"

"There are a thousand thesis topics in the area of historical causality! They're talking about opening a whole new department for it."

"I must have missed that," I said. "With Dr. Elk as the chair, I suppose."

"Who else? He'll need good grad students. And don't tell me you haven't enjoyed the project." She snuggled up to me on my couch, her faux leather silky smooth on my arm.

"I'm changing the subject," I said. "Are we dating yet?"

She leaned back, frowning. "Is it important to define our relationship?" She leaned in again and kissed me gently.

I looked into her blue eyes, ran my finger along her jaw, wondering why she was here with me. Then I kissed her back.

In the next millennium, Columbus started gobbling up North American city-states: New Orleans, Memphis, St. Louis, and Cairo, until just Minneapolis remained independent of a pan-American empire based in the Yucatan.

The centralized bureaucracy seemed to be favoring technological development, and in several placed iron working appeared to be under way. The bureaucracy was clearly using a logogram alphabet, though we didn't spend enough time to understand the language. Ages of history were closed off to us, never to be surveyed again as we barreled forward to the inevitable collision of Europe and America.

By 1000 CE, the Columbus Empire had collapsed, and in its place was an Alaska to Tierra del Fuego nation of seafarers, who hunted whales and caught fish, and traded up and down the western coast of the Americas, but never venturing beyond a dozen miles of shore. The Mississippi Valley was a confederacy of nation states, each governed by artisan syndicates, which drove technology forward. They had gunpowder, steel, and simple steam engines.

"When Europe meets America, they will be on equal footing. There will be no wide scale destruction of culture. We have made them equal players."

We moved the hole up the line. And suddenly the Americas were overrun by orientals. Skipping by half-centuries, we had missed the invasion. But in 1150 CE, our experimental subjects were serfs of a Chinese empire, ruled by eunuchs. The cities were gone, turned under into the ground. The artisans gone, now slaves. The Chinese were slowly burning the Amazon to the Atlantic.

"Those damn orientals!" Dr. Elk railed in the lab. "Why didn't they stay put like they did in our world? They've ruined everything."

Beth tried to soothe him. "We've gotten great data, Professor. We proved that a good domesticated grain will raise the continent's population by two orders of magnitude. We've shown independent technological development of language, gunpowder, steel . . ."

"It's not enough! We'll do it again," he said, and stormed out of the lab.

"Again?" I said.

Beth shrugged, then followed after Elk.

Spring break came, and Beth left for Fort Myers. She called once while she was down there, drunk, and in the background I heard male voices calling her back to the hot tub. She giggled and hung up. Hey, we weren't dating. Though I wasn't seeing anyone but her. We hadn't even slept together yet. She dissuaded my advances, but we had kissed a lot. She was beautiful, and smart, and not my type at all. But here I was all jealous and smitten.

Since the Chinese invasion, the class had turned into project prep time. Each student was doing a project based on the new universe's data, and my time as TA was spent checking standard deviations and logic, correcting bad grammar and unclear arguments. Dr. Elk let me devise, give, and grade the mid-term. Beth got an A+.

The week after spring break, Dr. Elk announced to the class that he had funding to build a new universe, enough funding to introduce a breeding pair of horses.

"If the Chinese arrive now, our Native Americans will have the horses for armies," he explained.

I whispered to Beth, "Where's he getting this money?"

She shrugged.

We started over, on an accelerated schedule. The maize was easy. The natives in all three areas took to it on the first try. The horses, donated by the Equine Science Department, were just-weaned mustangs. A special container was fashioned, ultra-light weight material. From birth the foals were trained to follow the high-pitched whine of a spyeye, so that once on the other side, the horses could be led to food or away from danger.

We released them on the Great Plains.

The news stations loved it, the horses peeking out of the container, sniffing the air. You've seen the videos, I know. They take one tentative step, look around, and then gallop full speed into the open, as if they *know* they have a whole continent to fill with babies. The spyeye sizzles to catch up, as they run for miles across the open plains. A beautiful sight.

The first successful transfer of living things between universes. I figured humans would be next.

We had a vet on call around the clock. But we needn't have worried. The horses were as happy as could be and birthed a foal the next spring. And another one the year after. Concerns of inbreeding were unfounded; the mustangs had clean genomes, no recessives.

In a decade there were fifty in the herd. By the end of the century there were thousands of horses across North America, in hundreds of herds. A few years after that, the first horse was domesticated by Native Americans.

We'd brought them maize and horses. I guess we could have dropped rifles in if we had the power to spare, but they would have used them as clubs. We'd done all we could do. If they didn't fend off the Europeans and the Chinese now . . . well, then they deserved to lose.

This time we kept tabs on Asia and Europe, but they seemed to be following the same path as they had in our world. Meanwhile in the Americas, empires rose and fell, population burgeoned, technology came and went, and sometimes stuck. The printing press, steam engines, tall sailing ships.

And then in 1000 CE, instead of waiting for the Europeans to discover them, our North Americans discovered Europe, in a single tall ship that plied the Atlantic in sixty-five days, landing in Bournemouth, England. We cheered and celebrated late into the night at the lab. Dr. Elk had a bottle of champagne which we drank in defiance of University rules; even Kyle had a drink.

Tipsy, I guided Beth back to my apartment and began removing her pantaloons and poofy shirt.

"No, Ryan," she said, as my mouth took her left nipple.

"Beth."

"No. I can't. Don't."

"You seemed interested enough in whoever you were with on spring break," I said, regretting it.

"That's none of your fucking business!" She pulled her shirt across her chest and fell back onto the couch.

"I know. Sorry. We never made a commitment, and I've just assumed —"

"Listen, Ryan. I like you. But we can't have sex."

"I have an implant," I said. "We can't get pregnant."

"I'm not worried about that!"

"Then what?"

She looked away, rubbed her face. "I was wild in high school, Ryan. I dated a lot of men. Older men. Men with many past lovers."

"Are you still seeing one of them?" I asked, confused.

"No! Don't you get it? I can't —"

She pulled on her shirt, dug for her pants on the floor.

"Beth." I took her hand, but she shook loose.

Then she was out the door, and gone. I'm slow sometimes, but then I got it. I remembered the tremors in her hands, the palsy in her arm. She had Forschek's Syndrome. "Oh, shit," I muttered. And I almost chased after her, and said we could use a condom, that it didn't matter, but at the same time I knew it did, that she could be days, weeks, or months away from the nerve-degeneration as the prions made there way from her sex organs, up her central nervous system to her brain.

It wasn't okay.

*

The next day, the entire class met in the MWD lab, and watched as we moved the hole up the line, three months at a time after the trans-Atlantic trip. Beth wasn't there, and it bothered me enough that I almost ran the spyeye into the rigging of the North American's ship.

After trading with the locals and provisioning, the ship turned around and headed back across the Atlantic, but not before taking a few of the English with them.

"Translators," Dr. Elk said. "The first step toward understanding. This is most excellent."

We watched the ship from high above, as it completed the two month voyage back home. But when it reached pseudo-Boston, we saw that the ship was battered and broken by sea storms; it barely limped into the harbor, and when we dove closer, we saw that half the crew was missing. And those that were left were diseased with a pox-like covering on their skin.

Disease.

I switched to the Bournemouth spyeye and was shocked to see the black smoke of funeral pyres clouding the sky. Plague.

"If we nuke pseudo-Boston, we can stop the spread," Dr. Elk said. "We can contain it."

Kyle and I shared a look.

"Dr. Elk, that's impossible," I said.

"I have enough money to send a bomb through."

"We can't nuke a city," I said. "Even one in another universe."

"We can't let them destroy this world!" he cried.

Kyle picked up the phone, and dialed a number. "We've got a problem with the Maize-2 universe," he said.

Dr. Elk ripped the phone from his hand and threw it against the wall.

I said to Kyle, "Move us ahead one year."

"No!" cried Dr. Elk. "We can cauterize the infection."

"You've caused the infection!" I said.

Kyle opened a new hole, and when the spyeyes went through, we saw that the entire world was filled with empty cities and ghost towns, both hemispheres devoid of civilization, and left with just a few scattered pockets of survivors.

The crowd diseases of America had been too much for Europe to handle, and *vice versa*. They had wiped each other out with their germs on first contact.

We had been party to 200 million deaths.

I stood, queasy, and left the lab, unable to look Dr. Elk in the eye. Unable to do anything but walk.

The sister who answered the door at the sorority house was cool. "Yes?"

"I'm looking for Beth Ringslaught."

The student frowned. "She's not here."

"Where is she?"

"At the hospital."

"Which hospital?"

"St. Anne's."

I took a taxi and found her in the isolation ward. They wouldn't let me in, but finally told me her status. The palsy had started months ago, but now the disease had reached her brain, and she had lost motor control of her body. She was unlikely to leave the hospital again.

"I'd like to see her," I said.

"Who are you, just a boyfriend?" the nurse asked, clearly wondering if I was infected too. Maybe I'd infected her.

"I'm a good friend," I said.

"Well, okay. Her family hasn't been here."

She was sleeping, so I sat beside her, took her hand in mine. She looked like she had the day before when we'd talked. But I knew she would start wasting away, that in a month she would be skeletal, her face a grinning rictus as the disease ate at her. I forced the thought from my mind, but it was never far away.

Her eyes fluttered open, filled with terror.

"Ryan," she said, softly.

"Beth."

"Sorry I missed the big day."

"It was anything but." And I told her that we had killed 200 millions of people.

She turned her head away and the tears fell down her face into her pillow.

"What did we do?"

"Nothing good."

"I wanted you to continue this work . . . after." She looked up at me, and I kissed her forehead.

"I'm sorry."

*

They shut the universe down. Dr. Elk didn't come back the next year; he disappeared completely, not just from academia, but from all contact with society. Perhaps the magnitude of his deeds penetrated his egotistical side.

The MWD was shut down for a year, and now there's legislation in place to govern transfers of material between universes. If we did now what we had done, we'd all be up on manslaughter charges. That's one good thing that's happened, advances in the rights of parallel people.

Beth died six weeks after she entered the hospital. Her family had disowned her. Her sisters didn't even send flowers. No one wants to have been associated with one of the Infected. Only a decadent lifestyle led to that disease.

But I was with her at the end. Three years later, she's still in my thoughts. My thesis is complete, and I've taken a professorship here at the University, adjunct to the Macro Quantum Mechanics Department and the History Department both. Yeah, I changed majors again.

Dr. Elk's senior project was the basis for my thesis in technological morality. It came at a heavy cost, 200 million and one lives.

We are rebuilding Dr. Elk's universe. We are helping the survivors, and I am directing the effort, making certain we do not play god again. Making certain we do not use entire universes as laboratories.

I wonder if someone farther ahead is watching us. I wonder if we are playing out some scenario to test someone's pet theory. I hope they're watching closely and they learn something from us. Something from our mistakes.

DOCTOR MIGHTY & THE CASE OF ENNUI

Doctor Mighty noticed the malaise right around the time he captured Auntie Arctic in her lair in the back room freezer at a local Giant Eagle. Actually it was the fifth straight time he'd captured her in a Giant Eagle. Every time she escaped from the Institute, her first stop was the freezer of grocery store, never a Kroger, never a Big Bear, always a Giant Eagle. First it was the one in Plymouth. Then it was the one on Grant downtown. Then in Crestview.

Mighty hadn't even bothered to decipher the clues that she was leaving at each of the tanning salons she destroyed with her freeze ray. He just went to the newest Giant Eagle in Roosevelt and confronted her and her two henchmen, Fahrenheit and Celsius. Rankin and Absolute had died several months earlier in a freon accident.

"Doctor Mighty! You've cunningly tracked me down to my lair!" Ms. Arctic cackled. "Get him, boys!" A fine sheen of ice crystals covered her skin, and he could see the blue veins in her neck as she screamed. She was a young aunt, trim in her tight, blue leotard and matching cape. Her dark hair framed her sharp, pale face. If she had been a woman he'd met at a party or in the produce section during his off-hours, he might have been tempted to ask her out or at least talk to her. Alas, he mused, she wanted her henchmen to kill him, and that wasn't a good basis for any relationship.

F and C didn't have superpowers, so Doctor Mighty had to carefully adjust the strength of his punches as he laid them low. They bounced across the non-skid surface of the freezer and thwacked into a pile of frozen lima beans and corn: succotash with a side of henchman. Ms. Arctic he dispatched with his hair drier. He'd figured that out a few months earlier, when Ms. Arctic had nearly speared him with a giant icicle, and only in desperation did his hand fall upon the bathroom appliance. If he'd latch onto his electric shaver, he'd have been dead.

"No!" screamed Ms. Arctic, as she shriveled up and fell to the ground. "You've foiled my plans to freeze all of Ohio . . . again!" Sweat burst out on her forehead, and she struggled to breathe.

Mighty didn't even bother to retort with witty banter. What did it matter when they would go through the whole maneuver again in six months? Hot enough for you? Evil fades before the warmth of justice, villain! My hair drier of law will feather your bangs of evil! It was good form, he knew, but it all seemed so lame.

He dragged her to the Mightimobile and drove her to the Institute for the Criminally Insane.

"Thanks, Doctor Mighty!" cried Doctor Gestalt.

"Do you think you can keep an eye on her this time?" Mighty asked.

"Uh, sorry. We'll try. She's slippery. Like, um, ice." Even the layperson wanted to get in on the witty banter. Mighty could have reported him to the Guild, but he chose to ignore the illegal witticism.

"This is five times so far this year. Can't you use a . . . a . . . heat lamp or something in her cell?"

"That would be painful for her."

Doctor Mighty threw up his hands and drove back to his lair, the abandoned hospital in Mechlinberg. There he crashed on an old gurney instead of programming the crime computer. The computer watched for anomalies in the price of butter, disappearances of key scientists, their daughters, or their current top-secret projects, and fluctuations in the listing prices of local supervillian lairs. The correlated information shined a spotlight on the doings of the criminally insane. Villains were so . . . so predictable.

Doctor Mighty folded his fingers behind his head and shut his tired eyes. He should have been up and at his heroic duties. There were newspapers to be scanned, parole hearings to attend, and The Violet Penumbra was taking a pension after forty years, and he needed to pick up a gift for the retirement party. So much to do, yet he just didn't feel like doing anything.

Sometimes Curt wished he'd opted for a surgical mask to hide his face. But when his powers had manifested during his first year of medical school, he'd felt no need for an alter ego. He'd just started fighting crime in some scrubs he'd picked up at a used clothes store. A mask had seemed such a bother. It constrained his field of vision, messed up his hair, and made it hard to brag at the singles bar about his deeds.

Of course, once he started getting good at superheroing, he'd seen the benefit of being able to walk down the street and not be mobbed by autograph seekers and old ladies who wanted to describe their pancreas for him.

"I'm not a real doctor," he tried to explain, but they always brushed that aside. He wished he could help them. He wished he did know what to do about that goiter.

"I dropped out of medical school," he said. "I don't have a degree." But still they described the pain in their arm when they moved it just so.

"Then stop moving it like that," he said, and they laughed.

What always worked though was, "Hark! I think I hear someone in peril!" And then he would sprint down the street until he was out of sight. No one knew he didn't have super-human hearing. In the parlance of the Guild, his was a uni-power. Unlike the Dread Snark who could jump fifty feet from a standing position and turn invisible, Doctor Mighty only had super strength. Multi-powers got much better endorsement deals and better match-ups with villains.

Curt wasn't interested in endorsements or cage-matches with the Angry Motorist or the Sharper Shooter. In fact, he wasn't sure what he was interested in all. It became such a bother going out that he started staying in all the time.

There were other superheroes on duty, heroes with multi-powers, heroes who enjoyed signing autographs and cutting ribbons. Let them handle the Split Infinitive and Dirty Dunkirk and Nuclear Winter. Then Curt could sleep in for once. Let Doctor Mighty take a break. He wasn't on call anymore.

"Don't you see?" said the Intern. "It's the Skinner Boxer's plan to get you to give up superheroing!"

"I don't think he has anything to do with it," Doctor Mighty said. Steve, dressed in burgundy scrubs, complete with booties over his shoes, had brought him a six-pack of KryptoLite and pizza. He'd had to wipe a six-inch layer of debris off the operating table to find someplace to put the pizza.

"Sure you don't. It's all part of his mind game. Well, I'm here as your trusty sidekick to help you snap out of it, man! He shot you with his doldrum ray, Mighty."

"Steve, you're not my sidekick. I thought you had something going with Alligator Joe? You were Crocodile Kid, or something." Curt had gone through a few sidekicks early on; there'd been the Human Ambulance, who was as big as an ambulance, but had trouble keeping up; he would arrive, heaving, at the scene after the villain had been subdued. Once they'd had to call an ambulance for him. Then he'd tried out the X-Ray Boy, but his vision only seemed to work through woman's clothing. The Defibrillator couldn't work near water or in the rain. Steve the Intern had no super power at all; he was a pure sidekick, which meant Curt spent a lot of time freeing him from traps, pushing him out of the way of death rays, and explaining the villains' plots slowly and in small words.

Steve the Intern looked stricken. "Did you know he uses real alligators to fight crime? You at least don't throw dirty syringes or iron lungs at people. I thought we could team up again, you know."

"Listen, Steve. I really don't feel like fighting crime today. It's not a plot of Boxer or Sigma Freud. I'm just . . . tired."

Steve the Intern seemed ready to argue, then he said, "Yeah, yeah, I understand. I feel that way sometimes too." He pulled his cape back on, and adjusted the drape of it in the glass window of the abandoned operating theatre. "Have you talked to someone about it? You know, maybe someone at the Institute could help you . . . whatever."

"I don't need anyone at the Institute to help me out, Steve."

"Well, you get some vitamin C, and you'll feel better. And stop by the Guild some night, okay? Have a few beers and some laughs with the heroes."

"Maybe," Curt said, but he didn't really want to face any other super heroes.

"See ya."

Doctor Mighty rolled over, grabbed one of the KryptoLites, and popped it open in a spray of foam. Vitamin C was not called for in this case. He needed some vitamin beer.

*

Doctor Mighty took to wandering the halls of the abandoned hospital, putting on dark phantom airs, and pulling rebar steel from the concrete walls and bending it into pretzels. He sent back the supervillain challenges he received through the Guild. He didn't bother programming the crime computer, but loaded an illegal copy of Tetris on it instead. Instead of patrolling the streets, he patrolled the hospital, bending steel in his bare and heavily calloused hands.

Curt found he could bend five bars at a time. Six was impossible, but five he could do every time. Loop, loop, twist, and he had a twenty pound pretzel.

Super-strength really was his only power, and he began to wonder if he could enhance it if he worked out. Maybe he could better himself as a superhero. It wasn't that he wanted to be a multi-power. He just wanted a change.

He started bending bars in the morning, five sets of eight pretzels, another three sets after lunch, and then five sets before dinner. He lifted the x-ray machine in a bench press. He drank a protein drink after every workout. It was good to have a routine. Doctor Mighty considered going after some more villains.

Then he realized after a month that he could still only bend five bars. His power was static, as is, unalterable. He was Doctor Mighty and no more.

He stopped working out, and just read comic books, played Tetris, and ordered pizza for every meal.

Doctor Mighty would have remained forever in the abandoned hospital if Auntie Arctic hadn't escaped from the Institute and managed to freeze his favorite pizza place. No one else would deliver to his lair.

He found her at the new Giant Eagle in Dublin, sitting in the refrigeration unit in the back room on a pallet of frozen strawberries, tossing bags of french-cut green beans into a box with amazing precision.

"Oh, hi," she said. "I was waiting for you to show up."

Doctor Mighty looked around for the henchmen, but the frozen food locker was empty except for the two of them. Auntie Arctic kicked the strawberries with the back of her booted heel in an arrhythmic patter.

"Where are your henchmen?" Curt checked the ceiling and glanced behind a stack of chicken breasts.

"I traded Centigrade to the Copyright Infringer for a death ray. F and C retired, said the business wasn't for them anymore. Moved to Arizona for the weather."

"Yeah, hot, but no humidity."

"Whatever."

Doctor Mighty stowed the hair drier in his belt and sat on a pallet next to Ms. Arctic. She was looking sad, the icicles on her elbows dripping a bit, the frost on her cheeks a little more blue than usual.

"You seem down," he said.

"You don't seem yourself either," she said.

"No, I . . ."

"Yeah, I know."

Curt found himself tapping his foot in time with Auntie Arctic's. He stopped his foot, worked up his courage, and said, "Hey, do you want to get some dinner before I take you back to the Institute for the Criminally Insane?"

She raised her eyebrows at him, then she smiled with blue lips, made bluer with cyan lip gloss.

"Yeah, sure. Can we get ice cream after?"

They got take-out and ate it in the Mightimobile, with the air conditioning cranked up on her side and the heat on on his.

"So, yeah, I did the whole career quiz thing, and my empathy was zero and my megalomania was like 100, so I went with supervillain," Auntie said around a mouthful of pad thai. "It was either that or homemaker. What about you?"

"I was in medical school . . . when the whole mess happened."

"Thus the name."

"Yeah. But it was just my first year, so I'm not really a doctor."

"Really. I always thought you were like an ER doctor when you weren't superheroing."

"No, I dropped out," Doctor Mighty said.

"Yeah? Radioactive scorpion? Blast of gamma rays? Glowing meteorite from another planet? Artifact of the Old Ones?"

"Well . . ."

"Come on, give. I told you all about how Empress Evil's perfect heat sink from her freeze ray got lodged in my sternum."

"Yeah, well. It's not a very . . . flattering story."

"Like getting speared between the tits with a superconductive brick is. I thought we were sharing here. Just take me back to the Institute now, if that's the way you're gonna be."

"No. Sorry," he said. "I was drunk, okay. I don't even know how it happened."

"Oh, boy."

"A bunch of us were out late the day after finals. We were drinking, then came back to the radiology lab. The last thing I remember is my buddy daring me to swallow the Strontium-90 sample. Then I woke up strapped to the x-ray machine with it pointed at my . . . er . . . gonads."

"It was on?"

"They said they hadn't turned it on. It was a joke. But it had been on all night. As near as the scientists at the Superhero Origins Facility can figure, the Rolling Rock and the Strontium were irradiated by the x-rays and started emitting s-rays that enhanced the fast-twitch muscle fibers in my body. I got super strength."

"You do have nice biceps," she said, giving his arm a squeeze. "So. How are the . . . uh . . . the little Mighties."

"They're fine, actually. As far as I can tell."

"Well, that's good. So you dropped out of medical school to be a superhero."

"Yeah, everyone was real happy that it had happened to me."

"Everyone?"

"You know, the school. They played down the beer part, and made it seem like they had a world-class superhero generation program or something." He poked a dumpling with his plastic fork. "We never could figure out the exact sequence of events that created the superstrength. We went through a lot of mice and monkeys trying."

She laughed, a maniacal, overzealous cackle that he found endearing. He actually felt better for telling this supervillain his woes. Perhaps it was because she wasn't a mundane, who always thought it was the coolest thing to have a super talent, and she wasn't a fellow superhero, who always seemed so on top of his emotions. If anyone could understand him, it was a supervillain. Supervillains had flaws; they appreciated imperfections and could sympathize.

"So," Auntie said. "Maybe you could turn me in tomorrow."

Doctor Mighty caught her eye, and his cheeks turned mighty red when he realized what she meant.

"I, uh, sure."

They made love gently in a series of bizarre positions that limited the amount of time he was near her heat sink and kept all her parts away from his clenching fists when he orgasmed.

The next morning he dropped her off at the Institute. As the guards shackled her into a sauna jacket, they awkwardly stood together.

"Um," he said.

"Yeah," she said.

"I hope you get better."

"Yeah."

"You know, maybe we could . . . team-up if you switched sides," he said. "Or something."

"Likewise."

"Yeah."

As they were dragging her away, she turned and said, "You know, Mighty. You ever think you weren't really cracked up to be a superhero?"

"Huh?"

"I know it sounds like a supervillain mind game," she said. "But maybe you need another career."

"I —"

"Thanks for the fuck!"

"I —"

"Thanks for not calling me frigid!" They dragged her around a corner.

Doctor Killdozer looked him up and down. "Perhaps you should join our superhero support group. Fraternizing is not a life-affirming action."

Doctor Mighty started attending Guild meetings again. He was glad he'd spent time talking with Auntie Arctic. He was even glad they'd spent the night together, though he hoped it didn't get out.

There were bylaws that covered that. But talking with her had made
him realize he spent too much time in the abandoned hospital. He
made an effort to get out.

Guild meetings were weekly affairs at the Hall of Beer and
Pretzels, more social than political. Sometimes they had seminars
on the latest villain trickery or discussed some new tactics on making sure bystanders survived superbattles. Their Guild post had the
smallest bystander death rate of any in the Midwest, just 713 so far
that year. At the meetings, usually the heroes broke up into groups,
along age lines, and bragged about their latest battles. For the geri-
atric superheroes, meeting night was a chance to get out of the old
folks lair and talk about battles of yore.

"Once that Kneehigh Nazi had me tied between four circus
elephants, one on each arm and leg —" the Bomber was saying as
Curt walked in.

"That's nothing. Evil Foo Ling Duck once hypnotized my sidekick to try to kill me with a poodle while I slept!"

Doctor Mighty walked past the geriatrics and tried to find Steve
the Intern, but he didn't see his former sidekick anywhere. To hide
his awkwardness, he ordered a Mxyzptlk at the bar.

He couldn't help but feel that the other heroes were looking
askance at him, but he never caught anyone whispering, or laughing, or even looking, except for the Human Frog who looked everywhere all the time anyway.

He hoped it wasn't because he'd slept with Auntie Arctic. He
knew that was against the bylaws, but he didn't think anyone had
found out. Would she blab? he wondered. Was she one to screw
and tell? What would a supervillain do? He'd always thought they
were predictable, but now that he had a relationship with one . . .
Was it a relationship? No, it couldn't be.

Gaseous Jorge had married his sidekick Flatulent Flo and the
Guild had snubbed them; the two had had to relocate. What would
the Guild do if they knew about what he'd done? Jorge and Flo had
been on the same side.

It was enough to make him reconsider visiting Ms. Arctic at the
Institute. He decided he'd better cancel the flower order too.

"Back in the saddle, huh?" asked the Yippee Ka Yay Kid, from
the stool two down from his. He twirled his lasso, whipped it around,
and caught his beer.

"What do you mean?" Doctor Mighty said, searching for sexual innuendo in the greeting. He scrutinized the Kid's face under his wide-brimmed cowboy hat.

"You know. Back to fighting the bad guys instead of moping in your old mental asylum."

"It's an abandoned hospital, and I wasn't moping."

"So then you're up for a wrangle with some of the Squid's Tentaclemen who are roosted over at the docks?"

Doctor Mighty hated fighting the Tentaclemen. He always ended up with hickies all over his arms and legs. But he would look like more of a moper if he said no.

"Yeah, I'll wrangle."

They did find a clutch of Tentaclemen, unloading smuggled boxes of counterfeit comic books on a wharf next to a rusted freighter of Albanian origin. The fake books were easily spotted by turning to page twelve where the Gallant Ghost was shown with his utility rope on his left hip instead of his right.

"Your exploitation of young comic readers across the city is over, Tentacleboys!" Mister Suds shouted, shaking the soapy canister on his back and pumping it up with the plunger at his hip. A spray of sudsy water splattered the Tentaclemen, and one slipped on his back with a thud.

"Ow! You didn't have to shoot!" the downed Tentacleman shouted. "It's not like we have workman's comp!"

Captain Corporeal, not to be outdone on slogans, warped through the solid freight container and substantiated his fist just as it met the jaw of another of henchman. "Copyright is sacred to a five-year-old, leech!"

Yippee lassoed two more with his rope and dragged them down the steps. Curt, watching from the back, flinched when he heard the leg of one them break. He shouldn't have come, he thought. He didn't like gang battles against henchmen. He poked his fingers in his ears as he saw the Screech advancing for his turn.

"Aaaaaaiiiiiiieeeeeeee!" the Screech yelled, and the henchmen who weren't roped, unconscious, or laying with thrown-out backs, clutched at their ears as their drums popped.

The four other heroes turned and looked at him. Curt shrugged and said, "I think you guys have it under control."

"Thanks," said the Tentacleman on his back. "We appreciate that."

"Hahahaha!" The Squid's laugh echoed along the wharf, and a heavy, wire mesh fell from a loading crane.

"It's a trap!" cried the four superheroes. Doctor Mighty, because he had hung back, was the only one to escape as the net fell upon henchman and hero alike.

Blue fire raced across the wire mesh of the net; it was electrified. Curt backed away in shock as the heroes and henchmen jerked and twitched. The Screech's cry drowned out the screams of the others.

He ran from the smell of burning flesh, dodging down the narrow passages between the shipping containers. He rounded a corner, and there were two henchmen guarding a flashing device; colored wires protruded along its length, solid carbon dioxide sublimed into cold fog, and a giant digital clock, mounted at its base, counted down to zero. All the signs said doomsday device.

Doctor Mighty landed two punches, breaking the jaws of the henchmen and regretting it. He studied the doomsday device for a moment, then yanked out the most crucial and removable component. As expected, the clock paused, at two minutes and twenty-five seconds, which was rather high by Guild standards; he should have let it run down a little more.

Doctor Mighty glanced around the shipping container, and there was the Squid, tentacles waving in the sky, gracefully sailing to the ground on the crane's lowering hook. He was too far to hear, but Curt was certain he was lecturing the downed heroes on his current scheme to take over the world.

Curt took the doomsday device part under his arm and ran down the aisle of shipping containers, trying to double around so that he could free the other heroes. As he neared the Squid, he heard snatches of his speech.

". . . totalitarian regime . . ."

". . . meritocractic syndicate . . ."

". . . Marx and Engel . . ."

At least the Screech had stopped screeching, though the Squid's lecture was almost worse.

"Bring in the doomsday device!" he cried, then paused, waiting. "Loyal henchmen, bring in the doomsday device!"

Mighty listened to his heavy tread as he walked down the wharf.

"Curse you, Doctor Mighty! What have you done to my doomsday device?"

Curt felt the retort bubbling up inside of him, but he clamped it down.

"Give it up, Doctor Mutty!" the Squid yelled. "My Tentacles are homing in on you even as we speak."

Doctor Mighty peered around the box he was hiding behind. No one. He had a clear line to the netted heroes, unconscious now.

"Here he is!"

A Tentacleman had snuck up on him from behind.

He kicked the sucker in the chest, cracking several ribs.

"Sorry."

He dodged down a narrow passage toward the heroes and emerged in a cluster of henchmen. He was trapped!

"Not a step closer, or I crush the doomsday device!" he cried.

"No!" cried the Squid. "I worked years on that doomsday device. Where will I get another thousand myopic bumblebees?" His waving tentacles slurped at the air.

"Yes! Let the heroes go! Or I crush the device."

"Never."

"I'm crushing it."

"Can't we come to some agreeable arrangement?"

"Such as?"

"You and me, masters of the world. What do you say? We'll split it fifty-fifty. A partnership."

Mighty looked over at his unconscious brethren. He didn't really like them that much. And, really, was good and evil diametrically opposed? If you squashed the axis of morality to a micron, superheroes and supervillains, ended up pretty close together.

"Okay."

"I don't know why I even ask, but still I ask. It's in the villain bylaws — Hey, what did you say?"

"Okay. Fifty-fifty," said Doctor Mighty. "But we have to let these heroes go."

"Let me see your fingers."

Doctor Mighty put the doomsday device down and wiggled his fingers.

"Really?" asked the Squid. "You want to be my . . . partner?"

"Sure." He wasn't sure why he'd said yes, but he knew he was tired of being a hero. And the Squid was revolutionary if nothing else, and revolution was something the world needed.

The Squid wrapped a rubbery arm around Doctor Mighty's shoul-

der. "Excellent!" he said. "I've never had a partner before. I'm
rather speechless."

"I don't want death and destruction," Doctor Mighty said. "I
want social reform."

"Eggs and an omelette, don't you know. But I agree, I agree.
We must discuss the works of Marx and Engel. I have some very
interesting ideas I want to bounce off you, Doctor Mighty." The
Squid paused. "That won't do. You'll need a new *nom de guerre*,
of course. And new clothes." He tugged at the shoulders of Curt's
hospital scrubs. "Practical, but not fashionable. As for a name, how
about the Proctologist?"

"No. Too evil."

"The Fearsome Forceps?"

"No."

"Ah! The Sinister Surgeon!"

They took over all of Ohio and part of Indiana in a bloodless,
Socialist coup involving a grass roots campaign and mind control de-
vices. Curt had talked him out of using the cobalt bomb. The Squid
handled the chortling and the brain wave devolver. The Sinister Surgeon made sure people didn't get hurt and kept the superheroes at
bay. It was relatively easy if you knew how a hero thought; feed the
crime computers bogus info, distract them with kidnapped gover-
nors, and suddenly you were living in the Socialist Buckeye Republic.

For awhile, Sinister found the whole supervillain business ful-
filling. Laws were easy to enact when the entire executive branch
was he and a cackling cephalopod. He was changing society, force-
fully and without democracy, true, but ultimately it was change,
change, he thought, for the better. And he was helping the farmers
and small townsfolk, while royally annoying the big businesses.

Hardly anyone got killed.

It was a good three months; at first, he was so busy with one-,
three-, and five-year plans, that he didn't notice the depression. He
started ditching the goose-stepping parades and the book-burnings.
The plan to take over Michigan by instigating the extreme right
militias didn't seem as fun as it had a month before. The cloning
vats held no charm. The three hundred foot marble statues of him
and the Squid overlooking the Squidopolis capitol didn't gleam like
they once had.

Something still wasn't right with him.

He wished he had someone to confide in, someone who understood the frustration of being a supervillain. He certainly couldn't confide in the Squid, who was alert for any sign of weakness. The common throng had no conception of his problems; all of them thought being a dictator was the end-all. The Sinister Surgeon had just spent several hours micromanaging the winter food shipments through the Ohio Valley, when he remembered other frozen foods.

He found Auntie Arctic in the gulag on Kelly's Island where they'd sent all the insane people. She was sitting by the window of the woman's hut watching the birds skipping across the waves. A line of drool rolled off her lip. She was dressed in shorts and a t-shirt even though it was a crisp March day.

He pulled down his mask.

She looked at Sinister for a few moments, then blinked and smiled. "Hi, Doc."

"Hi, Auntie." The cold seemed to roll off her in waves. "How are you?"

She didn't answer, and though he sat with her for half an hour, she didn't say anything more.

Back in the capital, Squidopolis, he signed an edict closing the gulags. Then he drugged the Squid's ink juice and shipped his body in a giant lobster cage to the Guild district office in Pittsburgh. He dropped his mask and surgical smock in a trash can and took a long vacation out west while their dictatorship was slowly toppled and Ohio was reaffirmed into its place in the Union.

"I thought it was you," the woman said. "So this is your secret identity."

Curt looked at the pregnant woman in the wheelchair. Her hair was black and straight instead of the blue-black ringlets he remembered. She had put on a few more pounds and her face was rosy.

"Auntie?"

"Gwen Ka Yay," she said with a smile. "Sorry, I didn't mean to blow your cover."

He rolled her into an examination room and took her blood pressure himself instead of letting a nurse do it.

"I don't do that anymore."

"You lost your power too?" She reached out to squeeze his biceps.

"You don't freeze anymore?" he asked, surprised. He stuck a thermometer in her mouth. Ninety-eight point six.

She shrugged. "I found a doctor who said he could remove the brick. It's in my freezer now. We don't even have to plug it in."

"Where's your —?" he pointed to her belly. "Mrs. Ka Yay? You?"

"My husband is the Yippee Ka Yay Kid. He's parking the horse." She blushed. "He was real nice to me once Sinister Squidtopia collapsed."

"That's good," he said, his heart in his throat.

"Oh! Oh! Oh!" she said. Curt noted the time of the contraction. "When was the last one?"

"Ten minutes, maybe? The Kid was writing it down. We were at a park doing tricks for the kids. I was a cow and he would lasso me."

"In your condition?"

"Well, I wasn't a running cow, more of an ambling cow." She laughed and rubbed both hands over her belly. "I'd rather be a supervillain sometimes than face what's coming."

"I think you'll be a fine mother," he said. "And the Kid will be a fine father."

"I'm worried that I won't know how to care for it. I've never really cared for anything at all."

"That's not true, and we both know it."

She wiped her fist across her face and looked at him.

"I remember seeing you on the island. Geez. I remember seeing a lot of things come up that beach. The Titanic. Jim Carey. The USC Marching Band. But I remember seeing you too."

Curt didn't say anything.

"Howdy, Pard!" the Yippee Ka Yay Kid shouted. "How's the little lady doing, Doc?"

He squeezed Curt's hand and Curt squeezed back.

"Ow! That's some grip you have there, Pard! Say! Don't I know you from somewhere?"

Curt shrugged, and glanced at Gwen. She smiled and said, "He's an old friend I knew once. You're an intern here, aren't you?"

"Yep."

"Finally finishing up school, huh?"

"You can read me like a book."

"You have a good bedside manner."

"I figure it's where I can do the most good."

"Are you happy?"

"I, um —" he said, having never thought about it. "No happier than before, but a little wiser. I guess."

She smiled and then squeezed her eyes shut.

Curt checked his watch. "Six minutes. I think we better get you ready."

He hung around until their OB showed up, then he went back to his rounds. No one ever thought they'd be able to care for something as defenseless and needy as a baby, but it usually worked out. He figured the Ka Yays had a good shot at figuring it out. He silently wished them the best of luck.

"Doctor Curt! There's a boy who caught his head in the stair rail. The firemen brought the whole banister!"

"Coming!"

He wasn't Doctor Mighty anymore. But sometimes it was easier to care when you had biceps of steel.

ALIEN FANTASIES

I keep practicing what I'm going to say when one of the aliens picks me. I know I said "when" but that's how I feel about it. I have a rapport, you know. Sooner or later, I'll look up from my desk at the bank, and see a leonine mane bobbing over the edges of the cubicles, weaving its way toward me. I just know it.

I think I'll play it cool, like aliens come by my desk every day and ask me to gallivant across the galaxy. I'll tip my glasses forward on my nose and ask in my best bureaucratic voice, "May I help you?" And he'll recognize and appreciate my coyness, since we'll both know why he's there. He'll smile with his large canines, toss his mane to the left, and ask, "Care to join me aboard the Mother Ship, Jennifer?" And I'll say, "Not tonight, I have to pick Gabrielle up from her ballet lessons."

No, that wasn't quite right.

I guess I always assumed Gabrielle would come along. The aliens must have some facilities for students: playgrounds and schools and such. Readjustment is always difficult on a teenager, with meeting new friends and getting used to no sun. But children are resilient. My parents moved seven times before I was out of high school.

Or I could leave her with Nick. But learning to live on the Mother Ship would be better than living with her father. I mean, he threw a glass of Coke in my face the last time we spoke. What would he do to Gabby? He ran out on us, after all. He's untrustworthy.

I have two bags packed: a smaller one I keep with me at all times, and a bigger one in the hall closet at home. I could make do with either, but the one at home has a summer and winter wardrobe in it. The aliens have been unusually reticent about their home world, so I have no idea how to pack.

In each bag I have a few of my old Heinlein juveniles. I don't know why I bother with that; the aliens have spent the most time, other than on talk shows, in libraries transcribing all the books to archives on the Mother Ship. I figure I won't need those books then, if they have the entire libraries of Earth in a boxed set. But I'd miss the smell of the binding and the yellowed pages. Gabrielle will appreciate that.

Not that I can get her to read or anything. Kids these days have different priorities. I remember that before I met Nick, I could spend all day with my nose in a book.

The day ends without incident, without Sylvia forcing me to account for all the time I spent daydreaming, I mean. I'm efficient when I work, I just don't like to work. The bus ride from downtown is the best part of the day. No demands, no customers, no boss, and no screaming teenager trying to find her tights.

As we pass over the Monongahela, I see the excursion vehicle hovering over the Incline. It is a smaller one — not like the one in Washington — but still the size of a small skyscraper. They're actually renting the airspace over the houses.

Maybe coy isn't the best way to play it. Maybe a subdued surprise, followed by tentative, then full-fledged acceptance. "The Mother Ship? Well, I don't know. Am I fit to be an emissary of my race? I am? Then, of course, take me! I'm yours!"

I smile innocently at the man I accidently jostled.

"Sorry."

Oops. I think I need a bigger pause between tentative and full-fledged.

When I get home, the dog is chewing on a pair of Gabrielle's tights, and it doesn't realize until I kick it that I am not playing tug of war.

"Gabby! Gabby! Get down here!" I yell up the stairs.

She appears, fists on hips, purposefully insolent, and I want to smack the smirk off her face. I wave the tights.

"Cosmo is eating your tights."

"So?"

"These are expensive. I can't afford to keep buying them."

"I don't want to take ballet, Mother," she says. "I can save a lot more money by not going."

"Gabby."

"Mother."

I sigh, suddenly not angry, just tired. "You remind me of me when I was your age."

"Well, I'm not pregnant," she says, and I am stunned.

"To your room," I cry, but she has already disappeared through her door.

We do not talk for the rest of the evening.

The planet-side commander, Labintine Os-Moss-Chor, is on Letterman tonight. Most people say they can't tell the aliens apart. I can. It all goes back to that rapport I have. Labintine is even more regal than the typical alien, with strands of silver running through his mane, his bulging musculature apparent even under his robes. For a race that averages four feet high, they are quite impressive.

"So, I hear humans and aliens can mate." Letterman gives Labintine a gap-toothed smile, full of innuendo. I feel a moment's embarrassment for the alien.

"Yes. Our races can interbreed."

"So, tell me how you know this."

Labintine cocks his head, then deadpans the camera with, "Trust me, I know."

Silence, followed by female tittering and then a roar of laughter.

Letterman grins again, waves his audience silent.

"I guess it isn't height that's important, huh?"

"Height? No," says Labintine, a slight smile creasing his features. Is it a smile? I don't know. "It's the size of the mane that matters. And not a single male on this planet has a decent one." He stands and twirls. The camera follows hesitantly, then quickly. He shows his full mane, running the length of his back, to curl prettily at his calves. The audience applauds in appreciation.

"Now, wait a minute, Labby. Even I know aliens and humans shouldn't be able to produce offspring."

"Your question is not well-defined," he replies. "The fallacy in your statement is the definition of 'alien.' As is supposed by several of your premiere scientific fiction writers, we have a common ancestor."

"I think it was my Aunt Violet."

"A little farther back. About seven hundred thousand years ago. Stock was taken from the gene pool at that time by another passing race that is also related to us, but much farther back. We have since been modified to include other genetic characteristics."

"Have you talked to the Vatican about this?"

"The Vatican is a geo-political entity that would probably not understand what I was saying to it."

Letterman gives the camera a cocked smile.

"Ha ha. Give an alien a straight line . . ." Paul chimes in.

"So," continues Letterman, "an alien of your race and an Earthling could conceive a child. What would he look like?"

"Well, a female of my species could not birth such a child naturally. The head would not fit through the birth canal. If the child was surgically removed, there would be no problem. All the female offspring of such a union would be sterile. The male hybrids would be able to produce viable sperm for either species."

"That's better than bisexuality: two whole races of females."

Labintine smiles softly as the rimshot plays. His dignity is as unscathed as ever. I had been worried for nothing.

"When we come back, a bonus top ten list! 'Top ten things to do the morning after you bring home an alien from Club Xeno.'"

I fall asleep before the commercial is over.

The morning is hectic, and I find myself hoping that an alien will come in the next few minutes. But he doesn't and I am forced to deal with Gabby's frantic search for clean jeans and missing my bus, so that I have to stand on the next one that comes.

The males of my race are so stupid, dumb, and ignorant. I glare at each one who refuses to give me his seat, until finally my eye catches the ship hovering over the Incline. It is abuzz with the little jet scooters each of the aliens drives, like gnats around a decayed apple.

A woman standing next to me is watching as well. "Awful busy now that they are about to leave."

My expression must speak volumes.

"Yeah, you didn't hear the news? The aliens are leaving, say they might be back in a few thousand years. Good riddance, I say. Take all our knowledge, give nothing in return 'cause it's against 'Human super-species' tradition — whatever that is — and then motor off again. A true family race would stay a little longer, and not be so rude. It's like when my sister-in-law . . ."

"When are they leaving?"

"Tonight. Now my sister-in-law, for instance . . ."

My mind has run through a thousand possibilities by the time I get to work, and I am firmly in denial. The woman obviously got the story all screwed up. The aliens are probably just leaving Pittsburgh, which is bad enough for me. How could they take me with them, when they have left the city I live in. But my Walkman confirms the news, and I begin to get nauseous like when I learned I was pregnant with Gabby at seventeen.

I am so broken up that my radar doesn't pick up Sylvia until she is standing in front of my desk, asking me why I was staring off into space instead of entering the customer service response card into the database.

"I'm, uh, not feeling so well," I say, hoping my disheveled look adds some credibility to the statement.

"You let Nick back in the house?" Sylvia asks. "He leeching of you again, 'cause . . ."

I cut her off, embarrassed by her sympathy. "No, no, stomach flu."

Sylvia nods and picks up the stack of questionnaires. "I'm light today. You can take the day off and I'll finish these up."

I try to nod in the disappointed relief of an employee who was willing to risk death to make it to work, but now realizes she should spend the day recuperating.

"Okay, Sylvia, thanks," I say, grabbing my coat. I am running by the time I reach the door.

I realize that it's time for the direct approach. No more waiting for the aliens to come get me. I'll show up there, and an alien will be leaning against the steel orifice into their ship. "It's about time," he'll say.

"You've been waiting for me?"

"Move your ass, lady!"

I am bumped by some guy running down the street. I stumble as he disappears into the bank, and I am left to pull the shoe off my foot. The heel is broken.

"Fuck," I say, leaning against the cool stone of the building. The morning crowd is beginning to thin.

The shoe is ruined so I take the other off. I step gingerly to the corner, to the newsstand there.

"Hey, where do I catch a bus over to the South Side?"

The withered old man looks up from an issue of *Esquire*. "Over there. The thirty-seven."

"Thanks."

"But, lady, it don't run but till nine-o-five."

I glance at my watch. I've missed it. "Damn."

I am suddenly exhausted, and I sit on the curb. The departure time was ten o'clock. Labintine had announced that the advance craft would converge on the Mother Ship over Washington and then leave the solar system. Gone for a thousand years.

Pity rolls off my body and collects in the gutter. I'm an idiot. I live in fantasy. What a fool I've been acting, ranting on about the aliens and going with them. I wish that I had the last six weeks to live over again. I wish that I had my whole life to live over again.

My wallowing is disturbed by an approaching chirp, and I finally recognize it as the sound of the alien single-person scooters. I glance up and see the thing drift by, driven by a small gray alien. He is scanning the opposite side of the road, and I jump up, ready to wave my arm, telling him that I'm over here.

But I stop, stand and turn toward the bus stop that will take me back home. I've been a fool, but I'll not be a hypocrite as well.

"Hey! Human lady!"

I turn to see the alien trotting towards me, and I am giddy with joy.

"I'm ready," I say. "Well, I have to grab my travel bag. I left it next to my desk. But all I have to do is go get it. Then I'm ready to go. Just give me a second. Hold on, okay?"

The alien, a short one, but still cute, furrows his brow and shakes his head. "No need to prepare for request. Just need sample."

"Huh?"

"Need sample of yellow-haired human lady."

"Oh. You don't need a live sample?"

"No. No authority to take live sample. Need fluid." He reaches into his pack and pulls out a small clear cylinder.

I finally notice the ratty clothing of the alien, the unkempt look, the yellow symbol on his sleeve indicating his student status. He's a geek alien. Just my luck. The aliens were leaving and he was on a last-minute quest to finish a homework assignment.

"Fuck you," I say, spinning on my heel. Tears begin to flow and I am mad, so mad at everything. I start running.

But he's faster than me in my stockings, and he catches me within a block, jumping in front of me. "Stop!"

"What? I gave at the office!" I yell.

"Seen leaving syndrome on other planets. Common among us. On every planet."

"'Leaving syndrome?'"

The alien shrugs. "Escapist syndrome. Wanderlust." He smiles slightly, pats my arm. "No better out there. No more hope than here. Less even."

I shrug, turn away, start walking down the street.

"No sample?" he calls. "Need to get back."

I pause, then I finally nod. "Fine. Pick an arm."

The alien places the plastic cylinder against my skin. I feel a warmth, and the cylinder begins to fill with my blood, bubbling red.

I wipe my tears away with my other hand. "I guess a part of me is going into space."

"Small part."

"You could clone me, maybe. Then it would be like I was there after all. I would grow up in your society, and it would . . ."

"No." He shakes his head slowly. His eyes are sad. "Still don't understand. You live on this planet, nowhere else."

I sigh. "I know."

He reaches into his pack and pulls out a small clipper set. "I take something of you, and you keep something of me." He snips a length of his gray-blue mane and hands it to me.

It is stiff and coarse and I am suddenly happy, and I hug him before he can react.

"Thank you." I have to bend over, but I manage to bury my face in his shoulder. I hear the murmur of a purr deep inside him. He pats my head.

"Got to go, human lady." Pushing away, he turns up the street trotting back to his scooter. "Good luck," he calls, and I wave.

In a daze, I wander to the bus stop, still clutching the small bale of hair. I brush the end against my cheek, feeling the prickly coarseness. I see that there is enough for me to braid a necklace, maybe two, and I decide I will make one for Gabrielle and I will make one for me.

THE SUMMER
OF THE SEVEN

In the summer of our fourteenth year, we weren't the only one to live with Mother Redd on the farm in Worthington. That was the year the Seven came to stay.

"After lunch, you'll need to clean out the back bedroom," Mother Redd said that morning at breakfast. One of her was busy frying eggs at the stove, while another was squeezing orange juice. Her third was setting the table. We had just come in from chores — picking diamond flowers, plucking sheep cloth, and, secretly, milking the beer bush for a few ounces of lager — and were lounging around the kitchen table.

Meda, my true sister and our pod's interface, asked the question we were thinking. "Who's coming to stay?" It wasn't a visit. For a visit, we wouldn't bother to clean out the bedroom; we'd just pull out the beds from the couch in the downstairs den and let the visitor sprawl around the first floor. Or, if it was more than one person, we'd lay quilts and pillows in the great room.

One of Mother Redd gave us a look that said we asked too many questions. "A guest," she said.

We all shrugged.

We spent the morning on calculus and physics. We were doing word problems: if you fired a cannonball from a train car and it lands on another train car, how fast are the train cars traveling apart after five seconds. Stuff like that.

Why would anyone mount a cannon on a train car? I sent.

Strom laughed. Bola, who understood force and motion intuitively, flashed us the image of the cannonball and its graceful trajectory. Then he added air currents, and gravity perturbations and other second-order forces. As he added in tidal effects and the pull of Jupiter, Quant sent, *Seven and a half centimeters per second.*

"At least let me write something down before you give me the answer," Meda said. She had the pencil, but Quant was solving the problems in her head.

"Why?"

"For the practice!"

"Why?"

Meda groaned. My sister is always so expressive; there's never any doubt what she's — or we're — feeling. That's why she was our interface.

"We have to show our work on the tests! We can't just write down the answer."

Quant shrugged.

Sometimes Quant won't be with us, I sent.

Moira!

I felt Quant's surprise and a moment's fear; we'd been together for almost fourteen years. Being cut off from the rest of us was what we most often had nightmares about. And if one of us had a nightmare, we all had it.

"Okay." I sent a smile and reassurance to Quant, and she relaxed and returned focus to the problem set. We worked through the rest of them on paper, Quant guiding us through the equations to the answer she already knew.

After lunch, we trudged up to the back bedroom and started moving boxes. We couldn't just throw the junk out the window and then haul it to the trash heap; Manuel had found a pipette set, and there were frames and pictures in some of the boxes. We had to be careful.

"What's this?" Meda asked, holding up a photo in an old plastic frame.

We saw the image through her eyes, well enough for me to recognize Mother Redd, a younger woman than she was now, and a quartet. Her hair was brown and bobbed, not long as she wore it now. And she was slender in the picture, not anything like the plump, huggable women we knew.

"That was before —" Meda said.

Yes.

Mother Redd was a trio now, but once, a long time ago, she had been a quartet. She had been a medical doctor, a famous one; we'd read a few of her papers and barely understood them, even though we were the highest order — a sextet — and specialized in math and science. Then one of her had died, leaving her three-quarters of what she had been.

Again, the fear of separation rippled through us, emotions that we would have to learn to check. Strom shivered, and I touched his hand. To lose one of ourselves, to become a quintet . . .

Meda looked closely at the picture. I knew what she was wondering, though I could only taste the curiosity. Which one of Mother Redd had died? I didn't think we could tell; she had been identical quadruplets. Meda put the picture away.

"Look at this," Quant said. She held up a tattered and old biology book. The date inside was 2020.

"That is so old!" Meda said. "Older than pods. What could that have that's any use?"

Quant thumbed through the pages and it fell open at a colored plate, a bisection of the female body.

"Now that's sexy," Manuel said. Arousal mingled with embarrassment. The stupidest things triggered desire in our male components. I sometimes wished that we were an all-female pod like Mother Redd, instead of an equally mixed sextet.

He turned the page, and there was a dissected frog, with overlays, so that you could flip from the skin, into the musculature, and then the internal organs.

"The spleen's in the wrong place," Bola said.

We had built frogs in biology class last year. Ours had been the best jumper.

As we were stowing the last of the boxes in the barn loft, we heard the whine of a jet car.

"Folsom 5X," Bola said. "Six-prop hydrogen burner."

It was actually a Folsom 3M, a converted older skybus, but we didn't have time to razz him for his mistake. The skybus landed on the airpad behind the farm house, and we ran to meet it.

Mother Redd waved us back, and we saw why. The bus had already discharged its passenger and was whining back into the sky. Another pod stood there next to Mother Redd, its interface shaking hands.

"Hi, I'm Apollo Papadopulos," Meda said. "Welcome to–"

The newcomer turned to us, and we counted: a seven-person pod, a septet. Our greeting hung in Meda's mouth. We gaped in wonder, stunned by the sight. We were a sextet; our order was only six.

*

"Everyone knows that the higher the order, the stronger the pod," Quant said.

"That's not true," Meda said.

We'd gotten over our voicelessness and had managed a polite greeting to Candace Thurgood. Meda had shaken hands with the leader of the septet, one of six identical females, skinny, blonde-haired, green-eyed girls. The seventh member was a male, taller, just as skinny and pale in skin and hair. We're three females and three males; Meda and I were identical female twins, while our other pod mates were of different genetic stock.

Then Strom came up with the idea that we still had chores in the barn, and we made a quick exit, watching as the seven of Candace and the three of Mother Redd walked to the house.

Yes, it is!

No, it isn't!

I shushed them with a whiff of baby pheromone, a poke at their childish behavior.

We all knew the history. The first pods had been duos, created almost fifty years ago, the first to use the chemical memory and pheromones to share feelings between two separate humans. Since then, the order of the pods and complexity of the chemical signaling had grown. We were a sextet, the largest order we'd ever seen. All our classmates were sextets. Everyone in the space program was a sextet.

"Because sextets are the largest order. They're the best," Strom said.

Not anymore! Candace is a seven, a septet!

It made sense. Genetic engineers were always trying to add to the power of an individual. Why wouldn't they try to build a seven? Or an eight?

"They succeeded in building one, finally."

"How old is she?"

"Younger than us. Maybe twelve."

I hope she's not staying all summer.

But we knew she was. We wouldn't have turned out the guest room if she wasn't.

Maybe we can make her leave.

I said, "We have to be nice. We have to be friends."

We have to be nice, but we don't have to be friends.

Why be nice?

I looked at Meda, and she said, "Oh, all right. Let's go be nice. At least there isn't eight of her."

Though how far away would *that* be?

We tried to be nice.

I was the one who'd advised it, and even I chafed at the manners of that arrogant septet.

"Fifteen point seven five three," Candace said, while we were still scribbling the problem. One of her was looking over Quant's shoulder as we sat at the great room table.

I knew that, Quant sent.

Still Meda wrote the problem down and we worked through to the answer, while Candace tapped seven of her feet.

"Fifteen point seven five three three," Meda said.

"I rounded down," she said. "One of us —" She nodded at the identical girl to her left — "is specialized in mathematics. When you have seven, you know, you can do that. Specialize."

We were specialized too, we wanted to say, but I sent, *Humble.*

She's specialized at being a git.

"You're very smart," Meda said diplomatically. I hadn't even had to remind her.

"Yes, I am." She was standing so close that the pungent smell of her chemical thoughts tickled our noses and distracted us. It was almost rude to stand so close that our memories mingled. We couldn't understand her thoughts, of course, just a bit of self-satisfaction from the pheromones. The chemical memories that we passed from hand to hand, and to some extent by air, were pod-specific, most easily passed by physical touch at the wrists where our pads were. Pheromones were more general and indicated nuance and emotion. These were often common across all pods, especially those from the same creche. So even though our thoughts didn't mix together, it felt weird for her to be so close.

She doesn't know any better, I sent, touching the pad on Manuel's left wrist. *She's young.*

We knew better at that age.

We should try to be friendly, I sent.

"Do you want to go swimming this afternoon?" Meda asked.

Candace shook her head quickly, then she paused for a consensus. We smelled the chemical thoughts, pungent and slick in the air, and wondered why she had to consense on going swimming.

"We don't swim," she said finally.

"None of you?"

Another pause. They touched hands, tap, tap, tap, pads sliding together. "None of us."

"Okay. Well, we're going swimming in the pond."

The smell was stronger. The heads turned inward, and they held palms together for ten seconds. What was so complicated about going swimming?

Finally, she said, "We'll come and watch, but we won't swim in dirty water."

Meda said, "Okay," and we shrugged.

After physics, we studied biology, and, in that, Mother Redd instructed us closely. The farmhouse was not just a farmhouse; attached were a greenhouse and a laboratory with gene-parsers and splicers. The hundred hectares of woods, ponds, and fields were all Mother Redd's experiment, and part of it she let us work on. We were rebuilding the local habitat, reintroducing flora and fauna in a close facsimile to what had been there before the Exodus and the Gene Wars. Mother Redd was building beaver pods. She was letting us build pods of ducks.

Candace followed us to observe our latest version of duck: a clutch of ducklings that had been gengineered to share chemical duck memories, supposedly. There'd been success in modifying some mammals for chemical memories, but none for other classes of *Chordata*. We were trying to build a duck pod for the Science Fair at the end of the summer.

We'd released our ducklings — two different modified clutches — by a pond on the farm, and every morning we went and watched how they worked together.

Bola slid between the reeds while the rest of us hunched down and listened to his thoughts on the wind. The chemical memories were fragile and diffused over distance, but still we could understand what he was seeing and thinking if we concentrated.

"Where are the ducks?" Candace asked.

"Shh!"

"I don't see them."

"You're going to scare them!"

"Fine." The seven of her folded her arms across her chests.

An image flitted across from Bola of the ducklings poking at the edge of the pond with their bills. They were still covered in yellow fluff that wasn't quite feathers yet.

"See? One of them saw that patch of moss and the others came over right away!"

Maybe she signaled with sound.

Maybe it was random.

We'd mounted pheromone detectors around the pond to pick up any intrapod memory-sharing among the ducks. So far we'd measured nothing, so we were using observation to try to prove that the ducks were thinking as one.

"Here, ducky, ducky!"

"Candace!" Meda yelled.

The duck, about to climb into her hand, scattered with its siblings.

"What?"

"Will you leave our experiment alone?"

"I was just going to hold it."

"We want them to be wild, not bonded to a human."

"Fine." She turned and left, and, in disbelief, we watched her go. This was supposed to be where we spent *our* summers. This was our farm.

It's going to be a long summer, Strom sent.

We went swimming by ourselves that day, and, when we got back, we found Candace in the lab building her own duck.

Great.

"Look!" she cried. "I'm building a duck too!"

We didn't want to look, but I suggested we at least feign interest.

She showed us the gene sequence she was using, a modified string used with the beavers.

"We've tried that already," Meda said.

"Yeah, I know. I looked at your notes. But I'm adding a different olfactory sequence."

She looked at our notes! Our notes were on our locked desktop.

I advised calm, but Meda's face twitched with rage.

"Good luck," she grated, and we left.

In the barn, Meda railed, too angry for chemical thoughts. Her emotions filled the loft and caused the pigs Mother Redd was building to oink and stamp at us. "She's stealing our project, and she's stealing our notes! She has got to go!"

"She just wants to fit in," I said.

No one else was buying that.

"We should give her the benefit of the doubt," I said.

Manuel growled, and snaked his fury through the air.

"Anyone can enter the gengineering competition at the Fair," I said.

We need to do something.

What?

No one was looking at me.

We need more ducks.

How many more?

A lot.

They all turned to me, and I smelled the consensus like fresh bread. I could have held out, but I didn't. I wanted to win the competition too.

"Fine."

We snuck all the incubators we could find from the lab into the barn. Candace had already tagged a couple for herself. Then we built a dozen more from spare parts.

For the genes, we begged cutting-edge sequences from Professor Ellis at the Institute — mammalian, reptilian, avian — anything that we could jam into the anatine DNA. We cooked eggs instead of doing our chores. We even cooked while we studied. By the time we were done cooking, we had over a gross of duck eggs incubating.

We figured that at least some of them would show *something* interesting that we could report at the Fair. Candace couldn't keep up with our volume of output either. We had her licked, no problem.

"Which egg has which genes?"

"Um," Meda said. Mother Redd was surveying the rows of duck eggs. We'd hidden the incubators in the empty stalls, but you couldn't miss the electric wires we'd strung across the rafters.

One of her eyed the code violations and tsked.

"None of these are marked," she said.

"Um," Meda said.

"Where's your control variable? Where's your lab books?"

We didn't bother to "um." Embarrassment coursed among us. I expected a well-deserved lecture, but instead, Mother Redd, said, "Come on. There's someone in the house I want you to meet."

We climbed down from the loft and followed Mother Redd across the yard to the house. I tried to force down the I-told-you-so deep inside.

Strom and Bola both threw me guilty looks.

Some scientist we were.

Candace and another pod were in the great room. The other pod was a quintet, in his thirties. One of him was examining one of Candace with a stethoscope; another tapped another of her on the chest.

"Doctor Thomasin. This is Apollo."

Four pods in the great room, large though it was, made the place pretty crowded, especially when one of us was a seven. We hung against the wall and let Meda shake hands with Doctor Thomasin's interface.

"Ah, Apollo Papadopulos! A pleasure to meet someone with your strong lineage."

"Um, thanks, I guess."

Who cares what our lineage is? We had been designed and built, then raised in Mingo Creche. As far as we knew, our lineage was just the result of some scientists somewhere mixing eggs and sperm together.

"I'm Candace's doctor. I built her," he said.

Several of Candace blushed.

He was young to be a human gengineer. But he must have been good to have succeeded at a septet.

Compare his and Candace's face, Bola sent.

I saw it the way Bola saw it: Thomasin was a genetic donor for Candace. He could have been her biological father if she'd been born that way.

Weird. We had no father or mother, though we understood the concept. Mother Redd took the title, but she was more a mentor than an actual mother to us.

"Congratulations," Meda said, though it seemed odd even as she said it.

"Thank you."

He turned and started discussing something regarding nanosplicing with Mother Redd, so we snuck out with Candace on our heels.

"Isn't he great?" she said.

"You have a nice father," Meda said, before I could cut her off.

"He's not my dad! He's my doctor."

"You look —"

Meda!

"How're your ducks doing?" she asked.

"I think they're gonna hatch soon!" she said. Bola pointed out that it was a different one talking than before; she'd changed faces when we changed topics. Meda was always our face; she did all our interfacing with other pods. "I've been varying the heating and light to simulate a real mother sitting on the eggs."

"Great," Meda said.

Another of Candace spoke up. How many faces did she use? "Did you know we had our first period? That's why Doctor Thomasin was here."

"Um." It was our turn to flush. I felt Strom's shock. He turned away from Candace and looked across the yard at the barn. Meda, Quant, and I had all had our first menses. We'd all had to deal with it, as well as wet dreams and all the other drawbacks of male and female puberty. But some things were best left within the pod.

"You know what that means, don't you?"

"Yeah, I think so," said Meda. "We're half female, you know."

"No. That isn't what I mean. Doctor Thomasin made me so I can breed true."

"What?"

"You know why all pods are gengineered."

"Yes!"

"If I breed with another of my type of pod, I can birth six members of a septet."

"If you breed with a six male, one female septet?"

"Yes!"

"Why do you need a septet? You just need one male to inseminate all of you and one more female to carry the seventh."

They have a male, Manuel sent.

That is so gross.

"Biological diversity, of course!"

We all felt foggy, the smell of confusion circling among us.

"But —"

"If *you* breed," she went on, "you'll just have normal human singletons who will still have to be coalesced into a pod. It won't happen naturally. With *me*, my children will be *born* as a pod!"

"But —"

"It's so much more stable biologically, don't you see?"

"But —"

"Until pods can reproduce more pods, we're just a genetic dead-end. This is all part of Doctor Thomasin's work."

"But —"

"But what?"

"You're not a new breed. You're still human."

She stared at us with her fourteen green eyes. "I'm more than human, Apollo."

"So you can only have babies with a pod just like you, another of Dr. Thomasin's septets. You can't have babies with just anyone."

"Oh, I see what you're getting at. Don't be silly! Procreation doesn't have to follow love. I'll have children for the sake of the species regardless of who I bond with," Candace said.

"Did Doctor Thomasin pick your mate yet?"

"No. I guess not. Maybe."

She paused to think. This time we saw the interface cycle into the pack and another of the identical females take her place.

Why is she doing that? Manuel asked.

Identity crisis, Bola replied.

"Even if he has," the new face said, "that's fine. Besides, any mate will have to be one that he made. No one else has succeeded in building a septet."

"So you don't know other septets?" we asked.

"No. Not really. But there are others like me, I guess. And I'd mate with whomever was necessary, to propagate the species."

"Pods aren't a separate species. We're all human beings," we said.

"Of course we're a separate species!" she replied. "Pods are much better than singletons. It's obvious. And I'm much better than a sextet or a quintet or a quartet."

"We're all human," we said again.

"Well, *you* may be human, but I'm another species," she said, walking off.

I'll say.

We rotated the eggs every day. We measured the humidity with a wet bulb. We determined temperature with sensors that logged to our desktop. The damn alarms kept failing and waking us in the middle of the night. We couldn't just roll over and go back to sleep, since the ducklings might really be freezing to death. After fifteen days of incubation, we opened the vents on the incubators and lowered the temperature a half a degree.

Mother Redd's words had stung us, and we started keeping better records. We marked the eggs with their genome tag, at least the ones we could remember. We tracked temperature and humidity hourly and graphed the data.

We watched the brood by the lake meticulously, though the pheromone sensors never picked up a whiff of chemical thought and our lab books were line after line of "No sign of consensus."

We avoided Candace when we could, which was tougher than it would seem on a farm of over a hundred hectares. Mother Redd had given her chores that seemed to overlap ours.

Candace's arguments, however, were something we couldn't avoid. I found myself researching her ideas. She was wrong about a lot of things and right about a lot of things too.

The classical definition of "species" still stated that pods were human. If Meda, Quant, or I had a child with an unmodified human, the child would be human. We weren't a new species. However, we weren't entirely standard human either. We had been modified by our predecessors to have pads on our palms that could transfer chemical memories among our podmates. We had glands at our necks to send pheromonal emotions and crude thoughts. We had enhanced olfactory capability to decode the scents. Unless closely inspected, we would not look any different than a human from a century ago.

But the fact that we were a pod, that we functioned as a single being in the fabric of our society, indicated that we were a radically different *type* of social organization, created by our biological technology and artificially sustained. If there were no creche-system and no genetic modification of embryos to add pod traits, pod society would disappear in a few generations, replaced by normal humans. Candace was right; if the Overgovernment fell and society crumbled, then pods would fall apart. There would be no pods without constant social manipulation. We were the most advanced animal on the planet, but behind that façade was a framework of scaffolding and wires.

There were three million pods in the world, which amounted to just over ten million people. Three decades ago, there had been over ten billion humans on the planet. The cataclysm was far from over. We pods had inherited the Earth, not because we were superior, but because we had failed to leave or die or advance with the rest of the Community. It was a fragile ecosystem we had inherited. Our own biology was fragile, and perhaps more desperate than we knew.

We spoke to Mother Redd.

"How stable is our society?" Meda asked one evening as we cleaned up after dinner. Candace was out turning her duck eggs.

"We have a representative democracy implemented by consensus-formed legislation. It is more stable than most," she said.

"No. I mean biologically and societal. If we lost our scientific knowledge, what would happen?"

One of Mother Redd stopped her drying to look at us, while the other two continued with the pots.

"A sage question. I don't know, but I expect that the next generation of humans would be normal. Perhaps we could form pods; perhaps the genetic changes we have implemented would breed true."

"Do we know if they will?"

She smiled. "Perhaps you should do a literature search."

"I did! I couldn't understand the results." Biology wasn't our strongest subject. Physics and math suited us.

"Technology gives us our individuality. That is the problem. And given that, we will not willingly give up our individuality, we can't see the path back," Mother Redd said. "We have passed our own singularity, just as the Community did. And you have hit upon the greatest problem of our world. How do we propagate?"

There were some who said the Exodus — the near instantaneous vanishing of all the billions of Community members — was a technological singularity, the transmogrification of normal humans to posthumans. Mother Redd was saying that the pod society had created its own parallel singularity, one we could not reverse without losing our identity.

"Candace is the future, isn't she?"

"Maybe. Doctor Thomasin's ideas are radical. Perhaps reproducing septets are the answer. There are others researching it, including ethicists."

"Why?"

"If our society and our biology are unsound, we cannot allow it to advance."

"But —"

Candace bounded in then, shouting, "One of my ducklings is hatching!"

We all went out to watch the wet and lizard-like bird peck its way through the shell. Our mind was on Mother Redd's words, and we kept touching hands, swapping thoughts, as we considered them. I realized then, as we watched the ducklings hatch, that there were those who were considering the elimination of pod society and biology as a desirable path into the future.

Doctor Thomasin visited again the next day. He was visiting every week now, examining Candace for hours. That evening, after he left, Candace hadn't shown for dinner, so Mother Redd sent us up to fetch her.

"Candace?" Meda called, as she knocked on the door.

"She needs to check the temperature on the ducklings, too," said Bola. We pretended we didn't care about Candace's project, but clearly we did.

We just don't want the ducklings to die!

"Yes?" Her voice was soft, and male. When had her male component done anything but stay in the background?

Meda pushed open the door.

Candace was sprawled on the beds, her faces flushed, her shirts wet at the pits. The room reeked of heavy thinking.

"Are you okay?"

The male was the only one sitting. "We'll be okay."

"It's dinner time."

"We're not feeling too well. I think we'll pass."

One of the females opened her eyes.

Didn't she have green eyes before?
Yes.
"Do you want us to check on your ducklings?"
"What ducklings?" she asked.
"Your Science Fair project!"
She grasped wrists, consensing.
"Oh, right. Thanks."
"Are you all right?"
"I'm fine. Really."
Maybe Doctor Thomasin gave her a vaccination.
She's old enough to make her own vaccinations.
We ate quickly, then went out to the lab to feed and check Candace's ducks. Ours were still a few days from hatching.

Her ducks had a fine layer of down and weren't too noisy nor too active, so the temperature was probably okay. We dipped bits of bread in water and dropped the food in the hutches.
Don't let them imprint on us.
Why not? That would be funny.
Because they wouldn't survive in the wild if they did. They need to imprint on each other.
Like we are.
We shared a glance. We were indeed imprinted on each other.

Two days later, our own eggs began to hatch. Twelve hatched that day, which wasn't so bad. Twenty-five hatched the day after. Then fifty-some the day after that. We were too frazzled to notice when the last fifty hatched.

The barn suddenly became a duck maternity ward, with assembly lines for soaked corn meal, temperature and humidity checks, and bedding manufacture.

We quickly found that the chicken brooders we'd planned to use for the ducks were too small, and had to build half a dozen more out of plywood and chicken wire. We kept one as a spare so that we could move a clutch at a time to clean the brooders.

"We should have kept better track of the gene sequences that we used," Strom said. He was scooping duckling after duckling from one brooder to another. He held up one that had a lizard's tail attached to its fluffy bottom.

Bola looked into the emptied brooder and held his nose. We

all felt his revulsion though we couldn't actually smell what he smelled.

"How long until they can forage on their own?"

Six weeks.

Not soon enough.

We had so many ducklings to take care of that we couldn't spend a moment watching for pod-like behaviors. Candace, however, loved to stop by the barn and provide details of her latest experiment and success.

"I separate one duckling," she explained to us, "and feed it a bit of food. The other ducklings start quacking within seconds."

"They smell the food," we said.

"Maybe. But it also works for pain stimuli."

"Pain stimuli?"

"Sure. When I pinch one of the ducklings, the others start making noise."

"You're pinching your ducks?"

"Just a gentle pinch. Besides, it's for science!"

"Right."

"I've got video of the process. It's very compelling," she said.

"You'll have a good presentation at the Science Fair then," we said.

"You have an awful lot of ducks."

We turned and stared at her, all six of us.

"We know."

"This one has dalmatian spots."

"We know!"

Her eyes are green again.

She looks pale.

"Are you still sick?"

She swapped faces, something she did all the time now. "A little still. Allergies, maybe."

"What are allergies?"

"Reactions to air-borne particles and pollen. It used to be very common. Doctor Thomasin thinks I have it, and it just manifested when I came to the farm."

"Hopefully he'll fix that in the next batch of septets he cooks up," Meda said.

"Yeah, I guess."

As she walked away, Quant showed us memories of her when she first arrived. *She's grown fifteen centimeters in a month.*

Growth spurt.

Bigger boobs. This was followed by a pheromone leer from Manuel.

"Stop it."

There's something wrong with her. Changing interfaces, allergies, forgetting things.

The rest of my pod shrugged at me.

What can we do?

Talk to Mother Redd.

We didn't have time to ponder Candace's allergies and growth chart, and we never talked with Mother Redd. The ducklings needed their food.

Two weeks later, we started letting the ducklings roam the farmyard for food.

Look! They re-form into the same subgroups if we separate them!

I didn't understand until Bola shared his memory of what he saw. Bola's specialty was spatial, and, in an instant, I saw how the nearly identical ducklings coalesced into groups when we removed them from the brooder.

It could be the group they imprinted to.

Perhaps imprinting is a crude form of pod-building.

Strom scattered the ducklings and we watched them re-form into their subgroups. We marked a few of them with paint on their backs and did it again and again, showing how a single group of six re-formed every time.

It seemed that we were on to something.

Unfortunately, so were the six ducklings with the paint on their backs. They followed Strom wherever he went. When he broke them apart, they re-formed and headed straight back to his ankles.

They've imprinted on you.

"Didn't they imprint on themselves already?" Strom asked as the ducklings clustered on his feet.

Apparently not. Dad.
Strom answered that with a sardonic smile.

Once we moved the ducklings to the lake, we actually had time
to do our chores and study. One hundred and fifty ducks, less the six
that would not leave Strom's feet, made for a crowded, messy lake,
and we still had to drag out bags of bread so the birds wouldn't
starve.

Candace continued to have luck with her clutch of ducks, while
we showed mannerisms that could easily be attributed to other
ducklike behavior patterns.

"This fair project is gonna suck," Quant said. "We've got nothing."

Negative results are still results.

"Negative results don't get the blue ribbon."

Before we knew it, the Science Fair arrived and we drove
over to the county fairgrounds with Mother Redd and Candace
in the farm bus. We left the ducks, though Strom's six quacked
pitifully.

"Can't we take the aircar?" Meda asked. "And can't we drive?"

"No."

The county seat was a good 100 kilometers away, a mere hop in
an aircar, but two hours in the old bus. It was a tight fit with three of
us in it. We opened the windows, and that helped.

In the three decades since the Exodus, there'd been little need
for the roadway infrastructure. With the smaller global population,
farms that had been critical to feed the masses had gone fallow. We
passed orchards where the clear lines of trees were now the start
of a chaotic forest, carefully tended hybrids gone wild. It was a
bumpy ride, over a decaying road.

"It's hard to imagine what was here twenty years ago," we said
to Candace.

She looked at us blank-eyed. "Yeah," she said, though we didn't
think she knew what we'd said.

"Are you nervous?"

She shrugged.

"Do you want to borrow a brush?" we asked. Her hair was
straggly.

"I'm okay!" she shrilled. "Leave me alone."

Just nervous. We had butterflies too.

"Sorry."

One of Mother Redd was driving, and the other two glanced at us. Manuel shrugged to show our confusion at Candace's overreaction, and Mother Redd turned back to the road.

Bola read the schedule for the Fair, while we watched the countryside.

One hundred junior presentations.

That was a lot. That was one for every student pod in the county. He read off some of the presentation titles.

"Hyper-efficient Hydrogen Engines with Platinum Catalyst."

We did that in Third Class.

"Vaccination Study for Rhinovirus AS234."

The cure for the uncommon cold, Strom sent.

"Cold Fusion Yields in Superconducting Amalgams."

That'll never work.

Nothing with avian genetics except for us and Candace.

"Harumph."

On our side of the bus, we passed a large tract of overgrown houses, small three-story homes, with just a few meters between them.

"Look at those. So many people in such a small space."

Mother Redd said, "Each of those housed a family, just four or five people." She must have smelled our puzzlement. "It's hard to believe that the population of the Earth dropped by three orders of magnitude in the course of just a couple years. You two were born just after the most cataclysmic events in human history. Before the Exodus, pods and multi-humans comprised less than a tenth of a percent of humanity. Now we are the stewards of the entire world. It is a grave responsibility."

Quant slid across the aisle to catch a glimpse of the Ring. Candace flinched as Quant neared her, and glared at us. The sky was pale blue and cloudless, and there, arcing across its dome, was the Ring, the symbol of the Community and now a lifeless reminder of their former glory.

"They failed," said Candace, not her face, but the male. "They're a dead-end."

"So are we," Meda said. "According to your theories. We can't breed true."

Don't bait her, I sent. *She's not feeling well.*

Meda glared at me. "Sorry, Candace," she said. "Do you want to talk . . . or something?"

She didn't turn; her eyes remained on the Ring.

It isn't worth trying, Manuel sent bitterly.

I couldn't really argue with him, and we turned away to watch the desolate countryside slip by.

The Science Fair was held in a huge building that dated to the previous century. It was crowded, almost like school, pods shoulder to shoulder with other pods; it was nearly impossible to think with all the interference in the air.

We found the junior pavilion, registered, and then wandered the Fair. Our presentation wasn't until the afternoon, and Candace's was right before ours.

Stealing our thunder again.

The junior pavilion was packed at three o'clock that afternoon, and not just with us student pods. Mother Redd was there and so was Doctor Thomasin. We recognized several professors from the Institute, including Doctors Thackery and Charona.

We were in the biology section, so we sat through a dozen mice-in-maze and build-a-better-chlorophyll presentations until Candace's turn finally came.

She climbed the steps to the speaker's platform, looking pale and slouched.

She's still sick, we thought, touching palms so we didn't disturb anyone nearby.

She plugged in her cube and the screen behind her erupted with the title of her project.

She misspelled ruficollis!

"Shh!"

"Sorry."

"I-I-I . . ." Candace started. "I'm, I'm Candace Thurgood."

Then she changed interfaces in front of everyone and started again.

"I'm Candace Thurgood, and my presentation is . . ." She looked at the words on the screen behind her and paused.

She changed heads again, and this time I smelled the thoughts swirling around the auditorium.

"I'm Candace Thurgood and this is the title of my pr-pr-presentation."

She was shaking. Her face shone with sweat. She tapped the

cube and the page started showing video of her ducks. If she was supposed to be narrating what was happening, she wasn't. She was just standing there.

Oh, no. She's frozen up!

Sixty seconds passed, and, finally, Doctor Thomasin stood up.

Candace stared at him as he climbed the steps; I smelled his calming scent from where I was. But I smelled Candace's fear too. She ran before her doctor reached her, dashing down the steps on the other side of the platform, heading for the door.

Let's go! I sent. *We need to help her.*

"The next presenter is Apollo Papadopulos."

Our presentation is next!

But, she needs . . .

We reached consensus and walked up to the platform.

It was just us and Mother Redd on the bus back to the farm that evening.

"I want to help look," Meda had said as we climbed aboard.

"Doctor Thomasin is doing everything that needs to be done."

"Okay." I was sure she caught our sullenness, mine especially. It weighed heavy on me that we had not gone after Candace. For all her annoying habits, she was still a friend going through a crisis, and no blue ribbon was worth a friend's pain.

She's not our friend.

I turned on Manuel and let loose with my anger. He shirked back from me, but held his call for consensus.

Even if she isn't our friend, she still needs our help! I sent.

I threw my ribbon at him. It missed and sailed to the front of the bus. Mother Redd glanced at it, then at us, but I didn't care, even when Strom filled the air with embarrassment.

No one else stood up to help in that whole auditorium. No one. We should have.

More embarrassment from Manuel and the others.

She was scared. And she ran, because there was no one to help. And now she's missing!

Finally they agreed. We sat in silence the rest of the way home.

At the house, there was a taxi bill in the house email account that we saw when we walked in the door.

"She's here. She took a taxi," Meda said.

We checked her room, and the rest of the house, but there was nothing. We checked the barn and the labs. Mother Redd called Doctor Thomasin, and we started to check the lake, but stopped when Strom's duck quacked to be let out. Then the clutch rushed off toward the lake.

"Where are they going?"

"Apparently they aren't imprinted on Strom anymore."

Candace wasn't at the lake either. We stood, looking in six directions for some sign of her, some clue to where she was hiding.

I hope she's okay.

"Look!"

There coming out of the forest was a flock of ducks — our ducks; *all* our ducks.

"What are they doing?"

They waddled right up to us and began swarming around our legs.

"Oh, great. More imprinted ducks."

They began to quack, not individual dissonant sounds, but in unison: Quack, pause, quack, pause, quack, with the tempo slowly increasing.

Then they rushed back toward the forest. We followed.

A flocking pod?

We followed the flock into the brush, struggling to keep up with their orderly and low-to-the-ground progression. They were waddling through the brush easier than we were walking.

Ahead, the woods broke into a clearing, and there was Candace, lying on the ground.

"Oh no!"

She was pale, every one of her, clammy to the touch. Her breathing was shallow.

Look how thin her face seems.

Her skin looks like paper. We could see the blue veins at her temples.

The ducks clustered around us as we checked her.

Let's get her back to the house.

We found an easier way back, and carried her to the house, three at a time, leaving the male for last. We hated breaking her up like that, but she was unconscious, and we had to get her to the house.

"Goodness!" Mother Redd said when she saw us. She directed us to the lab. It jolted us to see her behaving as a medical doctor; we thought of the quartet she had been as a doctor. The trio she was was an ecologist. I guess she was still a doctor, even though she had lost a quarter of herself. I wondered how much medical training had been lost when her fourth had expired. "Lay her on the table. Get the rest of her."

When we got back with the next three, Mother Redd had already begun running tests on her: hormone levels, blood tests, gene maps. When we got back with the last one, Mother Redd was on the vid to Doctor Thomasin.

"Her gene map has deviated from her norm. She appears to have applied transmogrifying sequences to herself, as recently as a week ago. The result is shock, renal failure, and seizures. Possibly shared memory degradation. I've called an ambulance."

His face looked shocked. "Why would she do such a thing?"

He's misleading us.

I don't know why I thought it, but as soon as I did, the consensus formed behind it. None of us had had an inkling of his prevarication, but now it seemed obvious. We were built for intuitive leaps.

"I'll be there in half an hour."

Meda said, "How would her own doctor not know she's monkeying with her genome? She's been sick all summer." She said it softly, but loud enough for Mother Redd to hear.

One of her turned and looked directly at us. We met the gaze. She nodded slightly.

To Doctor Thomasin, she said, "The ambulance is already here. We're going to the county hospital."

"I'll meet you there." He signed off.

Mother Redd said, "Wait in the house, please."

"But —"

"Wait in the house."

We did, and, to pass the time, we ran searches on the legal and medical ramifications of postpartum genetic manipulation. Our children were built; it is a fact of our society. But the individual — the pod — is sacred, once it has pod-bonded. For his own reasons, Doctor Thomasin, who had built Candace, saw the need to change her still, to modify his creation.

It's wrong.

There was no doubt in our mind.

When the ambulance arrived, Mother Redd directed it to the Institute hospital instead of the county hospital.

*

Mother Redd relented and allowed us to come with her as she followed the ambulance in the aircar. She wouldn't let us drive, though we were checked out on the car, and had about ten times better reflexes than she did.

We sat in the waiting room while she consulted with the physicians at the Institute. We'd been in the Institute hospital only rarely; we'd had a single anatomy class the year before in one of the auxiliary buildings. Most of our classes were in engineering, science, and we were rarely sick enough that we couldn't fix ourselves.

It was late, but we couldn't sleep. We kept checking with the floor AI to see if Candace's condition had changed. It hadn't.

Manuel gazed out the window at the dark buildings. The Institute looked desolate, and I doubted that anyone was on campus, certainly not students, and probably not teachers. Fall classes didn't start for another three weeks.

A door banged. We looked up, and there was Doctor Thomasin, pushing out of the stairwell. He'd run up the six flights of stairs instead of waiting for the elevator.

Without thinking, we formed up behind Strom, our defensive position.

He did a double take.

"I thought you took her to the county hospital," he said.

"We know what you did. Mother Redd knows," Meda said.

"What are you talking about?" Now that we knew how he lied, his bluffs were transparent.

"You have been modifying her DNA all summer. You almost killed her."

"It's some problem with the DNA, sure. But I didn't modify it. Where is she?"

He tried to step around us, but we repositioned ourselves in front of him.

"Get out of my way, student!"

"We're not your student. We're human beings with full rights just like Candace. But then you don't care about that, do you?"

For a second, I thought that he was going to strike at us, and I felt Strom determine the best defense, the best offense. For a moment, we were a matrix of possibility, a phalanx of potential.

"Gorgi, you better go."

It was Mother Redd, standing in the doorway of Candace's room.

"I just need to see her."

"No."

"I was just trying to make her *perfect*, don't you see?"

"I see."

"I have a responsibility to the future," he said. "We need to become a viable species. We're on the cusp. We're as near extinction as we've ever been, and I have got to save us!"

"Saving the human race through Candace is not your responsibility," Mother Redd said.

"You were responsible for Candace," we said. "But you failed." We were suddenly aware of all our responsibilities, to our friends, to ourselves, to our ducks: duties and relationships interwoven.

Doctor Thomasin looked at me. "I wanted to build something as good as you," he said.

"You did."

He held our look and we smelled his thoughts. After a moment, he nodded, then turned away.

We saw Candace once after she left the hospital. She came to the farm, and we showed her the duck pod: one hundred and fifty-seven ducks forming a single entity. We told her that we were going to publish a paper, and we wanted her to be coauthor.

"No, thanks. I don't have anything to contribute."

We nodded, embarrassed. We'd forgotten that she'd lost a huge amount of pod memory with the last genetic modification.

"What are your plans then?"

"I'm thinking about medical school. I'll have to start a lot of studies from scratch, but I think I'd like to do that."

"That sounds good. You'll do well."

Her interface and Meda hugged, and then she finished packing her stuff. On the air pad, we said another awkward good-bye. We made sure she had our ID so she could write, but I had a feeling that she wasn't going to. I doubted that she wanted to remember this summer at all.

We watched the aircar rise and depart.

Time to check the ducks.

It's always time to check the ducks.

SINGLETONS IN LOVE

M oira was sick, in bed with a cough, so Mother Redd shooed us out of the house. At first we just hung around the front yard, feeling weird. We'd been separated before, of course; it was part of our training. In space, we'd have to act as a quint or a quad or even a triple, so we practiced all our tasks and chores in various combinations. That had always been practice, and we'd all been in sight. But Moira was *separated* now, and we did not like it.

Manuel climbed the trellis on the front of the house, skirting the thorns of the roses that grew among the slats. As his hands caught the sill and pulled his head just over the edge, his hind legs caught a rose and bent it back and forth to break it off.

I see Moira, he signed.

"Does she see you?" I asked, aloud since he couldn't see me, and the wind took the pheromones away leaving half-formed thoughts.

If Manuel could see Moira and she could see him, then it would be enough for all of us. We'd be linked.

Just then the window flew open, and one of Mother Redd was there. Manuel fell backwards, but he righted himself and landed on the grass, rolling, sprawling until he was among the rest of us, the red rose still clutched in his toes.

I touched his shoulder, breathed him a thought, and he offered the rose to Mother Redd. I saw immediately it wasn't going to work.

"You *five*, go and play somewhere else today. Moira is sick, and it won't do us any good for you to get sick too. So vamoose!" She slammed the window shut.

We thought it over for a few seconds, then tucked the rose in my shirt pocket, and started down the front path.

We didn't have Moira, but we did have license to vamoose, and that meant the forest, the lake, and the caves if we were brave enough. Moira would have advised caution. But we didn't have Moira.

The farm was a hundred acres of soyfalfa that Mother Redd worked with three triples of oxalope. The ox were dumb as rocks by themselves, but when you teamed them up, they could plow and seed and harvest pretty much by themselves. The farm was a good place to spend the summer. Lessons took up our mornings, but they weren't as rigorous as during the school year when we studied all day and most of the night at the 'Drome. At school we learned to sleep in shifts, so four or five us were always awake to study. We'd spent summers at the Redds for sixteen years, since we were out of the creche.

Baker Road led west toward Worthington and the 'Drome or east toward more farms, the lake, and the woods. We chose east, Strom first like always when we were in the open with Manuel as a scurrying point, never too far away. I followed Strom, then Quant, and Bola last. Moira would have been after Quant. We felt a hole there, which Bola and Quant filled by touching hands too often.

Within a mile, we were relaxed, though not indifferent to Moira's absence. Bola was tossing rocks onto the tops of old telephone poles. He didn't miss once, but we didn't feel any pride in it. It was just a one-force problem, and Bola lobbed the rocks for diversion, not practice.

We passed a microwave receiving station, hidden in a grove of pine trees, just off from the road. Its paraboloid shape reflected the sun as it caught the beamed microwaves from the Ring. The Earth was dotted with such dishes, each providing a few megawatts to the Earth-side enclaves, more than we could use, now that the Community had left. But they had built the Ring and the solar arrays and the dishes as well. Decades later and the dishes still worked.

I could see the Ring clearly, even in the brightness of the morning, a pale arch from horizon to horizon. At night, it was brighter, its legacy more burdensome to those of us left behind.

Bola started tossing small twigs into the incoming microwave beam, small arcing meteoroids that burst into flame and then ash. He bent to pick up a small toad.

I felt the absence of Moira as I put my hand on his shoulder and sent, *No living things*.

I felt his momentary resentment, then he shrugged both physically and mentally. He smiled at my discomfort at having to play Moira while she was gone. Bola, in whom was hardwired all the Newtonian laws of force and reaction, had a devilishness in him. In us. Our rebel.

Once, the instructors had divided us up as two triples, male and female, and broken up our classmates as well along the same lines. The objective was an obstacle course, no gravity, two miles of wire, rope, and simulated wreckage, find the macguffin first. All other teams were enemy, no rules.

They hadn't given us no-rules games too often; we were young then, twelve. Mostly they gave us a lot of rules. That time was different.

Strom, Bola, and Manuel found it first, by chance, and instead of taking it, they laid in wait, set traps and zero-gee deadfalls. They managed to capture or incapacitate the other four teams. They broke three arms and a leg. They caused two concussions, seventeen bruises, and three lacerations, as they trussed up the other teams and stowed them in the broken hut where the macguffin sat.

Finally we came along, and the fiberglass mast zinged past, barely missing us.

As Moira, Quant and I swam behind cover, we heard them laughing. We knew it was them and not some other team. We were too far for pheromones, but we could still smell the edges of their thoughts: proud and defiant.

Moira yelled, "You get your asses out here right now!"

Strom popped out right away. He listened to Moira first no matter who else was there. Then Manuel left the hut.

"Bola!"

"Forget it!" he yelled. "I win." Then he threw the macguffin at us and Quant snatched it out of the air.

"Who's 'I'?" Moira yelled.

Bola stuck his head out. He looked at the five of us for a moment, then signed, *Sorry*. He kicked over and we shared everything that had happened.

The teachers didn't split us up like that again.

Baker Road swerved around Lake Cabbage like a giant letter C. It was a managed ecomite, a small ecosystem with gengineered inhabitants. The Baskins ran it for the Overdepartment of Ecology, trying to build a viable lake ecosystem with a biomass of twenty-five Brigs. It had everything from beavers to snails to mosquitoes. Lots of mosquitoes.

The adult beavers turned a blind eye to our frolicking in the lake, but the babies found us irresistible. They had been bioed to birth in quads, their thoughts sliding across the pond surface in rainbows like gasoline. We could almost understand, but not quite. In the water our own pheromones were useless, and even our touch pads were hard to understand. If we closed our eyes and sank deep enough, it was like we weren't a part of anything, just empty, thoughtless protoplasm.

Strom didn't like to swim, but if we were all in the water, he'd be too, just to be near. I knew why he was uncertain of the water, I knew his anxiety as my own, but I couldn't help deriding us for having such a fear.

We took turns with the beavers pulling rotten logs into the water and trying to sink them in the mud, until the adult beavers started chiding us with rudimentary hand signs, *No stop work. Messing home. Tell Baskins.*

We swam to shore and dried ourselves in the afternoon sun. Manuel climbed an apple tree and gathered enough ripe fruit for all of us. We rested, knowing that we'd have to head back to the farm soon. Strom balled up some memories.

For Moira, he sent.

Quant came alert and we all felt it.

A house, she sent. *That wasn't there before.*

She was up the bank, so I waited for the thoughts to reach me through the polleny humid air. It was a cottage, opposite the lake from the beavers' dam, half hidden among the cottonwoods which shed like snowfall during the summer.

I searched our memory of the last time we'd been at the lake, but none of us had looked over that way, so it may have been there since last year.

The Baskins put in a summer house, Strom sent.

Why, when their normal house is just a mile away? Manuel replied.

It could be a guest house, I sent.

Let's go find out, Bola sent.

There was no dissent, and in the shared eagerness I wondered what Moira would have said about our trespassing.

She's not here.

We leaped between flat stones, crossing the small stream that fed the lake.

Beneath the cottonwoods, the ground was a carpet of threadbare white. The air was cold through our damp clothes. We stepped across and around the poison oak with its quintuple leaves and ivy its triplet.

An aircar stood outside the cottage, parked in a patch of prairie, shaded by the trees.

Conojet 34J, Manuel sent. *We can fly it*. We had started small craft piloting the year before.

The brush had been cleared from the cottage to make room for long flower gardens along each wall. Farther from the house, in the full sun, was a rectangle of vegetables: I saw tomatoes, pumpkins, squash, and string beans.

"It's not a summer house," I said, because Quant was out of sight. "Someone's living here."

Manuel skirted the vegetable garden to get a good look at the aircar. I felt his appreciation of it, no concrete thought, just a nod toward its sleekness and power.

"What do you kids think you're doing in my garden?"

The door of the cottage flew open with a bang, and we jumped, as a man strode toward us.

Strom took a defensive posture by reflex, his foot mashing a tomato plant. I noted it, and he corrected his stance, but the man had seen it too, and he frowned. "What the hell!"

We lined up before the man, me at the head of our phalanx, Strom to my left and slightly behind, then Quant, Bola, and Manuel behind him. Moira's spot to my right was empty.

"Stepping on my plants. Who do you think you are?"

He was young, dressed in a brown shirt and tan pants. His hair was black and he was thin-boned, almost delicate. I assumed he was the interface for his pod, but then we saw the lack of sensory pads on his palms, the lack of pheromone ducts on his neck, the lack of any consensus gathering on his part. He had said three things before we could say a single word.

"We're sorry for stepping on your plant," I said. I stifled our urge to waft conciliatory scent into the air. He wouldn't have understood. He was a singleton.

He looked from the plant to me and to the plant again.

"You're a fucking cluster," he said. "Weren't you programmed with common courtesy? Get the hell off my property."

Bola wanted to argue with the man. This was Baskin land. But I nodded, smiling. "Again, we're sorry, and we'll leave now."

We backed away, and his eyes were on us. No, not us, on me. He was watching me, and I felt his dark eyes looking past my face, seeing things that I didn't want him to see. A flush spread across my cheeks, hot suddenly in the shade. The look was sexual, and my response . . .

I buried it inside me, but not before my pod caught the scent of it. I clamped down, but Manuel's then Quant's admonition seeped through me.

I dashed into the woods, and my fellows had no choice but to follow.

The undertones of their anger mingled with my guilt. I wanted to rail, to yell, to attack. We were all sexual beings, as a whole and as individuals, but instead, I sat apart, and if Mother Redd noticed, none of her said a word. Finally, I climbed the stairs and went to see Moira.

"Stay over there," she wheezed.

I sat in one of the chairs by the door. The room smelled like chicken broth and sweat.

Moira and I are identical twins, the only ones in our pod. We didn't look that much alike anymore, though. Her hair was close-cropped; mine was shoulder-length auburn. She was twenty pounds heavier, her face rounder where mine was sharp. We looked more like cousins than identical sisters.

She leaned on her elbows, looked at me closely and then flopped down onto the pillow. "You don't look happy."

I could have given her the whole story by touching her palm, but she wouldn't let me near her. I could have sketched it all with pheromones, but I didn't know if I wanted her to know the whole story.

"We met a singleton today."

"Oh, my." The words were so vague. Without the chemical sharing of memories and thoughts, I had no idea what her real emotions were, cynical or sincere, interested or bored.

"Over by the Baskins' lake. There was a cottage there . . ." I built the sensory description, then let it seep away. "This is so hard. Can't I just touch you?"

"That's all we need. Me, then you, then everybody else, and by the time school starts in two weeks, we're all sick. We can't be sick." We started training for the zero-gee classes that fall. Everybody said this was when the real culling began, when the teachers decided which pods were viable enough to crew our starships.

Moira nodded. "A singleton. Luddite? Christian?"

"None of those. He had an aircar. He was angry at us for stepping on his tomato plants. And he . . . looked at me."

"He's supposed to look at you. You're our interface."

"No, he *looked* at me. Like a woman."

Moira was silent for a moment. "Oh. And you felt . . ."

The heat crept up my cheeks again. "Flushed."

"Oh." Moira contemplated the ceiling. She said, "You understand that we are individually sexual beings and as a whole —"

"Don't lecture me!" Moira could be such a pedant, one who never threw a stone.

She sighed. "Sorry."

"'Sokay."

She grinned. "Was he cute?"

"Stop that!" After a pause, I added, "He was handsome. I'm sorry we stepped on his tomato plant."

"So take him another."

"You think?"

"And find out who he is. Mother Redd has got to know. And call the Baskins."

I wanted to hug her, but settled for a wave.

Mother Redd had been a doctor, and then one of herself had died, and she'd chosen another field instead of being only part of the physician she had been. She — there had been four cloned females, so she was a she any which way you looked at it — took over the farm, and in the summer boarded us university kids. She was a kind woman, smart and wise, but I couldn't look at her and not think how much smarter she would have been if she were four instead of just a triple.

Mother Redd was in the greenhouse, watering, picking, and examining a hybrid cucumber.

"What is it, sweetie? Why are you alone?" asked the one look-ing at the cucumber under the light microscope.

I shrugged. I didn't want to tell her why I was avoiding my pod, so I asked, "We saw a singleton over by the Baskins' lake today. Who is he?"

I could smell the pungent odor of Mother Redd's thoughts. Though it was the same cryptic, symbolic chaos that she always used, I real-ized she was thinking more than a simple answer would warrant. Finally, she said, "Malcolm Leto. He's one of the Community."

"The Community! But they all . . . left." I used the wrong word for it; Quant would have known the technical term for what had become of two-thirds of humanity. They had built the Ring, built the huge cybernetic organism that was the Community. They had ad-vanced human knowledge of physics, medicine, and engineering exponentially until finally they had, as a whole, disappeared, leaving the Ring and the Earth empty, except for the fraction of humans who either had not joined the Community or had not died in the chaos of the earth-bound Gene War.

"This one was not on hand for the Exodus," Mother Redd said. That was the word that Quant would have known. "There was an accident. His body was placed into suspended animation until it could be regenerated."

"He's the last member of the Community, then?"

"Practically."

"Thanks." I went to find the rest of my pod. They were in front of the computer, playing virtual chess with John Michelle Grady, one of our classmates. I remembered it was Thursday night, Quant's hobby night. She liked strategic gaming.

I touched Strom's hand and slipped into the mesh of our thoughts. We were losing, but then Grady was good and we had been down to four with me running off alone. Was that a trace of resentment from my fellows? I ignored it and dumped what I had learned from Mother Redd about the singleton.

The chess game vanished from our thoughts as the others fo-cused on me.

He's from the Community. He's been in space.

Why is he here?

He missed the Exodus.

He's handsome.

He's been in space. Zero-gee. On the Ring.

We need to talk to him.
We stepped on his tomato plant.
We owe him another.
Yes.
Yes.

Strom said, "We have some plants in the greenhouse. I can transplant one into a pot. As a gift." Strom's hobby was gardening.

"Tomorrow?" I asked.

The consensus was immediate. *Yes.*

This time we knocked instead of skulked. The tomato plant we had squashed had been staked, giving it back its lost structure. There was no answer at the door.

"Aircar's still here."

The cottage was not so small that he couldn't have heard us.

"Maybe he's taking a walk," I said. Again we were out without Moira. She was better, but still sick.

"Here, I think." Strom indicated a spot at the end of the line of tomato plants. He had brought a small spade and began to dig a hole.

I took out paper from my backpack and began to compose a note for Malcolm Leto's door. I started five times, wadding up each after a few lines and stuffing the garbage back in my bag. Finally I settled on "Sorry for stepping on the tomato plant. We brought a new one to replace it."

There was a blast, and I turned in a crouch, dropping the note and pen. Fight or flight pheromones filled the air.

Gunshot.
There. The singleton. He's armed.
Posturing fire.
I see him.
Disarm.

This last was Strom, who always took control of situations like this. He tossed the small shovel to Bola on his right. Bola threw the instrument with ease.

Malcolm Leto stood under the cottonwoods, the pistol pointed in the air. He had come out of the woods and fired the shot. The shovel slammed into his fingers and the pistol fell.

"Son of a bitch!" he yelled, hopping and holding his fingers. "Goddamn cluster!"

We approached. Strom faded into the background again and I took the lead.

Leto watched us, looked once at the pistol but didn't move to grab it.

"Come back to wreck more of my tomato plants, did you?"

I smiled. "No, Mr. Leto. We came to apologize, like good neighbors. Not to be shot at."

"How was I to know you weren't thieves?" he said.

"There are no thieves here. Not until you get to the Christian Enclave."

He rubbed his fingers, then smirked. "Yeah. I guess so. You bunch are dangerous."

Strom nudged me mentally, and I said, "We brought you a tomato plant to make amends for the one we squashed."

"You did? Well, now I'm sorry I startled you." He looked from the cottage to me. "You mind if I pick up my gun? You're not going to toss another shovel at me, are you?"

"You're not going to fire another shot, are you?" The words were more flip than was necessary for the last member of the Community, but he didn't seem to mind.

"Fair's fair." He picked up his pistol and walked through us toward the cottage.

When he saw the last tomato plant in the line, with the fresh dirt around it, he said, "Should have put it on the other end."

I felt exasperation course through us. There was no pleasing this man.

"You know my name. So you know my story?" he asked.

"No. We just know you're from the Ring."

"Hmmm." He looked at me. "I suppose the neighborly thing to do is to invite you in. Come on."

The cottage was a single room, with an adjoining bathroom and kitchenette. The lone couch served as Leto's bed. A pillow and blanket were piled at one end.

"Suddenly crowded in here," Leto said. He put the pistol on the table, and sat on one of the two kitchen chairs. "There's not enough room for all of you, but then there's only one of you anyway, isn't there." He looked at me when he said it.

"We're all individuals," I said quickly. "We also function as a composite."

"Yeah, I know. A cluster."

Ask him about the Ring. Ask him about being in space.

"Sit," he said to me. "You're the ringleader, aren't you."

"I'm the interface," I said. I held out my hand. "We're Apollo Papadopulos."

He took my hand after a moment. "Who are you in particular?"

He held my hand and seemed to have no intention of releasing it until I answered the question. "I'm Meda. This is Bola, Quant, Strom, and Manuel."

"Pleased to meet you, Meda," he said. I felt the intensity of his gaze again, and forced my physical response down. "And the rest of you."

"You're from the Ring," I said. "You were part of the Community."

He sighed. "Yes, I was."

"What was it like? What's space like? We're going to be a starship pilot."

Leto looked at me with one eyebrow raised. "You want to know the story."

"Yes."

"All right. I haven't told anybody the whole story." He paused. "Do you think it's just a bit too convenient that they put me out here in the middle of nowhere, and yet nearby is one of their starship pilot clusters?"

"I assume you're a test for us." We had come to assume everything was a test.

"Precocious of you. Okay, here's my story: Malcolm Leto, the last, or first, of his kind."

You can't imagine what the Community was like. You can't even comprehend the numbers involved. Six billion people in communion. Six billion people as one.

It was the greatest synthesis humankind has ever created: a synergistic human-machine intelligence. I was a part of it, for a while, and then it was gone, and I'm still here. The Community removed itself from this reality, disappeared, and left me behind.

I was a biochip designer. I grew the molecular processors that we used to link with the Community. Like this one. It's grafted onto the base of your skull, connects to your four lobes and cerebellum.

We were working on greater throughput. The basics were already well established; we — that is myself, Gillian, and Henry —

were trying to devise a better transport layer between the electro-chemical pulses of the brain and the chips. That was the real bottle-neck: the brain's hardware is slow.

We were assigned lines of investigation, but so were a hundred thousand other scientists. I'd go to sleep and during the night, some-one would close out a whole area of research. The Community was the ultimate scientific compilation of information. Sometimes we made the cutting-edge discovery, the one that changed the di-rection for a thousand people. Usually we just plodded along, up-loaded our results and waited for a new direction.

The research advanced at a pace we as individuals could barely fathom, until we submerged ourselves in the Community. Then, the whole plan was obvious. I can't quite grasp it now, but it's there in my mind like a diamond of thought.

It wasn't just in my area of technology, but everywhere. It took the human race a century to go from horses to space elevators. It took us six months to go from uncertainty cubes to Heisenberg AND gates, and from there twenty days to quantum processors and Nth-order qubits.

You're right. It does seem like a car out of control, barrelling down a hill. But really, it was the orderly advancement of science and technology, all controlled, all directed by the Community.

We spent as much time as we could in the Community, when we worked, played, and even slept. Some people even made love while connected. The ultimate exhibitionism. You couldn't spend all your time connected, of course. Everyone needed down time. But being away from the Community was like being half yourself.

That's what it was like.

Together, in the Mesh, we could see the vision, we could see the goal, all the humans of Earth united in mind, pushing, pushing, pushing to the ultimate goal: Exodus.

At least I think that was the goal. It's hard to remember. But they're all gone now, right? I'm all that's left. So they must have done it.

Only I wasn't with them when it happened.

I don't blame Henry. I would have done the same thing if my best friend was screwing my wife.

Gillian, on the other hand.

She said she and I were soulmates, and yet when I came out of the freezer twenty-six years later, she was as gone as the rest of them.

You'd think in the Community things like marriage would be obsolete. You'd think that to a group mind, group sex would be the way to go. It's odd what people kept separated from the Community.

Anyway, Henry spent a week in wedge 214 with another group of researchers, and while he was gone, Gillian and I, sorta communed on our own. I'd known Gillian almost as long as I'd known Henry. We were first wave emigrants to the Ring and had been friends back in Ann Arbor when we were in school. We'd met Gillian and her friend Robin in the cafeteria. He liked them tall, so he took Gillian. Robin and my relationship lasted long enough for her to brush her teeth the next morning. Gillian and Henry were married.

She was a beautiful woman. Auburn hair like yours. Nice figure. Knew how to tell a joke. Knew how to . . . Well, we won't go there.

I know, best man screwing the bride. You've heard that pitiful tale before. Well, maybe you clusters haven't. Trust me. It's pitiful.

I'm sure it didn't take Henry long to find out. The Community sees all.

But he took a long time plotting his revenge. And when he did — bam! — that was the end for me.

We were working on some new interfaces for the occipital lobe, to enhance visualization during communing, some really amazing things. Henry ran the tests and found out our stuff was safe, so I elected to test it.

It's funny. I remember volunteering to try it out. But I don't remember what Henry said before that, how he manipulated me into trying it. Because that's what he did all right.

The enhancements were not compatible with my interface. When I inserted them, the neural pathways in the cerebral cortex fused. The interface flash froze. I was a vegetable.

The Community placed my body into suspended animation while it rebuilt my brain. All things were possible for the Community. Only some things take a while, like rebuilding a brain. Six months later, the Exodus occurred, and still the machinery of the Ring worked on my brain. For twenty-six years, slowly with no human guidance, it worked on my brain, until three months ago. It revived me, the one human left over from the Exodus.

Sometimes I still dream that I'm a part of it. That the Community is still there for me to touch. At first those were nightmares, but now they're just dreams. The quantum computers are still up there, empty, waiting. Maybe they're dreaming of the Community as well.

It'll be easier this time. The technology is so much farther along than it was before. The second Exodus is just a few months away. I just need a billion people to fuel it.

On my hobby night, instead of painting, we spent the evening on the Net.

Malcolm Leto had come down the Macapa space elevator two months before, much to the surprise of the Overgovernment body in Brazil. The Ring continued to beam microwave power to all the receivers, but no one resided on the Ring or used the space elevators that lined the equator. No one could, not without an interface.

The news of Leto's arrival had not made it to North America, but the archives had interviews with the man that echoed his sentiment regarding the Community and his missing out on the Exodus. There wasn't much about him for a couple weeks until he filed suit with the Brazilian court for ownership of the Ring, on the basis of his being the last member of the Community.

The Overgovernment had never tried to populate the Ring. There was no need to try to overcome the interface access at the elevators. The population of the Earth was just under half a billion. The Gene Wars killed most of the people that hadn't left with the Exodus. It'd taken the Overgovernment almost three decades to build the starships, to string its own nanowire-guided elevators to low earth orbit, to build the fleet of tugs that plied between LEO and the Lagrange points.

No one used the quantum computers anymore. No one had an interface or could even build one. The human race was no longer interested in that direction. We were focused on the stars and on ourselves. All of us, that is, except for those in the enclaves that existed outside of, yet beneath, the Overgovernment.

The resolution to Leto's case was not published. It had been on the South American court docket a week ago, and then been bumped up to the Overgovernment Court.

He's trying to build another Community.

He's trying to steal the Ring.

Is it even ours?
He's lonely.
We need Moira.
He wants us to help him. That's why he told us the story.
He didn't tell us. He told Meda.
He likes Meda.

"Stop it!" I made fists so that I couldn't receive any more of their thoughts. They looked at me, perplexed, wondering why I was fighting consensus.

Suddenly, I wasn't looking at me. I was looking at them. It was like a knife between us. I ran upstairs.

"Meda! What's wrong?"

I threw myself onto the floor of Moira's room.

"Why are they so jealous?"

"Who, Meda? Who?"

"Them! The rest of us."

"Oh. The singleton."

I looked at her, hoping she understood. But how could she without sharing my thoughts?

"I've been reading your research. Meda, he's a potential psychotic. He's suffered a great loss and awoke in a world nothing like he remembers."

"He wants to rebuild it."

"That's part of his psychosis."

"The Community accomplished things. It made advancements that we don't understand even decades later. How can that be wrong?"

"The common view is that the Exodus was a natural evolution of humankind. What if it wasn't natural? What if the Exodus was death? We didn't miss the Exodus, we escaped it. We survived the Community just like Leto did. Do we want to suffer the same fate?"

"Now who's talking psychosis?"

"The Overgovernment will never allow him back on the Ring."

"He's alone forever then," I said.

"He can go to one of the singleton enclaves. All of the people there live alone."

"He woke up one morning and his self was gone."

"Meda!" Moira sat up in bed, her face gray. "Hold my hand!" As she held out her hand, I could smell the pheromones of her thoughts whispering toward me.

Instead of melding with her, I left the room, left the house, out the door into the wet night.

A light was on in the cottage. I stood for a long time, wondering what I was doing. We spend time alone, but never in situations like this. Never outside, where we can't reach each other in an instant. I was miles away from the rest of me. Yet Malcolm Leto was farther than that.

It felt like half the things I knew were on the tip of my tongue. It felt like all my thoughts were garbled. But everything I felt and thought was my own. There was no consensus.

Just like Malcolm had no consensus. For singletons, all decisions were unanimous.

It was with that thought that I knocked on the door.

He stood in the doorway, wearing just short pants. I felt a thrill course through me, one that I would have hidden from my pod if they were near.

"Where's the rest of your cluster?"

"At home."

"Best place for 'em." He turned, leaving the door wide open. "Come on in."

There was small metal box on his table. He sat down in front of it. I noticed for the first time the small, silver-edged circle at the base of his skull, just below his hairline. He slipped a wire from the box into the circle.

"That's an interface box. They're illegal." When the Exodus occurred, much of the interface technology that was the media for the Communion was banned.

"Yeah. But not illegal anymore. The OG repealed those laws a decade ago, but no one noticed. My lawyer pried it loose from them and sent it up." He pulled the wire from his head and tossed it across the box. "Useless now."

"Can't you access the Ring?"

"Yes, but it's like swimming in the ocean alone." He looked at me sidelong. "I can give you one, you know. I can build you an interface."

I recoiled. "No!" I said quickly. "I . . ."

He smiled, perhaps the first time I'd seen him do it. It changed his face. "I understand. Would you like something to drink? I've got a few fix'ns. Sit anyway."

"No," I said. "I'm just . . ." I realized that for a pod's voice, I wasn't articulating my thoughts very well. I looked him in the eye. "I came to talk with you, alone."

"I appreciate the gesture. I know being alone is uncomfortable for you."

"I didn't realize you knew so much about us."

"Multiples were being designed when I was around. I kept up on the subject," he said. "It wasn't very successful. I remember articles on failures that were mentally deficient or unbalanced."

"That was a long time ago! Mother Redd was from that time and she's a great doctor. And I'm fine —"

He held up a hand. "Hold on! There were lotsa incidents with interface technology before . . . well, I wouldn't be here if it was totally safe."

His loneliness was a sheer cliff of rock. "Why are you here, instead of at one of the singleton enclaves?"

He shrugged. "There or in the middle of nowhere, it would be the same." He half-smiled. "Last of a vanished breed, I am. So you're gonna be a starship captain, you and your mingle-minded friends."

"I am . . . We are," I replied.

"Good luck, then. Maybe you'll find the Community," he said. He looked tired.

"Is that what happened? They left for outer space?"

He looked puzzled. "No, maybe. I can almost . . . remember." He smiled. "It's like being drunk and knowing you should be sober and not being able to do anything about it."

"I understand," I said. I took his hand. It was dry and smooth.

He squeezed once and then stood up, leaving me confused. I was sluggish on the inside, but at the same time hyperaware of him. We knew what sex was. We'd studied it, of course. But we had no experience. I had no idea what Malcolm was thinking. If he was a multiple, part of a pod, I would.

"I should go," I said, standing.

I was hoping he'd say something by the time I got to the door, but he didn't. I felt my cheeks burn. I was a silly little girl. By myself I'd done nothing but embarrass my pod, myself.

I pulled the door shut and ran into the woods.

"Meda!"

He stood black in yellow light at the cottage door.

"I'm sorry for being so caught up in my own troubles. I've been a bad host. Why don't you —" I reached him in three steps and kissed him on the mouth. Just barely I tasted his thoughts, his arousal.

"Why don't I what?" I said after a moment.

"Come back inside."

I — they — were there to meet me the next morning as I walked back to the farm. I knew they would be. A part of me wanted to spend the rest of the day with my new lover, but another wanted nothing more than to confront myself, rub my nose in the scent that clung to me, and show me . . . I didn't know what I wanted to prove. Perhaps that I didn't need to be a composite to be happy. I didn't need them, us, to be a whole person.

"You remember Veronica Proust," Moira said, standing in the doorway of the kitchen, the rest of us behind her. Of course she would take the point when I was gone. Of course she would quote precedent.

"I remember," I said, staying outside, beyond the pull of the pheromones. I could smell the anger, the fear. I had scared myself. Good, I thought.

"She was going to be a starship captain," Moira said. We remembered Proust; she'd been two years ahead of us. Usually pods sundered in the Creche, with time to reform, but Veronica had broken into a pair and a quad. The pair had bonded and the quad had transferred to engineering school, then dropped out.

"Not any more," I said. I pushed past them into the kitchen, and as I did so, I balled up the memory of fucking Malcolm and threw it at them like a rock.

They recoiled. I walked upstairs to our room and began packing my things. They didn't bother coming upstairs and that made me angrier. I threw my clothes into a bag, swept the bric-a-brac on the dresser aside. Something glinted in the pile, a geode that Strom had found one summer when we flew to the desert. He'd cut it in half and polished it by hand.

I picked it up, felt its smooth surface, bordering the jagged crystals of the center. Instead of packing it, I put it back on the dresser and zipped up my bag.

"Heading out?"

Mother Redd stood at the door, her face neutral.

"Did you call Dr. Khalid?" He was our physician, our psychologist, perhaps our father.

She shrugged. "And tell him what? You can't force a pod to stay together."

"I'm not breaking us up!" I said. Didn't she understand? I was a person, by myself. I didn't need to be part of a *thing*.

"You're just going to go somewhere else by yourself. Yes, I understand." Her sarcasm cut me, but she was gone before I could reply.

I rushed downstairs and out the front door so that I wouldn't have to face the rest of me. I didn't want them to taste my guilt. I ran the distance to Malcolm's cottage. He was working in his garden and took me in his arms.

"Meda, Meda. What's wrong?"

"Nothing," I whispered.

"Why did you go back there? We could have sent for your things."

I said, "I want an interface."

It was a simple procedure. He had the nanodermic, and placed it on the back of my neck. My neck felt cold there, and the coldness spread to the base of my skull and down my spine. There was a prick, and felt my skin begin to crawl.

"I'm going to put you under for an hour," Malcolm said. "It's best."

"Okay," I said, already half asleep.

I dreamed that spiders were crawling down my optic nerve into my brain, that earwigs were sniffing around my lobes, that leeches were attached to all my fingers. But as they passed up my arms, into my brain, a door opened like the sun dawning, and I was somewhere else, somewhen else, and it all made sense with dream-like logic. I understood why I was there, where the Community was, why they had left.

"Hello, Meda," Malcolm said.

"I'm dreaming."

"Not anymore," his voice said. It seemed to be coming from a bright point in front of me. "I've hooked you up to the interface box. Everything went fine."

My voice answered without my willing it to. "I was worried that my genetic mods would cause a problem." I felt I was still in my dream. I didn't want to say those things. "I didn't mean to say that. I think I'm still dreaming." I tried to stop speaking. "I can't stop speaking."

I felt Malcolm's smile. "You're not speaking. Let me show you what's possible within the Community."

He spent hours teaching me to manipulate the reality of the interface box, to reach out and grasp it like my hand was a shovel, a hammer, sandpaper, a cloth.

"You do this well," he said, a brightness in the gray-green garden we had built in an ancient empty city. Ivy hung from the walls, and within the ivy sleek animals scurried. The dirt exuded its musty smell, mingling with the dogwoods that bounded the edge of the garden.

I smiled, knowing he could see my emotion. He could see all of me, as if he was a member of my pod. I was disclosed, though he remained aloof.

"Soon," he said, when I pried at his light, and then he took hold of me and we made love again in the garden, the grass tickling my back like a thousand tongues.

In the golden aftermath, Malcolm's face emerged from within the ball of light, his eyes closed. As I examined his face, it expanded before me, I fell into his left nostril, into his skull, and all of him was laid open to me.

In the garden, next to the ivy-covered stone walls, I began to retch. Even within the virtual reality of the interface box, I tasted my bile. He'd lied to me.

I had no control of my body. The interface box sat on the couch beside me as it had when we'd started, but pseudo reality was gone. Malcolm was behind me — I could hear him packing a bag — but I couldn't will my head to turn.

"We'll head for the Belem elevator. Once we're on the Ring, we're safe. They can't get to us. Then they'll have to deal with me."

There was a water stain on the wall, a blemish that I could not tear my eyes away from.

"We'll recruit people from singleton enclaves. They may not recognize my claim, but they will recognize my power."

My eyes began to tear, not from the strain. He'd used me, and I, silly girl, had fallen for him. He had seduced me, taken me as a pawn, as a valuable to bargain with.

"It may take a generation. I'd hoped it wouldn't. There are cloning vats on the Ring. You have excellent stock, and if raised from birth, you will be much more malleable."

If he had me, part of one of the starpods, he thought he'd be safe from the Overgovernment. But he didn't know that our pod was sundered. He didn't realize how useless this all was.

"All right, Meda. Time to go."

Out of the corner of my eye I saw him insert the connection into his interface, and my legs lifted me up off the couch. My rage surged through me, and my neck erupted in pheromones.

"Jesus, what's that smell?"

Pheromones! His interface controlled my body, my throat, my tongue, my cunt, but not my mods. He'd never thought of it. I screamed with all my might, scent exploding from my glands. Anger, fear, revulsion.

Malcolm opened the door, fanned it. His gun bulged at his waist. "We'll pick up some perfume for you on the way." He disappeared out the door with two bags, one mine, while I stood with the interface box in my outstretched arms.

Still I screamed, saturating the air with my words, until my glands were empty, spent, and my autonomous nervous system silenced me. I strained to hear something from outside. There was nothing.

Malcolm reappeared. "Let's go." My legs goose-stepped me from the cottage.

I tasted our thoughts as I passed the threshold. My pod was out there, too far for me to understand, but close.

With the last of my pheromones, I signaled, Help.

"Into the aircar," Leto said.

Something yanked at my neck and my body spasmed as I collapsed. I caught sight of Manuel on the cottage roof, holding the interface box.

Leto pulled his gun and spun.

Something flew by me, and Leto cried out, dropping the pistol. I stood, wobbly, and ran into the woods, until someone caught me, and suddenly I was in our mesh.

As my face was buried in Strom's chest and my palms squeezed against his, I watched with other eyes — Moira's eyes! — as Leto scrambled into the aircar and started the turbines.

He's not going far.

We played with his hydrogen regulator.

Also turned his beacon back on.

Thanks for coming. Sorry.

I felt dirty, empty. My words barely formed. I released all that had happened, all that I had done, all my foolish thoughts into them. I expected their anger, their rejection. I expected them to leave me there by the cottage.

Still a fool, Moira chided. Strom touched the tender interface jack on my neck.

All's forgiven, Meda. The consensus was the juice of a ripe fruit, the light of distant stars.

All's forgiven.

Hand in hand in hand, we returned to the farm, sharing all that had happened that day.

STRENGTH ALONE

I am strength.

I am not smart, that is Moira. I can not articulate, like Meda. I do not understand the math that Quant does, and I cannot move my hands like Manuel. My world is not the fields of force that Bola sees.

If to anyone, you would think I am closest to Manuel; his abilities are in his hands, in his dexterity. But his mind is jagged sharp; he remembers things and knows them for us. Trivial information that he spins into memory.

No, I am closest to Moira. Perhaps because she is everything I am not. She is as beautiful as Meda, I think. If she were a singleton, she would still be special. If the pod were without me, I think, they would be no worse off. If I were removed, the pod would still be Apollo Papadopulos, and still be destined to become the starship captain we were built to be. We are all humans individually, and I think my own thoughts, but *together*, we are something different, something better, though my contribution is nothing like the others'.

When I think this, I wall it off. Bola looks at me; can he smell my despair? I smile, hoping he cannot see past my fortifications. I touch his hand, our pads sliding together, mixing thoughts, and send him a chemical memory of Moira and Meda laughing as children, holding hands. They are three- or four-years-old in the memory, so it is after we have pod-bonded, prior to Third State, but still in the creche. Their hair is auburn, and it hangs from their heads in baloney curls. Moira has a skinned knee, and she isn't smiling as largely as Meda. In the memory, in the distant past, Meda reaches for Bola, who reaches for Manuel, who reaches for Quant, who touches my hand, and we all feel Meda's joy at seeing the squirrel in the meadow, and Moira's anger at falling down and scaring it off. Here on the mountain, there is a pause in our consensus, as everyone catches the memory.

Moira smiles, but Meda says, "We have work to do, Strom."

We do, I know we do. I feel my face redden. I feel my embarrassment spread in the air, even through our parkas.

Sorry. My hands form the word, as the thought passes among us.

We are somewhere in the Rocky Mountains. Our teachers have dropped us by aircar, here near the tree line, and told us to survive for five days. They have told us nothing else. Our supplies are those we could gather in the half-hour they gave us.

For seven weeks, we and our classmates have trained in survival methods: desert, forest, jungle. Not that we will see any of these terrains in space. Not that we will find climates of any kind whatsoever, except for deadly vacuum, and that we know how to survive.

On the first day of survival training, our teacher, Theseus, had stood before us and screamed in volleying bursts. He was a duo, the most basic form of pod, just two individual humans bound together.

"You are being taught to think!" yelled Theseus on the left.

"You are being taught to respond to unknown environments, under unknown and strenuous conditions!" continued Theseus on the right.

"You do not know what you will face!"

"You do not know what will allow you to survive and what will kill you!"

Two weeks of class instruction followed, and then, week after week, we had been transported to a different terrain, a different locale, and shown what to do to survive. But always with Theseus nearby. Now, in our final week, we are alone, just the students on this mountain.

"Apollo Papadopulos! Cold-weather survival! Twenty kilos per pod member! Go!" one of Theseus had yelled at us from our dormroom doorway.

Luckily, the parkas were in the closet of our dorm room. Luckily, we had a polymer tent. Hagar Julian has only canvas coats with no insulation, we know. They will have a harder time of it.

Twenty kilograms is not a lot. I carry sixty kilos of it myself, and distribute the rest to my podmates. In the aircar, we note that

Hagar Julian and Elliott O'Toole have split the load evenly among themselves; they are not playing to their strengths.

Strom! Once again, Meda chastises me, and I jerk my hands away from Manuel's and Quant's, but they can still smell the embarrassment pheromones. I can not stop the chemical proof of my chagrin from drifting in the frigid air. I reach again for my place in the consensus, striving to be an integral part of the pod, trying to concentrate. Together, we can do anything.

Chemical thoughts pass from hand to hand in our circle, clockwise and counterclockwise, suggestions, lists, afterthoughts. Some thoughts are marked by their thinker, so that I know that it is Bola who has noted the drop in temperature and the increased windspeed, which causes us to raise the priority of shelter and fire. Consensus forms.

We have to rig our shelter before dark. We have to start a fire before dark. We have to eat dinner before dark. We have to dig a latrine.

The list passes among us. We reach consensus on decision after decision, faster than I can reason through some of the issues: I add what I can. But I trust the pod. The pod is me.

Our hands are cold; we have removed our gloves to think. In the cold of the Rockies our emotions — the pheromones that augment our chemical thoughts — are like lightning, though sometimes the wind will whisk the feeling away before we can catch it. With gloves on our touch pads and parkas over our noses and neck glands, it is hard to think. Almost, it is like working alone, until we finish some sub-task and join for a quick consensus, shedding gloves.

"Strom, gather wood for the fire," Moira reminds me.

I am strength, so the tasks that require broad shoulders fall to me. I step away from the others, and I am suddenly cut off from them: no touch, no smell. We practice this, being alone. We were born alone, yet we have spent our youth, from first state to fourth state, striving to be a single entity. And now we practice being alone again. It is a skill. I look back at the other five. Quant touches Moira's hand, passing a thought, some shared confidence. The spike of jealousy must be the face of my fear. If they have thought something important, I will know it later, when we rejoin. For now, I must act alone.

We have chosen an almost-flat tract of land in a meager grove of wind-stunted pines. The rock slopes gently away into a V shape, a catch for wind and snow. The shallow ravine drops sharply into a ledge of rock, the side of a long valley of snow drifts and rock that the aircar passed over as we arrived. Above us is a sheer wall, topped with a mass of snow and ice. I can not see the peak from here; we are many hundreds of meters below it. Stretching in either direction are lines of jagged mountain tops, their white faces reflecting the afternoon sun. Clouds seem to bump against their western sides.

The snow is thin enough on the ground here that we can reach the rocky ground beneath it. The trees will shelter us from the wind and provide support for the tent lines, we hope. I walk down the gentle slope, along the line of pines.

We have no axe, so I must gather fallen logs and branches. This will be a problem. We cannot have a good fire with half-decayed logs. I file the thought away for later consensus.

I find a sundered pine branch, thick as my forearm, sticky with sap. I wonder if it will burn, as I drag it back up to the camp. I should have climbed up to find wood, I realize, so that I could drag it down to the camp. It is obvious now and would have been obvious before if I had asked for consensus.

I drop my wood in the clearing the others have made and start to arrange it into a fireplace. I draw stones into a U shape, the open end facing the wind down the mountain for a draft. The stones at the sides can be used for cooking.

Strom, that is where the tent will go!

I jump back, and I realize that I had been working without consensus, making decisions on my own.

Sorry.

Confused and embarrassed, I drag the stones and wood away from the tent clearing. I think that I am not well, but I suppress that as I sweep snow away and place the stones again.

We decide to gauge our classmates' progress, so I climb the trail above the tree line to see how the rest of our class is doing. There are five of us on survival training, all of us classmates, all of us familiar with each other and in competition. It is how it has always been among us.

Each is destined to be a starship pilot. Or so we think. How many master pilots can the *Consensus* have? Not more than one. Will there be other ships for the rest of us to pilot? None are being built. Will the rest of us be allowed a lesser rank or position in the ship? Would we want it? These are questions we have asked ourself often.

How the rest are doing is important.

Above the tree line and to the west half a kilometer away, I see our classmate Elliott O'Toole's tent already up, with the pod inside it. To the east, a few hundred meters away, I see another student — Hagar Julian — working in the snow, instead of on an area of rocky slope. They are digging into a drift, perhaps to form a snow cave. They will have a long time to dig, I think. Hollowing out a space for six will expend much energy. They can't have a fire.

The other two pods are hidden in the trees beyond Hagar Julian. I cannot determine their progress, but I know from experience that our greatest competition will be from Julian and O'Toole.

I return and pass the others memories of what I have seen.

We have begun pitching the tent, using the nearby pine trees to support it. We have no ground spikes, removed from the packs to reach the twenty-kilogram-per-person limit. There are many things we have removed to make our weight limit, but not matches. I kneel to start the fire.

Strom!

The scent call is sharp on the crisp wind. The pod is waiting for me to help pull and tie the tent support lines; they have consensed without me. Sometimes they do that. When it is expedient. I understand; they can reach a valid consensus without me easily enough.

We pull the spider-silk lines taut, and the tent stretches into place, white on white, polymer on snow, a bubble of sanctuary, and, suddenly, our shelter is ready. The thrill of success fills the air, and Bola enters and comes out again, smiling.

"We have shelter!"

Now dinner, Manuel sends.

Dinner is small bags of cold, chewy beef. Once we have the fire going, we can cook our food. For now, it's cold from the bag. *If we were really on our own in the mountains, we would hunt for our food*, I send. The image of me carrying the carcass of an elk over my shoulders makes Moira laugh. I mean it as a joke, but then I count the bags of jerky and dried fruit. We will be hungry by the end of the test. It is my job to see to the safety of the pod, and I feel bad that we did not pack more food.

"Another test," Bola says. "Another way to see if we're good enough. As if this mountain is anything like another world! As if this will tell them anything about us!"

Sometimes we feel manipulated. I know what Bola means. Everything we face is another test to pass. There is no failure, just success, repeated, until it means nothing. When we fail, it will be catastrophic.

"We can watch the sunset," I say.

We have loosened hoods and gloves in the tent, though it is still just above freezing inside. But the difference between inside and out becomes even more severe as the sun now hides behind the western peaks. The sunset is colorless, the sunlight crisp and white. It reflects off the bottom of the Ring, making the slim orbital torus brighter than it is at noon. Wispy clouds slide across the sky, moving fast, and I note to the others the possibility of snow. Before our five days on the mountain are over, we will see more snow, that is certain. Perhaps tonight.

Elliott O'Toole has managed to light a fire, and we smell the burning wood. He probably hasn't finished his tent, but he has a fire. The smell of roasted meat drifts on the wind.

"Bastard!" Quant says. "He has steak!"

We don't need it.

I want it!

I say, "This is only about surviving, not luxury."

Bola glares at me, and I sense his anger. He is not alone. I cave before this partial consensus and apologize, though I don't know why I do. Meda has told me that I hate strife. I assume that everyone does. We are six and I am one. I bow to the group consensus, as we all do. It is how we reach the best decision.

With dinner finished and night upon us, we finish what chores we can outside: a fire, if we can start it, and a latrine. Manuel and I work on the fire pit, moving stones, breaking tender, building up a steeple of wood. The wind is too strong, I realize, for a fire tonight. The flatness of the plateau made it a good place for a tent, but the wind whips down the ravine. The tent ropes sing.

We smell fear on the wind, child pheromones, and I think one of us is in danger, but then we smell it as a foreign fear: one of our classmates is in danger. Then, as the wind dies for a moment, we hear the heavy breathing of someone running through the snow drifts. The pod condenses around me, as it does in times of crisis. We touch, assess, but we have only the smell and the sound to base consensus on.

I move forward to help whoever it is. I smell the caution in the air, but ignore it. Now is the time to help. Sometimes we spend too much time being cautious, consensing on things. I would never share such thoughts.

It is one of Hagar Julian, just one. I don't know her name, but she is running in the cold, her hood down, her head exposed. She doesn't see me, but I catch her in my arms and stop her. In her terror, she would have run past us into the dark night, perhaps over the cliff.

The smell of her is alien. I force the hood over her head. The head is a heat sink; you must always keep it covered in the cold. That and the hands. Perhaps this is why the instructors have chosen the mountains for our final test; the organs that make us a pod are nearly useless in the cold.

"What is it? What's happened?" I ask.

She is heaving, releasing fear and nothing else. I don't know how much of her fear is from being separated from her self or from something else that has happened. I know that Julian is a close-knit pod. They seldom separate.

The night is black. I can't see O'Toole's fire, nor Julian's ice cave anymore. It is a miracle that she reached us.

I pick her up over my shoulder and carry her slowly through the snow drifts to the open area around our tent. She is shivering. I push through the questions of my pod. Now is not the time for questions. Quant pulls open the tent for me.

Snow falls out of the woman's gloves. I take them off her hands, which are blue, and exchange them for my own. I check her boots and coat for more snow, and brush it out. By then, the rest of my pod has joined me, and I use them to access our survival instruction.

Hypothermia.

The shivering, the disorientation, and the lack of response are all signs of body-temperature loss. Maybe some of the disorientation is from being separated from her pod.

Hospitalize.

One of us glances at the transceiver in the corner of the tent. It is defeat to use it.

"Where's the rest of you?" I ask.

She doesn't even look at me.

I take a coil of spider-silk rope and begin cinching it to my coat.

No.

"Someone has to see what happened to the rest of her," I say. *We can't separate now.*

I feel the pull to stay and consense. To wait for rescue.

"Keep her warm. Huddle close to her. Don't warm her quickly."

I pull the tent door open and close it, but not before Quant follows me out.

"Be careful. It's beginning to snow," she says. She takes the rope end from me and ties it to one of the D-rings on our tent. The end wraps around itself and knits itself together.

"I will."

The wind whips the snow into my face, needles of cold. I hunch over and try to make out Julian's tracks from her camp to ours. Snow has already started to fill in the prints. The moon glooms through scudding gray clouds, making the mountainside gray on gray. I continue, making this task my focus, so that I do not remember that I have left my pod behind. Even so, I count the steps I take, marking the distance of our separation.

I have to keep my face up to follow the tracks, and when I do, the wind freezes my nasal passages. The cold is like a headache. There is no smell on the wind, no trace of Hagar Julian.

The woman has walked across a slide of broken slate. Her footprints end on the jagged mounds of rock. I pause, knowing I am close to their campsite; they had been no farther than three hundred meters when I'd spied them.

I turn my back to the wind and tuck my head a moment. Still the snow finds a way into my eyes. The weather is worsening. I take a moment to memorize the feeling, the sting, the sound for later.

I trudge on across the slate, slipping once and falling to one knee. The slate ends in a river of gray snow. I don't remember seeing this before. Then I realize that it's new. The snow bank above has collapsed, burying Hagar Julian's campsite in an avalanche.

I stand there, ignoring the cold.

I take one step onto the snow and it crunches under my boots. An hour ago, this area was clear, and now it is under a flood of rocks and snow. I look up at the mountain, wondering if more will follow, but swirling snow obscures it.

I climb up the side of the hill of snow. Ten meters into the slide, I see a flap of cloth, half covered. I pull at it, but the rest is buried too deep for me to extract it.

"Julian!" Sifting flakes muffle my voice. I yell again for my classmate.

I hear no reply, though I doubt I would have heard anything either, unless the speaker was next to me.

I pull my hands out of my pockets, hoping to catch a whiff of something on the pads on my palm. Nothing but needling cold. I am cocooned in a frozen, white mask. As isolated as the one part of Julian who made it to our camp.

I turn back. We will need digging equipment and many people to find Julian's corpses. I do not see how they could have survived. Except for the one.

But then I see something black against the gray of the swept snow. Just a smudge that catches my eye as I turn.

I stop and take one step up the slope, and I see that it is an arm. I am clawing at the ice, snow, and rock, hoping, praying that below is a breathing body.

I scoop huge armfuls of snow behind me and down the slope, tracing the arm down, reaching a torso, and finding a hooded head. I try to pull the body out, but the legs are still trapped. I pause, and slowly pull back the hood. Male, a part of Julian, face and cheeks splotchy pink, eyes shut. The snow swirls around his mouth, and I think that it means he's breathing, but I can't be sure. I pass my palm under his nose, tasting for any pheromone, but there is nothing. I feel for a pulse.

Nothing.

My mind struggles to remember how to revive a victim with a stopped heart. Moira would know. Quant would know. They all would know. Alone, I know nothing.

I panic and just grab the body about its torso and heave backward, trying to free it from the snow. I pull but the body remains embedded. I sweep at the man's hips, feeling the futility of it. I'm useless here. Strength is useless now. I don't know what to do.

But now he is free to his knees, and I pull again. He comes free in a cascade of snow. I stagger under his weight, then lay him down.

I kneel next to him, trying to remember. My hands are red and stinging, and I stuff them into my pockets, angry at myself. I am useless alone. Moira would . . . Then it comes to me, as if Moira had sent it to me in a ball of memory. Compressions and breathing. Clear the throat, five compressions and a breath, five and a breath. Repeat.

I push at the man's coat, unsure if I am doing anything through the bundles of clothing. Then I squeeze his nose and breathe into his mouth. It's cold, like a dead worm, and my stomach turns. Still I breathe into his mouth and then compress again, counting slowly.

The cycle repeats, and his chest rises when I breathe into him. I stop after a minute to check the pulse. I think I feel something, and I wonder if I should stop. Is that his own diaphragm moving or just the air I've forced into him leaving his lungs, like a bellows?

I can't stop, and bend to the task again.

A cough, a spasm, but a reaction, and then he is breathing. Alive!

The pulse is fast and reedy, but there.

Can he move? Can I get him back to the tent to warm him?

Then I hear the whine of the aircar, and realize I won't have to carry him. Help is on the way. I fall back into the snow. Alive!

The whine of the car rises, and I see its lights coming up the valley, louder, too loud. I wonder at the fragility of the layers of snow on the ridges above and if the shrill engines will cause another wave of snow.

I can do nothing but wait. The aircar reaches the edge of our camp and lowers itself behind the trees.

The engines die, but the sound does not. There is a deep rumble all around me, and I know what is happening. I know that the snow is coming down the mountain again. The first avalanche has weakened the ledge of snow.

I stand, unsure. Then I see the wave of white in the aircar spotlights.

"No!" I take one step toward the camp, then stop. The Julian here will die if I leave him.

The snow slams into my pod's campsite, flies up where it strikes the trees surrounding the tent. I see the twirling lights of the aircar thrown up into the air. My pod! My body tenses, my heart thudding. I take one step forward.

The rumble is a crashing roar now. I look up at the snow bank above me, fearing that ice is about to bury us. But the outcropping of snow that has fed the first avalanche has uncovered a jagged ledge that is shielding us. The river of snow flows twenty meters away, but comes no nearer. If it had taken me, I would not have cared. My pod is in the torrent, and my neck tightens so that I can barely breathe.

I see something snaking on the ground and think that the snow is chasing me uphill. I am jerked off my feet.

Dragged across the rock and ice, I realize that it is the line attached to my waist. The other end is attached to our tent, and it is dragging me down the mountain. Five, ten, twenty meters, I struggle to untie the rope, to find the nodule that will untwine the knot, but my chaffed, useless hands can grip nothing.

I fall on my face, feel something smash into my nose, and in a daze I slide another few meters, closer to the avalanche. I thought it was slowing, but this close, it still seems to be a cascade of flying rock and snow.

I stand, fall, then stand again and lunge toward the avalanche, hoping to slacken the rope. I run, and I see a tree, at the edge of the river. I dive at it, haul myself around it once, then once more, wedging the line.

I pull and brace, and then the line is steel-taut.

My legs are against the trunk and I am standing against it, holding on, or else I'll be sucked into the vortex with my pod.

For a moment, the desperation whispers the question: how bad would that be? Is it better to die with my pod or live on alone, a singleton, useless? A moment before, I had been ready for the avalanche to take me too.

But I cannot let go. A part of Julian still needs my help. I hold on, listening for the rumble to lessen.

Seconds, and then a minute, then two. Still I hold on, and the storm of snow slows, and the pull on my arms decreases. Sweat rolls down my cheeks, though the air is frigid. My arms shake. When the rope finally falls limp, I slump down and lie below the tree, unable to move. I am spent, and it takes minutes for me to recover enough to remove the rope. My fingers are raw and weak, and the spider-silk will not separate. Finally, the end unknits.

I stand and fall.

I shove my face into the snow to cool it, then realize how foolish that is. I stand again, and this time I make several steps before my legs shudder out from beneath me.

The snow is as soft as a feather bed, and I resolve to rest just a few moments.

It would be easy to sleep. So easy.

But I don't. The man is still on the mountain. A singleton just like me. He needs me. He needs someone strong to carry him down the mountain.

I glance at the rope. At the other end is my pod. How could they have survived the torrent? I stand and take one step onto the debris, but a cascade of tumbling snow drives me back. The snow ridge above is still unstable. I wipe my eyes with my raw hands, then turn and follow the trail I made as I was dragged down the mountain. It is easy to see the trail of blood I have left. I touch my lip and nose; I hadn't realized I'd been bleeding.

The Julian is still there, still breathing. And I cry aloud to see him alive, bawling like a child. I am anything but strength.

"What . . . what are you . . . crying for?"

The Julian is looking up at me, his teeth chattering.

"I'm crying because we're alive," I say.

"Good." His head drops back into the snow. His lips are blue and I know the chattering is a response to the cold and a precursor to hypothermia. We need to get him medical attention. We . . .

I am thinking as if I am still a pod. I cannot rely on Manuel to help me lift him. I cannot rely on Bola to show me the quickest way down. I am alone.

"We need to go."

"No."

"You need to get to warmth and medical aid."

"My pod."

I shrug, unsure how to tell him. "They're buried under here."

"I smell them. I hear them."

I sniff. Maybe there's a trace of thought on the wind, but I can't be sure.

"Where?" I ask.

"Nearby. Help me up."

I pull him to his feet and he leans against me, groaning. We take a step; he points.

I see the flap of cloth buried in the snow that I had noticed before.

He had survived several minutes in the snow. Perhaps his pod is trapped below. Perhaps they are in an air pocket, or in their hollowed-out snow cave.

I kneel and begin to scoop away the snow around the cloth flap. He rolls next to me and tries to help clear. But he slumps against a mound of snow, too weak, and watches me instead.

The cloth is a corner of a blanket and it seems to go straight down.

For a while the going is all ice, and I claw at it with my numb fingers, unable to move more than a handful at a time. Then I am through that and the digging is easier.

Clods of snow bounce off my hood, and I am leery of more snow falling on top of us. I take a moment to push away all the snow from around us.

Two more scoops and suddenly the snow gives way, and I see a cavern of ice and snow and canvas, and within the cave, three bodies, three more of Julian. They are alive, breathing, and one is conscious. I pull them one by one out of the cave and put them next to their podmate.

The two that are conscious cling to each other and lie there, gasping for breath, and I am so tired I want to collapse into the hole.

I check each one for hypothermia, for breaks and contusions. One of them, a female, has a broken arm, and she winces as I move her. I have a loop of rope on my belt, not spider-silk, and I bind her arm across her chest. The fourth is unhurt.

"Wake up," I say. "Come on." The fourth one opens his eyes, begins to cough. The third, with the broken arm, is still unconscious. I gently slap her face. She comes awake and lunges, then gasps as the pain hits her. Her pod, what is left of it, surrounds her, and I step back, fall back on the snow, looking up into the sky. I realize that the snow is coming down harder.

"We have to get down the mountain," I say. If another aircar comes, it will start another avalanche. If another avalanche comes, we are doomed.

They don't seem to hear me. They cling together, their teeth chattering.

"We have to get down the mountain!" I yell.

Despair floods the air, then a stench of incoherent emotions. The four are in shock.

"Come on!" I say and pull one of them up.

"We can't . . . our . . . podmates," he says, words interspersed with chemical thoughts that I don't understand. The pod is degenerating.

"If we don't go now, we will die on this mountain. We have no shelter, and we are freezing."

They don't reply, and I realize they would rather die than break their pod.

"There's four of you," I say. "You are nearly whole."

They look among themselves, and I smell the consensus odor. Then one of them turns away angrily. They can't do it. No consensus.

I collapse onto the snow, head down, and watch the snow swirl between my legs. I am one who was six. The fatigue and despair catch me, and my eyes burn.

I am strength; I do not cry. But still my face is washed with tears for my pod, buried in the snow. My face is fire where the tears crawl. A splash falls into the snow and disappears.

We will sleep here in despair and die before the morning.

I look at them. I must get them down the mountain, but I don't know how to do it. I wonder what thoughts Moira would pass me if she were here. She would know what to do with these four.

They are four. Mother Redd was a four. Our teachers are fours. The Premier of the Overgovernment is a four. Why do they cry when they are no worse off than our greatest? I am allowed to cry, but not them.

I stand up.

"I've lost my pod too, and I am only one!" I shout. "I can cry, but *you* can't! You are four. Get up! Get up, all of you!"

They look at me like I am mad, so I kick one, and she grunts. "Get up!"

Slowly they rise, and I grin at them like a maniac.

"We will reach the bottom. Follow me. I am strength."

I lead them across the snow to the spill of the other avalanche. With the nanoblade on my utility knife, I cut a length of the rope that disappears into the snow. At the other end of the rope is my dead pod. I take a step onto the gray avalanche; perhaps I can dig them out as I have dug out Hagar Julian. I hear a rumble as the snow shifts beneath me. More snow tumbles down the mountain. It has not settled yet; more snow could fall at any moment. And I know that it has been too long now. If they are trapped under the snow, their air is gone. If I had turned at once, if I had followed the rope when the avalanche had stopped, perhaps I could have saved them, but I didn't think of that. Quant wasn't there to remind me of the logical choice. Bitterness seeps through me, but I ignore it. There are the four who are left to take care of.

I hand each of them a section of the rope, looping us together. Then I lead them down the mountain. It is nearly black, save the light reflected by the moon that splashes upon the snow. The ledge and gaping holes are obvious. It is the hidden crevasses that I fear. But every step we take is better than lying asleep in the snow.

Our path leads to a drop, and I back us up quickly, not wanting the four to gaze into the abyss. I begin to wonder if there is no way down. We were dropped off by aircars that morning. Perhaps the location is so remote that aircars alone can reach it. Perhaps there is no path down the mountain. Or worse, we will pass through the path of an avalanche and die under the piles of snow.

The snowfall is steady now, and in places we are up to our hips. But the effort is warmth. To move is to live, to stop is sleep and death.

The trees all look alike, and I fear we are stumbling in circles, but I know that if we continue downward we will reach the bottom. I see no signs of animal or human. The snow is pristine until we tramp through it.

The line jerks and I turn to see that the last in the line, the one with the broken arm, has fallen.

I go to her and lift her onto my shoulder. The weight is nothing to the ache I already feel. What is another sixty kilograms? But our pace is slower now.

Still the others lag, and I allow rests, but never enough to let them sleep, until the fatigue is too much and I let my eyes droop.

Oblivion for just a moment, then I start awake. To sleep is to die. I rouse the four.

The four. I am thinking of them no longer as a pod, but as a number. Will they refer to me as the singleton? The one? There may be a place for a quad in society. But there is no place for a singleton.

After the Exodus of the Community, after the wars that followed, it was the pods who had remained in control. The pods are now the care-takers of the earth, while the normal humans who are left — the singletons — are backward and luddite. The pods, just a biological experiment, a minority before, are the ones who survived cataclysm. Only now I am no longer a pod; I am a singleton, and the only place for me is in the singleton enclaves. Alone I can not function in pod society. What could I contribute? Nothing. I look at the four. There is one thing I can contribute. These four are still a pod, still an entity. I can bring them to safety.

I stand up. "Let's go," I say, but gently. They are too empty to protest. I show them how to put the snow to their lips and drink it as it melts.

"We need to go." The one with the broken arm tries to walk. I walk beside her with a hand on her good arm.

The pine forest gives way to denser deciduous trees, and I feel warmer, though the temperature cannot have risen much. But the trees think it's warmer, so I think so too. The snow is less heavy here. Perhaps the storm is letting up.

"This mountain," I say, "is less than seven kilometers high. We can walk seven kilometers easily, even in the cold. And this is all down hill."

No one laughs. No one replies.

The wind is gone, I notice, and with it the snow. The sky is gray still, but the storm is over. I begin to think that we might not die.

Then the last in our line steps too close to a ravine, and he's down the side, sliding from sight. The next two in line, unable or unwilling to let go, slide after him, and I watch the slithering rope.

Again, I think. Again with this damn rope pulling me away. I let go of it, and the rope disappears into the gray below. The woman at my side doesn't even know what is happening.

The ravine is three meters down, lined by a steep, but not vertical, slope. I see the three who have fallen at the base. I have no way to get them out, so I must follow.

I take the woman over my shoulder, and say, "Hold on." I slide down the hill, one arm to balance me, one arm to hold her, and my legs folded beneath me, lowering myself down the slope.

No hidden tree branches, I hope. There are none, and sooner than I think, we are at the bottom of the ravine.

The three others are there, sprawled at the edge of a small, unfrozen stream. Sometime in the past, water has carved a cave-like trough into the ravine wall. The woman on my shoulder has passed out, her face gray, her breathing shallow. How bad is her fracture? I wonder. How much worse have I made it? Manuel would have known an elegant way to get her down.

The air is warm here, in this grotto that is nearly below the ground. It is like a cave; the ground is a constant temperature a few meters below the surface, regardless of the blazing heat or the blowing snow. I squat. It may be five degrees.

"We can rest here." We can even sleep, I think. No chance of frostbite. We can't get wet; the stream is too shallow.

A few meters down the streambed, I find an indentation. It is dry rock with roots overhanging. I carry the woman there and lead the others one by one to the cave.

"Sleep," I tell them.

My body is exhausted, and I watch the four fall asleep at once. I cannot. The female is in shock. I have made her arm worse by slinging her over my shoulder. She is probably bleeding internally.

I look at her gray face, and console myself that she would be dead if we were still a thousand meters up the mountain.

Unless they had sent another aircar.

I sit there, my heart cold, not sleeping.

I have always been strong, even when we were children, before we first consensed. I was always taller, stronger, heavier. And that has always been my weapon. It is obvious. I am not about deception. I am not about memory, or insight, or agility. I am quick when threats are near, yes, but never agile.

I never thought I would outlive my pod. I never thought I'd be the one left.

I don't want to think these things, so I stand up, and use my utility knife to cut two saplings that are trying to grow in the gully. Using the rope, I fashion a travois. It will be easier on the female.

"You should have left us on the mountain." It is the one who I had first found in the snow. His eyes are open. "You're wasting too much energy on a broken pod."

I say nothing, though I could acknowledge the truth of it.

"But then you wouldn't know that. All your thinking parts are missing."

He's angry, and he is striking out at me because of it. I nod.

"Yes, I am strength and nothing more."

Maybe he wants to fight, I think, so I add, "I saved your life today."

"So? Should I thank you?"

"No. But you owe me your life. So we will walk down this mountain in the morning, and then we are even. You can die then, and I won't care."

"Pig-headed."

"Yes." I can't argue with that either.

He is asleep in moments, and I am too.

*

I am stiff and cold in the morning, but we are all alive. I squat on the stones and listen for a few moments. The trickle of the water muffles all sound. I can't hear the whine of a rescue aircar. I can't hear the shouts of searchers. We have traveled so far that they will not look for us in the right spot. We have no choice but to continue on.

A wave of doubt catches me unaware. My choice has doomed us. But more than likely staying on the mountain would have done the same, only sooner. These four want that, I know. Perhaps I should too.

I touch my pockets one by one. I am hungry, but I already know there is no food. I was just stepping out of the tent for a moment. I had not prepared myself for a long journey in the cold. I check the pockets of the injured one, but she too is without food.

"Do you have food?" I ask the male, the one who argued with me. "What's your name anyway?"

"Hagar Jul —" he starts to say, then stops. He glares at me. "No food."

I squat next to him. "Perhaps I can lead you back up the mountain, and then you'll forgive me for saving you."

"'Saving' is a debatable term."

I nod. "What's your name?"

We have been classmates for ten years, and yet I do not know his individual name. We have always interfaced as pods, never as individuals.

He doesn't say anything for a long moment, then says, "David."

"And them?"

"Susan is the one with the broken arm. Ahmed and Maggie." These three are still asleep on the ground.

"The others may still be alive," I say, and as I say it, I know it is what I wish for myself. But I saw the river of snow that carried them away.

"We didn't find Alia and Wren," he says, and then he coughs. It is to hide the sob.

I turn away, not wanting to embarrass him, and I say, "One of them found our tent. She may still live."

"That was Wren. Alia was near me."

"A rescue party —"

"Did you see a rescue party?"

"No."

"A body will survive for an hour in the snow if there's air. If there's no air, then it is ten minutes." His voice is savage. The other three stir.

"It was like swimming in oil. Like swimming in a dream while smothering," David says.

"David."

It is Maggie. She pulls him close, and I smell the tang of consensus. They gather near Susan and sit for minutes, thinking. I am glad for them, but I walk down the stream several meters, not wanting to be reminded. I am a singleton now.

The creek twists and turns. I pull myself across a rotten pine tree blocking the way, banging loose a rain of brown needles. My breath hangs in the moist air. It is not cold anymore, and I feel like a thaw has passed through me.

The stream widens and opens up over a rocky basin where it spills in white spray. I see the valley before me, shrouded in mist. A kilometer below, the stream merges with a river. The ground to the river is rough and rocky, but not as snowy as we have traveled until now. Nor is it as steep.

We'd left for the survival trip from a base camp near a river. I can only suppose that this is the same river. Following it would lead us to the camp.

I hurry back to the four.

They stand apart, their consensus concluded. David hoists Susan's travois.

"Are you ready?" I ask.

They look at me, their faces relaxed. This is the first time these four have consensed since their pod was sundered. It is a good sign that they can do it with just four.

"We're going back to find Alia and Wren," David says.

I stand for a moment, voiceless. They have reached a false consensus. It is something that we are trained to detect and discard. But the trauma and loss they have suffered has broken their thought processes.

David takes my silence for agreement, and he pulls Susan up the streambed.

I stand, unable to resist a valid consensus, unable to stop them from climbing back up the mountain. I take one step toward them, perhaps to fall in line with them, but I stop.

"No!" I say. "You'll never make it."

The four of them look at me as if I am a rock. It's not false consensus; it's pod instability. Insanity.

"We need to re-form the whole," David says.

"Wait! You've reached false consensus!"

"How could you know? You can't consense at all." The biting words jolt me.

They start walking. I run to intercept, placing a hand on David's chest.

"You will die if you go back up the mountain. You can't make it." Ahmed pushes my arm away.

"We have to get back to Alia and Wren."

"Who was your ethicist?" I say. "Was it Wren? Is that why you're making faulty consensus? Think! You will die, just like Wren and Alia are dead."

"We had no ethical specialist," Maggie says.

"I saw the river from the end of this gully. We're almost to the camp! If we turn around, we will never find our way. We will be on the mountain at night. We have no food. We have no shelter. We will die."

No response but a step forward.

I push David hard, and he stumbles. Susan screams as the travois slams onto the rocks.

"You have reached a faulty consensus," I say again.

Pheromones flood the air, and I realize much of it is mine: veto, a simple pheromone signal we all know but rarely use. David swings at me, but I stop his fist. He is not strength.

"We go down," I say.

David's face is taut. He spins and the four fall into consensus.

I push David away from his podmates, breaking their contact. I push Ahmed and Maggie onto their backs.

"No consensus! We go now!"

I pick up Susan's travois and drag her down the streambed. Fast. I look back once and the three are standing there, watching. Then they come.

Maybe I am reaching false consensus too. Maybe I will kill us all. But it is all I can do.

The trek down the gorge is not easy on Susan, as the snow has disappeared in spots and the travois rides roughly across the ground. I find myself issuing soothing thoughts, though I know she cannot understand them. Only crude emotions can pass between pods, and sometimes not even that if they aren't from the same creche. I change the thoughts to feelings of well-being. Perhaps she can understand the simple pheromones.

Each time I glance behind, I see the other three trailing. I have broken their re-formed pod again with trauma, and I hope that I have done no irreparable damage to them. The doctors of the Institute will be the judge of that. Perhaps they can save them. I am a useless case and will probably have to emigrate to one of the singleton enclaves in Europe or Australia.

A line of boulders face me, surrounded by smaller stones and rocks, too large for the travois to travel freely across.

"Take one end each," I say to Ahmed and David. The travois becomes a stretcher. If I walk slowly, we make awkward progress.

The forest has changed. The pines are gone, and we are surrounded by maples. I keep checking the horizon for any sign of search parties. Why aren't they frantically trying to find us? Had we passed too far beyond the search pattern? Do they already know where we are? Perhaps they found us in the night, noted that we were broken pods and left us to fend for ourselves.

The paranoia drowns me, and I stumble on a loose rock. Even they would not be so callous. Everything is a test, Moira says. Is this just another? Would they kill a pod to test the rest of us?

That I cannot believe.

At the edge of a four-meter drop, our stream falls into the river, adding its small momentum to the charging rapids. I see no easy way down; we are forced to unlash Susan and help her down the jagged slope.

The rocks are wet and slimy. I slip, and we are flying to the ground, falling less than a meter, but the wind is knocked from me. Susan lands atop me, and she screams in pain.

I roll over and try to breathe. Then Ahmed and David are there, helping us up. I don't want to stand up. I just want to lie there.

"Up," David says. "More to go."

Everything is hazy in my vision, and I feel dizzy. The pain in my chest is not going away. I have a sharp sting in my ribs, and I prod myself. I have broken ribs. I almost collapse, but Ahmed pulls me up.

Susan manages to stand too now, and we limp along the flat stones of the shrunken river bed. In a few months it will fill the entire wash.

We are an ad hoc pod, all of us clinging together as we walk, step after step down-river. I am no longer strength. I am weakness and pain.

We pass a boulder and the smell hits me as we see it.

A bear, almost as big as the boulder. No, three bears pawing through the slow water for fish. We are not five meters from the biggest and closest.

Fear sweeps through the air; my fight response kicks in, and the pain washes out of me like cold rain.

We have surprised the bears.

The closest rears up on its hind legs. On all fours, it came up to my chest. Standing, it is a meter above me. Its claws are six centimeters long.

We back away. I know we cannot outrun a bear in this open terrain. Our only hope is to flee alone.

Separate, I send, then remember that the four are not of my pod. "We need to separate and run," I say.

The bear stops coming toward us. I think for a moment that it is reacting to my voice, but then I remember the smell I had caught as I passed the boulder. Pheromones.

The bears aren't a natural species.

Hello, I send, in the simplest of glyph thoughts.

The bear's jaws snap shut and it lands on its four legs again.

Not food, it sends.

The thought is more than simple. I can taste it like my own podmates' thoughts.

Not food. Friend.

The bear considers us with liquid brown eyes, then seems to shrug before turning away.

Come.

I start to follow, but fear emanating from the four stops me. I realize that they have not tasted the bear's thoughts.

"Come on," I say. "They aren't going to eat us."

"You . . . you can understand it?" David asks.

"A little."

"They're a pod," he says, wonderingly.

My shock has faded with recognition. On the farm with Mother Redd, we have gone swimming with the bioengineered beavers. We have ourselves modified clutches of ducks into clusters. Now that I know, I can see the glands on the backs of the bears' arms.

At the neck are slits that release the chemical memories. And to receive them, the olfactory lobe of their brain will have been enhanced.

That they are bears, that they are wild things, seems at first incongruent. The experiments on composite animals have been all on smaller, manageable beasts. But why *not* bears?

They amble along the riverbed, and I jog to follow them, though my ribs hurt. In a moment, I am among them, and I smell their thoughts, like silver fish in the river. Intelligent, not simple at all.

Sending *Friendship*, I reach out and touch the side of the bear who confronted us.

His fur is wet from his splashing at fish, and the smell is thick, not just pheromones and memories, but a wild animal's smell. I think I must smell worse. His mane is silver-tipped; his claws click on the stones.

I rub his neck just above the memory glands, and he pushes against me in response. I smell his affection. I sense deepness of thought and playfulness. I feel the power of his body. This is strength.

I catch images of topography, of places where fish swarm, of a dead elk. I see assessments of danger, and choices of path and best approach. I catch the consensus of decision. These three are a functioning pod.

The thoughts swirl through my head, but they shouldn't. I should not be able to catch their thoughts, but I can. Even humans can't share chemical memories between pods, just emotions sometimes.

I send an image of the avalanche.

The bears shudder. I understand their fear of the river of snow. They have seen it; it is part of their memories.

I ask them where the camp is. They know, and I see it on the edge of this river, near the rotten stump with the tasty termites.

I laugh, and they echo my joy, and, for a moment, I forget that I am alone.

Come on, they send.

"Come on," I call back to the four. Hesitantly, they follow.

The bears lead us through the trees, and, abruptly, we push through onto a trail, smashed flat by hikers' boots, a human trail. They sniff once, then amble across it and vanish into the brush.

I want to follow. Why shouldn't I? I have fulfilled my duty to Hagar Julian. Surely the bears would allow me to join them. My body shudders. I would still be a singleton. I would still be alone.

Goodbye, I send, though I doubt they are close enough to catch it. The chemical memories can not travel far.

I lead Susan down the trail, supporting her. I hear the sounds of camp, the voices, the whine of an aircar, before we round the last curve of the trail. We all stop. David looks at me, perhaps with pity, perhaps with thanks, then he leads the remainder of his pod into the camp.

I stand alone.

I fall to my knees, so tired, so weak. My strength can get me no farther.

Then I feel a push at my back, and it is the bear. He nudges me again. One arm around his steel-like neck, I stand, and we walk together into the camp.

The camp is awhirl, twice as many tents as when we left it, a bevy of aircars, and everyone stops to watch me and the bear.

Everyone but my pod, who are rushing at me, alive, and I feel them before I touch them, and we are one. Sweet consensus.

I see everything that has happened, and they see everything that I have done, and in one moment it is I who surfed the avalanche, dangling on the line Strom tied to a tree trunk, and it is we who walked down the mountain and communed with bears.

You saved us, Strom, Moira sends. Bola shows me how the tent dangling on my line of spider-silk, rode the top of the cascade of snow instead of plunging down the mountain. I hug Meda, Quant, and Manuel to my chest, squeezing. It hurts my ribs, but I don't let go.

"Careful!" Meda says, but she buries her face in my chest.

I am strength again, I think, as my pod helps me to the infirmary, not because they are weak, but because we are all strong.

DYSFUNCTIONAL
FAMILY CAT

I 'm leaving," said Tricia, punctuating the words with three short sneezes. She dug into the pocket of her flannel shirt, found a used tissue, and wiped her nose.

"All right, dear. Have a nice time." Her mother's glazed eyes never left the television as it blared the bantering dialogue of a late-afternoon talk-show.

"No, Mother. I'm leaving home."

"All right, dear. Have a nice time anyway."

"Have you been drinking again, Mother?" Tricia held her nose close to her mother's lips. Sour, yes, but no whiff of alcohol. Tricia realized that her mother wasn't watching the television, but that her eyes were fixed on the central speaker above it.

"Jesus, Mom. You're fried."

"Honey, you sound all congested. Do you have a cold?" Her mother's gaze wandered from the TV to Tricia's face.

"No, Mother, I'm just fucking allergic to cat hair."

"That's too bad, dear, now that we have Plonk."

"Well, here's a thought. Maybe we should get rid of the cat."

"Oh, no, we couldn't do that. Send it out into the world? Alone? Oh, never."

"That's what I thought. Goodbye forever."

"Bye, dear."

Tricia shrugged on her backpack and walked down the hall to her younger brother's room. Timo was sprawled across his bed, naked except for some tattered shorts, staring at the ceiling.

"I'm leaving home."

"Bye."

"Hey! I said I'm outta here for good. Don't you want this for your report?" For his seventh-grade social studies class, Timo was doing a case study on dysfunctional family units, using his family as the basis. His thesis was that since 57% of all family units were dysfunctional, the definitions of normal and abnormal could be reversed.

"Naw. I'm bored with that."

"What the fuck is wrong with this family?"

"Read chapter one through four in my report."

"What is wrong with you?"

"I'm going through one of my depression swings. They come and go."

"Timo, you are not suffering from bipolar disorder. You're just a moody preteen."

"You're just jealous of my creativity and its mystical link to my manic-depressive problem."

"I'm not jealous. Anorexia is a valid psychological disorder, too." Tricia paused, smiling sadly. "I'm gonna miss you."

"Then don't go."

Tricia sneezed. "It's either me or the cat."

"Oh. Okay. Bye."

Tricia rolled her eyes. As she turned to leave, Timo shouted, "Hey, if you see Plonk, could you bring him up here?"

Over her shoulder, Tricia snarled, "If I see it, I'm gonna kick it."

"Hey! You're kidding, right? You wouldn't . . ." Timo's voice faded as she ran down the stairs. In the den, her stepfather and stepbrother Chad sat in their two recliners watching the sports channel. In Chad's lap sat Plonk, a ball of white fluff, like an overweight, albino gerbil. Tricia sneezed, and Plonk looked up at her, pink eyes in a snow white face.

A phlegmy snore slithered from Chad's half-open mouth. Both of them were asleep, Tricia realized. She walked behind Chad's recliner and lifted an eyelid. The pupil beneath was huge and glazed, like a greased marble. Around Chad's nostrils and mouth were tiny white hairs. Tricia sneezed three times in succession.

"You need some monoxidil, cat," she said. Her eyes were tearing and her lungs felt like they were the size of beanbags. "Fuck it. I'm outta here."

She stood in the hall at the base of the stairs. She yelled, "I'm running away from home! I told you it was me or the cat. And now I'm leaving." Silence, punctuated by the sporadic drone of the TV's sports announcer. "Next time you'll see me, I'll be on Oprah!" Tricia paused a moment, her hand on the knob. No one rushed down the stairs to stop her. She half expected someone to tell her to bring back a gallon of milk.

Plonk wandered out of the den, pausing to rub its face against the doorway. Tricia looked down at the animal then kicked it in the stomach. "I hate cats," she said as she slammed the door shut.

She dumped the contents of her backpack out on the bus stop bench. Her inventory was sparse: thirty-seven dollars, a pack of gum, a can of mace, her address book, an emergency Kotex, a copy of *The Catcher in the Rye*, and her mother's Visa card. She noted each item, then sighed. Now that the drama of the act was over, despondency washed over her. She stuffed everything into her backpack, deciding to go wherever the next bus went.

Tricia waited on the sun-warmed bench, sitting in the red-violet of the sunset. The warmth seeped into her, calming her. Her sinuses cleared, and she took pleasure in the simple act of breathing.

Across the street, a young, poorly-dressed man stumbled down the sidewalk. In one hand he clutched a staple gun and in the other a ream of red paper. He paused at the light pole on the corner, then dropped the paper on the ground. He pulled at his earlobe, shook his head, and snorted like a horse. Taking the sheet from the top of the ream, he stapled it to the pole with four randomly-placed kerchunks.

The man stood back from his work, pulled at his earlobe again, and then crossed the street. He spotted Tricia, aimed himself at her.

"Have you seen my cat?"

The man waved a flyer in Tricia's face. She took it from him, glanced at it, and threw it on the ground. The man surged to pick it up again, but Tricia placed her foot squarely on the flier. The man pulled at it, ripped it in half. He stood straight up, then let the piece flutter away.

"A-a-a simple yes-or-no would have sufficed," he muttered, again pulling at his earlobe.

Tricia noted the man's red eyes and jittery manner. She'd seen the symptoms in her mother. He looked like he was coming down off something hard. His clothes were in disarray, his shirt untucked, socks unmatching, pants too short. His hair was uncombed, and his breath was foul. A badge clipped to his shirt pocket labeled the man as Dr. Jerry Wilder of Genomads Inc.

"How much of a reward?"

"A hundred dollars. You should have read the flier."

"A thousand, and I'll take you right to him."

"A thousand? That's . . . Wait! You know where he is? Tell me." Jerry grabbed Tricia's shirt and pulled her to her feet. "Where is my cat?"

Tricia calmly reached into her backpack and maced him.

"Are twenties all right?"

"Yeah. Fine. And don't forget the extra five hundred for not pressing charges."

Jerry handed the cash to Tricia as fast as the machine would spit it out. She was impressed with the limit on his bank card.

"All right. Let's go." The two walked back to Jerry's car. As Jerry pulled out his keys, Tricia stood in front of the driver's side door and held out her hand. "I'm driving."

Jerry paused, eyed her wearily, then shrugged and handed the keys to her. "You have a license?"

"Well, a permit. But that's pretty much the same thing, right?" she said as she heavily dropped the car into gear.

Tricia sped the car out of the strip-mall parking lot, narrowly avoiding a collision with a shopping cart. Unfortunately, she saw no one she knew on the way home. With a scraping of metal against concrete, she bounced the car into her driveway.

"Come on, Jer." Tricia popped the door open with a flick of the knob. "I'm home!" she called up the stairs.

Jerry pushed past her, stumbling on the step. "Mendel! Here kitty-kitty! Come here, Gregor!"

"Hey, Sis. Who's the geek?" Chad stood in the doorway to the den, scratching his crotch.

"This is Plonk's owner."

"Really? Cool. Thanks for letting us keep him, man."

Jerry noticed Chad for the first time. "He's my cat. I've come to take him back."

"The fuck you are, man. He's ours now." Chad turned around. "Hey, Dad, this fuck wants to steal our cat."

Tricia refrained from laughing and wandered into the kitchen where she filled a bowl with milk. Behind her, she heard her father join the argument.

"Anyone who's so irresponsible as to lose a cat doesn't deserve to own one," he said. "I think you better just leave before we call the police."

"He's m-m-my cat, sir. I en-en-en . . . raised him from a kitten. I couldn't live without him."

"Well, you ain't getting him out of this house," said Chad. "'Cause there's two of us and only one of you."

"What's going on down here?" Tricia's mother had joined the fray. "And who is this young man? Are you a friend of Tricia's? Is she finally showing an interest in men?"

"Dream on, Mom," Tricia said, walking into the front hallway. She had left the bowl of milk on the kitchen counter. "This is Plonk's owner, Jerry Wilder."

"Gregor Mendel," Jerry corrected.

"How do you do, Mr. Mendel?"

"Uh . . . No. The cat's name is Mendel. My name is Jerry Wilder, and I've come to get my cat." He pulled at his earlobe.

"No, no, no. Plonk's name . . ."

Tricia leaned close to Jerry. "Why do you keep pulling at your earlobe?"

Jerry whirled on her, turning his head so that his left earlobe was out of view. "Nervous habit."

"You've got some sort of bump, man," Chad said. "Bad piercing, dude?"

Jerry whirled again, then backed up to the front door. "It's just-just-just . . . a pimple."

Tricia edged closer to the man, intent upon his lobe. Jerry stood, back against the door, eyes dancing like butter in a hot skillet. Tricia jumped forward and squeezed the earlobe between her finger and her thumb.

Jerry screamed like a madman, and leaped away. Tricia jumped on his back, wrapping her legs around the man's chest. She squeezed his lobe, feeling something wet and soft squirm under the pressure.

"You're gonna OD me!" Jerry yelled. "Let go! Let go! Let gooooo." Jerry fell face first onto the carpet of the front hall. "I am soooo high, man," he muttered, then started to giggle.

"That was pretty cool, Sis," said Timo from where he stood on the stairs. "I'm glad you're back."

Tricia smiled at Timo. "Just for a few laughs."

"So what's with the geek?" asked Timo as he bounded down the steps. He and Chad rolled Jerry over.

"Oh, what's that smell?" said Tricia's mother in a nasal voice.

"He pissed himself," said Chad.

Jerry found that exceptionally humorous and began to giggle again.

"I think he's got a drug gland in his earlobe."

"Drug gland?" Timo, Chad, and her stepfather leaned close to Jerry's head.

"Can you do that with a beer, dude?"

Jerry paused in his fit of giggling. "Nawwwww!" He gulped in breath for a moment, then added, "Just en-en-endolphins! Endorphins! Enporpoises!" Drool rolled out of his mouth as he giggled.

"He works for a genetic engineering company. I think he made that drug gland to keep his fix nearby and ever-ready," said Tricia.

"Hey, that's pretty cool," said Timo.

"I think he engineered the cat too."

"Yeah, I did." Jerry sat up, coughing. He seemed to have partially recovered from the spurt of drugs into his system. His eyes were still glassy, and his voice was slightly slurred. "I made him to make me happy. Like God." He vomited on Chad's shoes.

"Shit. What a waste," said Chad. He wiped his shoe on Jerry's shirt. "Being such a loser you have to build your own friend." He paused. "Can you do me a chick?"

"Fuck you. I want my cat."

"Hey, wait a minute," Timo said. "Why are we so obsessed about a stupid cat?"

"Yeah," added Tricia.

"He's modified," said Jerry. "His odor is a mild euphoric. Well, actually, it's a highly addictive depressant."

"We're addicted to a cat?" asked Timo.

"Cool, beer-in-a-cat," said Chad.

"So why don't you just make yourself another cat?" asked Tricia. "Why don't you just make a gland to give you the drug? And why not a cute puppy next time?

Jerry shook his head. "It was a mutation. I can't reproduce the recombination sequence. I thought it was the retrocomb of the iris allele, but when I try to duplicate it, all I get is abortions. I was trying to breed him when he got away from me." He held his head in his hands and began to cry. "My one big success is a fluke."

"Here's a tissue, young man," said Tricia's mother.

"Well, I think that earlobe thing is pretty cool," said Chad.

Jerry sniffed. "I stole that from a colleague."

"You really are a fuck," said Timo.

"Well, I just stopped to bring Jerry by," said Tricia. "I'm outta here now." She waved at her family. "Bye."

"Bye, now Tricia, dear," called her mother.

Her stepfather said to Jerry, "Here's a solution, Jerry; you can move in with us. We got a room empty now."

"Really? That would be so . . . so . . . nice of you."

"See ya, Sis," said Timo.

Tricia stopped. "Come with me, Timo," she said softly. "We don't belong in this family."

Timo smiled. "I wish I could." He shrugged. "I'm stuck now."

Tricia nodded, then walked back to the kitchen. Holding her breath, even though she knew it wouldn't work, she plucked Gregor-Plonk-Mendel off the counter top and exited out the kitchen door into the backyard.

She managed to stifle the sneeze until she reached Jerry's car. Seven straight sneezes left the windshield speckled with mucus.

"I hate cats," she said to her companion, who blinked pink eyes at her.

Tricia gunned the car, flying out of the driveway. She threw the car into drive, and floored it with a screech of tires. In minutes she was in downtown Ormdon, headed for the interstate.

Tricia made one stop on the way.

"Oh, he's so cute," Wendy Morse said, taking Plonk into her arms, and squeezing him. Tricia knew Wendy from her gym class.

"Could you take care of him for just a few days? We're going on vacation."

"He's neutered, right? He's safe to put with Princess Gwen?"

"Oh, yeah. I think they'll be great pals."

"All right. I hope you and your family have a nice vacation."

Tricia turned around as she pulled open the car door. She smiled and said, "Thanks. I'll try."

Tricia adjusted her Raybans. She wondered how long it would be before the world was full of Plonks, then shrugged. As she sped up the highway, she rolled down the windows and inhaled the fresh air.

FALLOW
EARTH

The spaceship crashed through the tree tops, splintering the boughs of a gangly locust, and landed in the Olentangy River on top of Mr. Joyce, which was okay with Nick and me, since Mr. Joyce was drunk most of the time and liked to flick matches at Nick when we waited for the bus.

Nick looked up from his pile of skipping rocks, then back down again. I dropped my reel, tossed my ponytail over my shoulder, and watched the six-inch wave slide down the river. Splinters of wood spun through the air, while steam rose from beneath the spaceship.

It was built to resemble an old Volkswagen Beetle. The paint job was good; they'd even added rust around the wheel wells. If I hadn't seen the vapor trail and heard the sizzling as it sliced through the atmosphere and crashed on top of Mr. Joyce, I'd have thought it was some old car Harry and Egan had rolled down the hill below the Case Road bridge.

I slipped down the slope to the bank where Nick was piling his skipping rocks. I followed the bank upriver to within fifty feet of the ship, then I had to step into the deep part of the river. I heard Mama's voice in my head, and I felt her husband Ernie's swat on my butt as my shoes sank into the mud of the Olentangy. They'd have a fit if I tracked dirt into the trailer.

The Olentangy was a broad, slow river. I could walk it from the trailer park to the reservoir dam, two miles north, stepping from flat rock to flat rock without getting the tops of my knees wet. Up by the spillway was where the sporting fishermen cast, catching the occasional walleye. Down here by the trailer park, we got mostly small bass and bluegills.

The water hissed from beneath the Volkswagen spaceship. Its single occupant, a figure slumped over the steering column, looked like a man. He had a head with hair, not at all what an alien should have looked like.

Dirt swirled in the water, masking the river bottom, and I flung my arms out to balance myself, finally grabbing the door frame of the Beetle. I saw Mr. Joyce on the other side, face-up in the river. The ship hadn't landed on him after all, just near enough to the old drunk to knock him down and out. He hadn't drowned because he'd landed on his back on a wide, slimy stone.

The window of the Bug was open. I peered in and caught the odor of old vinyl. The alien's Volkswagen was well made. I popped the lock and pulled the door open.

The driver was dressed in tan slacks and a light tan jacket. He had on Nike shoes and a black belt. Horn-rimmed glasses, like the ones my real dad used to wear when he was young, were tilted across his face.

I leaned him back and noted where the skin had fallen away from his face to reveal red flesh. An alien, as I suspected.

"What the hell was that?"

I recognized Harry's voice up the slope, heard the rustle of brush as he and Egan came to investigate. Harry was fifteen, a year older than me, but because he'd flunked the fifth grade he was going to be a freshman just like me in the fall. Harry had started some nasty rumors about me because I let him touch my breast during truth-or-dare the summer before. That wasn't the only reason I hated him. I sure didn't want him finding the alien. Harry had once forced three younger kids to hollow out a pile of concrete blocks; he'd threatened to beat the kids up unless they spent the day hauling rock for him. They'd done it too. Harry was a user, with no conscience. I decided to help the alien out, at least until he could take care of himself. Maybe I could help him with his mission or something. This was the most interesting thing that had happened all summer, and I wasn't going to let Harry spoil it.

"Come on, fella," I said, tugging at the alien's arm. "Let's get you outta here." I didn't want to see the alien cited for hit-and-run. He needed to be someplace safe until we could clear this all up, get him back to the mother ship.

He groaned, but he moved, his eyes half-open. His legs splashed in the water and he nearly fell, but he leaned on me and we managed to stumble away from the spaceship.

Nick watched us for a moment, then returned to piling the skipping stones. We called them skipping stones, not that he'd ever throw them; he just collected them. He'd had me throw one once. I slung a beauty, fifteen skips at least before it sank to the bottom of the Olentangy. But then he became angry when he realized it was gone. I'd had to wade in and find a stone that looked reasonably close to the original. Now, we didn't throw them at all. He made piles.

I dragged the alien onto the bank, where he slumped onto the muddy sand. From the other shore, I heard voices. Harry was just beyond the tree line. I saw his red-and-white middle school jacket between the vines and short maples.

"Nick, help me get this guy up the bank," I said.

Nick didn't look at me, but I knew he heard. He can fool Ernie, but I know him too well. I kicked him on the butt with my wet tennis shoe.

He grunted. "Help me," I said.

Together we rolled the alien up the gentle slope and over its far side. When the river was high, it would flow around the little peninsula where I liked to fish. On the far side were rocky puddles where a few crayfish lived.

"What the hell!"

Harry was wading into the river toward the car.

I picked up my pole and cast a line into the river.

Harry circled the spaceship while Egan sat on the shore tossing rocks onto its hood. Harry peered into the front seat. He reached in and touched his finger against something on the steering wheel: blood.

Then he looked around and saw me.

"What happened, Priscilla? Did Mr. Joyce drive his car into the river?"

"Dunno, Hairy." He knew I was mispronouncing his name, though I didn't say it any differently. When he'd started those rumors, I'd made sure everyone knew what I thought of him. Egan snorted.

"Cars don't just fall outta the sky, Cilly," he said. He took a step toward me.

I reeled in my line and didn't reply.

"Where's the driver?" He took another step.

"Dunno, Hairy," I said and cast my line toward him. He jerked as the red-and-white bobber fluttered in the river a few yards from him. After our truth-or-dare adventures, he'd tried to press his advantage down by the river. My hook had caught his cheek just under the eye. He still had a puckered, pink scar where I'd yanked it out. "Screw you, Cilly," he said. "Don't you wish, Hairy," I said. He slinked back to the shore then disappeared into the woods with his slouching pal.

The alien was sitting up. He had smoothed the skin back into place, and there was no mark where the cut had been. He smiled brightly and I would have been convinced that he was some ugly guy who'd driven his Volkswagen into the Olentangy if I hadn't seen his gnarly red flesh.

There were other things that marked him as an alien. His face was lumpy below the cheeks and his neck seemed to be thicker at the top than the bottom. He looked human enough, and you'd just think he was ugly if you passed him on the street.

"Thank you, little boy,"

"Save it for the Galactic Council," I said. "I know what you are."

"What do you mean, young man?" he said.

"I'm a girl, you dork. Any human male would know that."

His shoulders fell. "Oh."

"Yeah. So, you might as well 'fess up. You here for First Contact?"

"No. I'm on Earth illegally."

I refrained from the pun. If I'd said it at the dinner table, Mama would have snorted milk out her nose and then Ernie would have choked on his pork chop and then Nick would have started laughing because everyone else was.

"So, there's no take-me-to-your-leader thing that you have to do?"

"No, I need to talk with your scientists. I need to redirect . . ."

He was staring over my shoulder. For a second I was worried that Harry had snuck back to spy on me, but it was just Nick. He was piling his rocks next to the limp elm that had rooted itself on the peninsula.

"Hey. Redirect what?"

"Is . . . is . . . he *broken*?"

I stared at him, unsure what he meant, until I realized. "Yeah, Nick is slow. So what?"

"I knew about . . . I just never . . ."

"Don't you have retarded aliens?" I was getting annoyed with this guy. I figured that a representative from an advanced civilization would know how to behave around someone like Nick. I expect Harry and his friends to make fun of the little yellow school bus, but from aliens I guess I expected a little more.

"No, of course not. I'm sorry. I . . ."

Nick wasn't paying too much attention to the alien. But the alien was all eyes for Nick. I snapped my fingers.

"So what are you doing here? You need to talk with Earth's scientists. You need to warn us about a supernova? Help us stop war? What?"

"No, nothing like that. I've got to change the direction of Earth's research."

"Are you bringing high-tech gadgets that will give us cold fusion, nanotechnology, quantum computers?" My real dad had given me one gift in the past ten years, but it was the best gift ever: a subscription to *Discover*. I'd been paying for the subscription myself for the past three years, but I still thought of it as Dad's gift. If it weren't for him, the deadbeat bastard, I'd never have gotten in the magnet school.

"That's exactly the sort of technology I need to steer you away from!"

"What sort of alien are you, anyway?"

"I'm a . . . teacher."

I glanced over at the Beetle. "You get shot down?"

"Yes."

"Air Force? NATO?"

"The . . . Farmers tried to stop me."

"Farmers." I sat back on my heels. I had the image of Hubert Erskine taking a pot shot at Herbie as it sailed over his soybean fields. "You mean something else than what I think 'farmer' means."

"Yes. Earth's protectors."

"Uh huh," I said. My alien had run a blockade to get here. Interesting, but still a little lame. I was half-tempted to put him back in his car and let Harry find him. "So, what exactly is it you want to do here on Earth?"

"I need to write anonymous letters to leading scientists, asking certain questions that will direct their thoughts toward key areas."

I looked him up and down. It was a slow summer, and this seemed like a pretty good diversion.

"So you'll need a place to hole up."

"Yes. And stamps."

The Mingo Concrete company had a factory about a mile from the trailer park. It was a small factory where they cast sewer segments, six feet long and interconnecting.

Some time ago, lost in local kid history, someone stole a steel wire reinforcement cylinder from the factory. They'd rolled it away from the factory site and into the woods, in what must have been a daring feat. Then they'd put it on its end and used plywood and plastic to build a two-level fort. These kids had grown up, left for college, and the fort had become overrun with thorn bushes, until you couldn't tell it was there.

Now it was Nick's and my fort. Maybe other kids knew about it, but I never saw anyone else there. We'd found it when I'd first got the Boy Scout handaxe I'd sent away for; it had cost twelve bucks, which was half a summer's worth of lemonade stands, lawn-mowing for Nick (under my guidance), and dog-walking. I'd used Nick's name on the order form since I wasn't sure about the correctness of a girl buying a Boy Scout gadget. When it came, we were eager to chop something down, anything, and had set out for the woods.

We'd found a maple with a trunk three inches in diameter and set to chopping. It was harder work than we'd thought and we got only a quarter way through before we gave up. We decided to look for something easier, and, seeing the thorn patch, we started blazing a trail. Unfortunately, the bushes were as hearty as the maple, not coming off in instant bails, but leaning against each other with clasped thorns.

After we cut a few bushes and pulled their carcasses out, I spotted the shape of the fort. We suddenly had a destination for our trail. The work became a little easier.

The fort was rusted, moldy, but instantly desirable. We cleared the orange shag carpet, limp, moldy Playboys, and Rolling Rock bottles out, and made it over into our own place, with a nine-volt radio, a homemade telescope, and sporks from KFC.

It seemed to suit the alien too. We gave him paper, pen, envelopes, and a roll of stamps I stole from Ernie's night stand. We borrowed our sleeping bag for him to sleep in. He used the lower, darker level for sleeping, and the upper, cramped level for his correspondence.

Each day, he wrote out long letters on a legal pad, with tight print. We collected them and left them in our mailbox for pickup.

He wrote a lot of letters. To MIT, Caltech, Harvard, and Princeton. We had to get airmail envelopes for his letters to Cambridge and the University of Tokyo.

When he wasn't writing, he'd talk with me. He never spoke to Nick. We learned his name was Bert. He liked classic TV, especially *Gilligan's Island*, because he used the show to teach the futility of organized action among classist herds. He was one of a long, well-known line of aliens. He liked warmer weather. He didn't agree with the Farmers.

"So why did the Farmers shoot you down?"

"The Earth is our restricted planet."

"Your restricted planet? No one told *us*."

"It's one of the fallow planets for this portion of the galaxy."

"Which means you ignore us."

"Oh no," Bert said. "We do not ignore you. How do you think I know English? It's our common language."

"English is the galaxy's common language?" Wouldn't Mrs. Moore, my composition teacher, be surprised.

"Just a small part of it. You're our source for a lot of things."

"Beer? Cows? Women?" What could we humans provide that these aliens didn't already have? "Comedy. It must be comedy."

Bert looked at me flatly. No, it wasn't comedy. He licked the envelope with his too thin tongue and handed it to me. "Tomorrow's post, please."

I handed the letter to Nick, and Bert recoiled as if it hurt him that something he'd touched had then been touched by something broken. He never looked at Nick, never talked to him, not even out of politeness.

"Don't you have slow people where you're from?"

He shook his head.

"Must be nice to be from an alien society."

He seemed to recognize my sarcasm. "It's not like that. We have problems. That's why I'm here."

"What problems could you possibly have?" I considered a world where Nick was whole.

Bert was more animated than I'd ever seen him. "We are all the same! We have everything we need and no cares for our own survival. There is no drive for growth, no need to create. We are as dead as he is." He pointed at Nick.

"Fuck you!" I yelled. "Nick is alive. You may wish he was dead, but he's alive!"

He blinked at me, then looked down. "I am sorry."

"Yeah, see ya tomorrow." I'd seen a lot of reactions to Nick, but the alien's was something new.

When Ernie came to live in the trailer with Mama, he never called Nick any names. He didn't ignore him; he sorta looked at him as a toy. He'd hold out his hand and say, "Slap me five." When Nick would try, Ernie'd pull his hand away. Nick would laugh every time, until Ernie said, "Now you hold out your hand." Nick didn't have the sense to move his hand from the snake-like strike. He'd smile a little, then look at me as he rubbed his hand. "Hold out your hand, Nick," Ernie would say again, and I'd have to distract them, somehow.

"Hey, Ernie, I think NASCAR is on," or "Nick, is that the school bus?" or "You guys want another Coke?" I hated thinking about what happened when I wasn't there.

I'd mailed about a dozen letters over a week's time when the Farmers showed up. You'd think they were insurance men or Jehovah's Witnesses, but I knew what to look for. Their cheeks were bumpy in the wrong place like Bert's, and their necks were too wide at the top.

I was coming out of our trailer, down the black metal stair specked with rust, when I heard Harry say, "That's her, there." The two Farmers fastened their gaze on me, and I stood like a statue. I hated Harry more, which I'd thought was impossible.

"We understand you saw the car land in the river," one of them said.

"Nope." The gravel of the driveway seemed to poke through my shoes.

"Yes, she did," Harry said.

"Nope."

"We're looking for the driver," said the first alien.

"To ask him some questions," added the second.

"Or her," I said. "Could'a been a woman driver. Them being the worst type of drivers." They faced me with blank stares. No senses of humor, just like Bert.

"We're very interested in what you saw."

"Nothing," I said, but they were crowding close.

"Could you talk with us in our car, please?" The second took my arm. "We can offer a cash reward."

Just then, Nick clomped down the stairs of the trailer, and I slipped free. "This is my brother, Nick. Have you met him, yet?" I shoved Nick into them, and his arms came up around his head. They didn't like it either, once they realized they were dealing with a broken human. They couldn't tell a boy from a girl, but they spotted a broken human right away.

"We're sorry," they said as they backed off.

Nick and I watched them get into their car and drive down the stone gravel road. I gave Harry the finger.

"I know you know something, Cilly."

"That'd be the only thing you do know, pudd'n head."

He sauntered off.

That day, the Farmers hired Bubba to tow the car. We watched from the woods. Bubba'd brought the smaller truck, the one with the tilting flatbed. The Farmers must not have explained it to him, since he started cursing when he saw the VW in the middle of the river. He cursed the whole time he waded across the river.

Harry and Egan watched from across the river. Harry had his eyes on the Farmers. I wondered if he could see the oddly shaped necks, the too-high cheekbones? Probably not. Harry was keen on the weaknesses of others but nothing else.

Well, that wasn't true. Once we'd worked on a project together, Harry and I and a group of people. We'd been in the sixth grade, and we'd gone over to the USDA facility and used their electron microscope to look at spores. We'd made a couple of trips into the woods to find samples, and Harry, off by himself, had found the best ferns, long, arcing, feathery plants, like green fire. He was brushing the back of them gently with a collection tray, intent, when I walked up. He turned, saw me watching, smirked, capped the sample, and tossed it to me. He'd thrown it so hard, I'd juggled it, and almost dropped it. He pretended he didn't care about it, but I'd seen how he'd carefully gathered the spores.

That was a long time ago, long before the truth-or-dare incident. Harry had changed since then. I watched him watching the Farmers, scheming.

Mr. Joyce was there too, pestering the Farmers about his back pain after the Volkswagen had fallen on him. The spaceship hadn't caused his problems; cheap bottles of Mad Dog 20/20 had done his back in, as well as the rest of him.

"Farmers came to look for you. And they towed your spaceship."

Bert nodded. "I knew they would. But I'm safe here, I think."

"Yeah, they don't like retards either."

"You're being purposefully cruel. I knew it was possible among outsiders, but not those of your own family."

"He's my brother, and I can do what I want with him." Nick was below, piling his skipping stones. He'd carried two jeans pockets full of them from the river.

Bert frowned, then returned to writing his latest letter.

"What're you writing?" I'd asked before, but he wouldn't show me.

"A letter to Doctor Robert Cutter at Vanderbilt University."

"What are you talking about in your letter?"

He didn't respond at first. "I'm asking questions that will expand his research into key areas."

"What areas?"

"I can't explain."

"You're writing a long enough letter to Doctor Cutter. How come you can't explain it to me?"

He said nothing.

"What's wrong with where we're going now? Robots, computers, nanotechnology. What's wrong with that direction?"

"We already *have* advances in those areas," Bert said. "We need advances in other areas."

"What other areas?"

He folded his sheets of paper into an envelope, sealed it, and handed it to me.

"I come from a tightly woven family. We have a long lineage, well-known for our teaching," he said. "When I was young, I lost my father. This is not a common thing. We have long lives, made longer and safer by technology. We should have lived long lives together, son, father, father's father, and several generations, in a chain. This is how our people live.

"When I was just a student, an accident severed the chain. Certain rites did not occur. Certain things did not happen because of his death. Our culture is more ritualized than yours."

"Like graduation?" We'd had a small graduation ceremony at middle school in June. They'd played music and made us walk in line with a double half step instead of a full step.

"Yes. Every day is like graduation. The grandfathers tried to make do, but I felt my father's absence strongly. Each father is a bridge to the past. My link was sundered.

"I came here . . . to find help."

I looked at the letter in my hands, confused. "There's no help here for that."

His eyes were fierce and glassy. "Yes, I know there is hope, and my hope is here on this fertile, fallow planet." He pulled out his legal pad and began addressing a new letter.

"Come on, Nick," I said.

Bert had such faith in human technology. He believed that we could solve his father's death. But we couldn't solve death. Mama took us to church sometimes, but I could see that was hogwash. What god would allow a person like Nick to exist? None that I cared to worship.

We passed the tree that we had once tried to chop down. It was brown, dead. We'd severed the trunk enough to kill it; it stood leafless while the trees around it were emerald green and full. Nick pressed his hand into the gray mouth we had cut.

I slapped the letter against my palm. How could we help Bert? What did he think we could do for his father now?

Halfway to the trailer, I opened the letter. I was so engrossed as I read it, that I must not have noticed Harry.

"What the hell is this?"

I stood on the ladder leading to the upper level of the fort. Bert looked at me blankly. I'd scrambled through the briars to get there, and there was a huge thorn poking through my jeans into my shin. I ignored it as I waved the letter in his face.

"Those are my private correspondences with leading scientists of your world."

My mouth wouldn't work, I was so angry. Finally, I held the paper in front of my face and read, "'I respectfully ask how one might gauge the magnitude of spiritual manifestation based on ganglion density in the cortex? Clearly a dog has less ghostly presence than a human. Is it tied to brain size? Is it linear? Is it related to some other parameter, such as sexual audacity or emphatic quotient? Find attached a chart of data that I have compiled.' What the hell is this? What do you think scientists will do with this crap?"

"I hope to direct their thoughts toward areas of fertile research."

"You'd rather have them studying ghosts than computers?"

"We already have computers."

"What about medicine?"

Bert looked away. "That has no impact on us."

"Then do your *own* research! Let us alone! Why use us for this crap? This won't help us."

"We can't do our research. We're . . . sterile, while your planet is not bound by our culture, by our ritual. We have medical advances. We have nanotechnology. We have no disease or . . . retardation. And we pay for that in stagnation. You're wild, alive. You have no bounds, no millennia of civilization to bind your minds.

"When one of us wants something, we ask for it and it is given to us by machines that care for themselves and us. If you want something, you have to build it. You have drive, while we have stasis. You have —"

Nick had stopped playing with his skipping stones. He moaned softly, peering out the door. A thorn had grazed his cheek as he'd lunged after me through the gateway.

I saw a shape moving beyond the thorn bushes.

"Cilly . . . I know you're in there."

To Bert, I said, "Hide." To Harry, I shouted, "Beat it, you sack of goat vomit!"

"What're you hiding in there?" he sing-songed.

"Your penis, but it was so small I lost it in a thimble."

Egan and he were crawling on their bellies toward the fort. "We got you now, Cilly. You can't hide your friend any longer." His face was stretched up, grinning.

"Back off, Hairy," I said, glancing around. I couldn't run without leaving Nick and Bert alone. Bert I didn't care about anymore, but Nick was no match for cruelty. And there was no easy way through the thorn bushes, except for the way Harry was coming.

"Leave us be, young men," Bert said.

"I told you to hide, you freak!" I said.

"Is that the driver of the car?" Harry asked. "Why are you hiding him here?" He was almost to the point where he could stand up.

"He's an alien spiritualist," I said.

"Yeah, right. I don't care what he is. Those guys said they'd give us a hundred bucks if we brought him to them."

"You can't count to a hundred," I said.

"Keep talking, Cilly," he said, standing, pulling a knife out of his belt.

Behind me Nick, or maybe Bert, was keening.

Something whizzed by my head, and Harry yelped. He dropped the knife and reached for his forehead where a red welt had appeared. Another rock flew at him, and he ducked.

"Ouch!"

I turned as Nick flung another skipping stone at Harry. The sharp edge caught his wrist and he shrieked like a kid. He turned and dived on Egan, trying to evade the rocks.

Nick threw one at Egan and caught the corner of his eye. Egan buried his face in his hands and started scrambling back the way he'd come. The two of them disappeared into the brambles, then ran when they could stand.

Nick threw rock after rock until I knocked the pile of stones away from him.

I screamed at him, "Those are skipping stones, you retard!" And then I dove through the thorn bushes, ignoring the thorns and ran for the trailer.

Ernie and Mama shared a pull-out bed in the living room. Nick and I shared the bedroom in the back. Above the door in our room was a small storage alcove that you could reach from the top bunk. I threw the box of old games onto the floor and climbed into the space, hunching my shoulders.

Screw Hairy, screw Bert, and screw Nick, I thought as I jammed my knees into my chin. Screw the goddamn Farmers. And screw me for believing in . . . what?

Fairy godmothers. I was on my own. Just like the whole Earth was. We were some Amazon rain forest to be mined for valuable technology. An Amazon brain forest. And they wanted us to invest in studying ghosts.

They lived where Nick could never happen, like gods. Then they came here to have us look for ghosts instead of doing medical research that could help our own.

I wasn't any happier in my hiding place. I was just angrier. I slid down, walked around back of the trailer to the train tracks. Every night at two in the morning, a freight train barrelled down the tracks, headed for Columbus. I could sleep right through it, without a twitch. They probably didn't have loud trains on Bert's planet.

I followed the tracks, stepping from tie to tie until I reached the trestle. Graffiti stretched across the iron i-beams and concrete pylons to every spot reachable by a spray can and an outstretched arm. In the shade of the trestle down by the river, Harry and Egan lounged.

Harry pressed a tissue to his forehead.

I dropped down, hanging by my arms from the trestle, and landed between them.

"What the hell do you want?"

"Those guys give you their number?"

He looked at me, then said, "Yeah. So?"

"Give it to me."

"No."

I picked up a skipping stone, prepared to throw it. Nick had done this same thing — threatened someone with a rock — and I had yelled at him. I felt disgust. The stone slipped out of my hand, and I turned to go. It was time to find Nick, tell him I was sorry, and get him home for dinner.

"Wait," Harry said. "Why do you want it? He's worth a hundred to us."

I said, "I'll split it with you."

Harry looked at me a moment longer then nodded at Egan. He handed me a card with a handwritten number.

We called from the bait shop.

Egan had to cut out for dinner, but Harry stayed with me until the two Farmers showed up. Their black Lincoln raised a white cloud of dust as they entered the trailer park.

"You have information regarding the driver?" one asked Harry.

"I do," I said. "I can hand him over to you."

"Where is he, little boy?" he asked.

"I'm a girl, you moron."

"Of course," he said.

"Come on," I said, and we led the pair into the woods near the casting factory.

They balked at crawling under the thorns, their bodies too stiff to bend, but finally they got on their bellies and shrugged their black suits through the dirt. Nick and Bert were standing at the front of the fort, both with the same blank expression.

"The Farmers are here," I said.

Bert nodded.

They stood without dusting themselves off, staring at Bert. One motioned at Bert. He stepped forward like a fish on a hook. They turned to crawl back out.

"Hold on," I said.

"Yes?"

"There was a reward," I said.

One of the Farmers pulled out a wallet and reached toward me with a smooth hundred dollar bill.

"No. I want more."

The alien's arm stopped, frozen. Bert looked at me.

"Little girl, the agreed amount —s"

"You made a deal with *him*," I said nodding toward Harry. "And I know what you are."

They didn't reply.

"I know what *he* is. I know all about what you're doing to us."

"Give her two hundred," the other said.

"No," I said. "I know you're Farmers. I know our world is fallow."

They just stared at me, but Bert's face had the start of a smile.

"I know your secret, and my silence is expensive. What do *we* get out of this arrangement? Short lives, poverty, mental retardation. Did we choose this? Don't we deserve the same lives as you? Doesn't *Nick*?"

I pointed at my brother. He stood watching the aliens. Sometimes there was something behind his brown eyes. Sometimes he understood, and it all made sense to him. It was like looking into the center of the sun with the RayBans melting off your face, and then it was dark again. Empty, like there'd never even been a spark. But sometimes . . .

The aliens' gazes touched him and turned away.

"Nick wouldn't exist in your world. There's no broken things, and you take all our best ideas." My throat was hoarse. "You don't even pay the price!" I shouted. "*We* pay the price and we have all the costs! You owe us! You owe *me*!"

I poked Bert in the chest. "You can't use us for your own ends and not *pay*."

"We're sorry," Bert said.

"Yes, aliens are very advanced in the field of apologies," I replied.

We stood for several minutes, silent, even Harry, until they nodded. "How much for your silence?" one said.

"A million," I whispered, so Harry couldn't hear, snatching the two hundred dollar bills from his hand. I gave one to Harry.

"Agreed." I watched as they led Bert through the brush.

Harry looked at me, then at the bill in his hands. "Those were aliens," he said. He'd never understand, I thought, as I took Nick's arm and dragged him home for dinner.

It's hard for a fourteen-year-old to explain several hundred pounds of gold, so Nick and I slipped away after burying most of the thin sheets of metal under the fort.

The aliens hadn't bought my silence. They couldn't take away the fact that I knew they were there. Nick didn't care, or maybe he did. He got on well in the programs I could now afford. I let him be. I wanted to be his protector, but I knew he'd have to make his own way.

I wrote letters of my own, to all the people Bert had sent them to, and others, undoing the damage. Maybe they thought I was a crackpot too, but I think I changed some course of thought. Somewhere.

And if not someone else's mind, my own was changed. It was *our* field to plant, ours to harvest, no matter who was looking over our shoulders.

DEATH OF THE EGG KING

D r. Rocque was dead — shot in the forehead with a small caliber handgun — and my first concern was whether he had signed my thesis.

The manuscript, in loose leaf form, lay open on his desk to the middle of Chapter 5. Rocque sat in his chair, head back, seemingly taking a moment to rest before continuing on with my masterpiece. That image was fine, if you ignored the dot in the middle of his brow.

I carefully flipped to the cover page. Empty, the slot for his signature in the lower left hand corner was empty. All the other signatures were there: mine at the top, then Dr. Forest's and Dr. Olivia-Yordan's and Dr. Khomeli's. But not Rocque's, and I had been sure the bastard was going to sign. Just to be rid of me after six years.

I heard the heavy drip-drop of blood and looked behind his chair at the pool of red. It was obvious what had happened; he'd been popped before he could sign. The row of eggs that usually lined his shelf were gone.

I grabbed his fountain pen, a gift from a Duchess during his Nobel Prize trip, and, after a quick glance at his signature on a student petition on his desk, signed his name for him. I'd done it before on a grant proposal.

The thesis was thick and heavy, and I was quite proud of the amount of material I had managed to regurgitate concerning my last six years in the Department of Aromatic Chemistry. Rocque had been less thrilled, but the bastard survived by keeping dumb graduate researchers like me in indentured servitude. The last time Rocque had been in a lab was when he was a graduate assistant. I thumped the thesis against his desk, squaring the pages.

With a look into the outer office, I exited and shut the door. I dropped the signed thesis in Thelma's in-box and departed for a well-deserved beer.

The Man Hole was empty, except for some rough boys in the back playing pool. Fernando was tending the bar and gave me a toothless grin.

"Hey, Stot. What'll it be, man?"

"Hey, Fernando. How much does it cost to get in here?"

He grinned again. "You know there ain't never any cover at the Man Hole."

"You never get tired of that joke, do you? Corona."

He handed me my beer and I handed him a twenty.

"How long have I been here?"

"An hour, Stot, at least. We been talking about your Grammy and the good cookies she used to bake for you."

"I've been here at least two. Remember? The bells of Saint Clemens rang five times when I entered."

Fernando bounced his palm off his forehead. "How could I forget, Stot? Oranges and lemons."

I grinned, then took a sip from my beer. I liked to avoid the Man Hole in daylight hours. At least at night the grunge sort of blended in. The wooden floor was pitted and warped. The odor of the place was this year's sweat mixed with last year's beer. The moulded metal on the ceiling made the acoustics shitty. Don't ask me why I spent so much time there.

I did notice the placement of Fernando's egg at the end of the bar, close to the door where everyone who entered would pass it. I'd told Fernando he could have put it under the bar and it would have done him just as well. The aromatics filled the whole room pretty much equally. Instead he'd put it out there in the open, and worse, under a ceiling fan. Any decent defense attorney would add a time variable of plus or minus one hour for data taken out of that egg.

It was a Singaporean rip-off of one of Rocque's first models. With a mass spectrometer and a neutron activation system, a good aromatic chemist could determine to the hour who was in the bar for the last twenty-four hours. I, with university equipment and newly decreed Ph.D., could figure it for the last forty-eight hours. Cheaper than a security system and more verifiable than video, the egg was a perfect crime deterrent. Unless the thief or murderer took the egg with him.

The egg had won Rocque his Nobel Prize and now it had won me my Ph.D. I downed my beer, and said, "You can call me Dr. Aristotle, now."

Fernando laughed, and brought me another beer. "This one's on the house, Doc."

I took it and went off to flirt with the rough boys in the back.

About an hour later, Russell walked in and we hissed at each other.

"There aren't enough gay bars in this town," I said.

"Well," he said in his ultra-lispy voice that he used in public, "when you've had as many boys as I've had, there could never be enough bars in this podunk town where I wouldn't run into somebody I'd done. And believe me, Aristotle, you're one of many." He looked me up and down and then shook his head.

Russell was my first lover when I came to graduate school, but not my first lover ever, even though I had let him think that for a few weeks. We'd parted in what I thought was an amicable way about a year earlier. Russell had seen it differently, and been a public nuisance to me since.

I was feeling nostalgic however, and said, "Let me buy you a drink, Russell."

"I thought you'd never ask," replied Russell. "Oh, Bar Wench! Bar Wench! A strawberry daiquiri, please." I passed the pool cue to one of the rough boys.

Fernando rolled his eyes at me as he turned on the blender. I flashed him a smile and took the stool next to Russell's.

"I got my doctorate. Handed in my thesis yesterday."

"It's about damn time, Aristotle. I figured you to be turning gray before you got that shingle. In celebration, if you buy me two more rounds, I'll buy you one."

"You are truly a gentleman."

"Stop flirting with me." Russell took the drink from Fernando. "I heard Adrian dumped you. How's it feel to be on the other end for a change?" I sensed a real anger behind Russell's mocking venom. Adrian had been my lover after Russell and until a week ago.

"He knew I was leaving. He knew we couldn't stay together."

"So you still fantasize about leaving our little community? We're spoiled here, you know? This little college town is the most liberal place in the world. Thirty-two percent of all students and faculty are gay in our little politically correct haven." He began to play with his umbrella. "Where do you think Fernando lost all his teeth? In the real world, out there among the straights." He paused to finish his drink. "Weren't you and Adrian a registered couple?"

I shrugged. Russell was beginning to piss me off. He knew me too well, knew what screws hurt when turned. I had yet to go down to the courthouse and un-register Adrian and me. I decided to do that before I left the next day.

"Well, speak of the devil," Russell said.

I turned and saw Adrian enter with a leather stud. He was dressed in tight jeans and a denim jacket. He'd added dark rouge to his eye to enhance the shiner he had. We had played rough before, but he had obviously decided to embrace the SM life-style fully. He saw me and gripped his stud tighter.

"Oh, ouch. Such immature displays of spite. I'm glad you never did that to me when you dumped me. He's such a bitch, Stot." Russell edged closer to me. "Why don't you come on home with me and forget about Adrian? I'll even be your punching bag, if you want."

I stood up suddenly, shaking loose Russell's hands. "No thanks, Russell. I've gotta pack. I'm leaving tomorrow."

"Well, okay," said Russell, already eyeing one of the rough boy pool sharks. "See you later, Doctor. Then again maybe not."

I slipped past Adrian and out the door.

The pounding of Police Sergeant Claudia Clarke's fist on my door woke me the next morning. I saw it was her through the front window, so I answered the door naked.

"I just love a woman in uniform."

"I'm gay because of you, Aristotle."

"Are you sure you're not het? That crew cut makes you look scrumptious."

"Open the screen door and get some clothes on, Stot. This is serious."

I pulled on a robe and we sat at the kitchen table. She kicked at a pile of boxes. "Going somewhere?"

"Yeah. I got my doctorate. I'm outta here." I put a cup of coffee in front of her. "What's the deal, Claudia? Last minute police work you need us for?" The university aromatic chemistry equipment was a leap better than the city's and on a number of occasions, I'd helped out deciphering an egg that had come from a particularly tough scene.

"Dr. Rocque is dead."

I frowned, tried my best to look shocked. Unfortunately my cynicism is my only defense mechanism. "He ate far too much butter. Success did him in; the Nobel Prize gave him too much spending money, raised his standard of living too high. You have to be born to upper class or the food will kill you."

Claudia smiled blandly. "It wasn't butter. It was a bullet. Through the forehead and out the back."

"Guns and butter are always linked." I nodded and looked down at the cup of coffee. "Dead, huh? He wasn't a bad sort. That's too bad. Did you dissect his egg?"

"Stolen. All seven of his eggs, including the one hidden under his desk. Did you know about that one?"

"All his students did. All the faculty did. Maybe he had one that no one knew about."

"Not in that office." Claudia sipped from her mug. "What was Rocque working on?"

"He's been pushing a new theory at the Government, using high-energy gamma tomography . . ."

"No. On Sunday, when he was murdered. Why was he in on a Sunday evening?"

I shrugged. I knew exactly what he had been working on, but I wasn't going to draw attention to that. "A grant. Grading papers. Anything."

"I ask because whatever he was working on was stolen."

"It was a murder-theft?"

"Apparently. We noticed it when we went to take samples from his desk. Even though the bullet came from the front of the desk, the ensuing cloud of blood, brains, and gore should have left a fine dusting of Dr. Rocque's innards all over the office. One of the forensics boys went to take a sample from the most convenient spot — Rocque's desk — and came up empty. He came up empty in a rectangle approximately forty centimeters wide and thirty centimeters long. There were smears at the twenty centimeter mark in the wide direction."

"Homework. He was grading homework, and some insane student came and blew him away. He was too tough a grader."

"Do you have a listing of all of Rocque's students, cross-referenced to their psychological stability index?"

"That was going to be my next Ph.D. thesis."

"Too bad." Claudia stood. "So you have no idea what Rocque was working on?"

"None."

"Okay. You know the routine. If you think of something before you leave, let me know." She handed me her card.

"Will do."

As I walked into the aro-chem building, Vladimir Rostov called to me. "Hey, Stot, man!"

"Hey, Vlad."

"We're throwing a 'Rocque is Dead' party. You coming, man? My place, tonight."

Vladimir had worked for Rocque for two years on the theoretical side, coming from Moscow University to study with the man. Vladimir had switched advisors, incensed by Rocque's inability to grasp any of his more subtle theoretical points. I had to admit that some of them were quite beyond my grasp as well. But my work was experimental.

"Isn't it rather morbid to have a party celebrating a man's death?"

"I will dance on his grave, when he is buried. Until then, I will toast his brains leaking out the back of his head."

"Well, I can't go. I'm leaving. My thesis is done."

"Hey! It's done? Congratulations. It's about time. Well, all right. I wanted to invite you. I knew you and Rocque weren't best pals."

I shrugged and headed to Thelma's office. The inner door to Rocque's office was roped off with yellow and black tape.

"It matches our school colors."

"What? Eh?" Thelma's head lolled lazily towards the door. "Yeah, sure Aristotle." She burped under her breath. "It does."

"How are you this morning?"

"Shitty. Just shitty." Her words slurred only slightly. She was a true veteran.

"Did you send my thesis off to reproduction, Thelma?"

"First thing, Aristotle. First thing. And they were back at noon."

She pointed to a box standing next to her filing cabinet. "Twenty quick copies with paper covers. Five stayed behind for leather binding, to be delivered next week. He was the only man I ever had an affair with."

"Do you have the original?"

She opened a file and handed me the original. "It was twenty-two years ago. A beautiful June night. He took me, all of me, I gave of myself freely. He never said a word about it. Not for twenty-two years."

"Then it's tough for you now that he's dead?"

"Hell, no. I'm glad." She wiped her nose with a tissue. "And I miss him already. Do you understand, Aristotle?"

I shook my head. "Heterosexual love just confuses me."

"I would guess so."

"Good-bye, Thelma."

"Bye, Aristotle."

I then looked up the surviving three members of my graduate committee, dropping off a copy of the thesis for each.

"So he actually signed it? Son of a bitch. I was sure he'd dig his heels in and push you for another year. I couldn't see why. You have some good stuff in here." Dr. Emil Forest leaned back in his chair, peering far too closely at the cover page. In a moment, he turned to the interior. "Congratulations, Aristotle. What are your plans?"

"Taking the summer off, then I'll start pitching my resume. A couple of police departments have already expressed interest."

"Ha! The last aromatic chemist we graduated took one-hundred-twenty thousand from the LAPD. Don't settle for a penny less."

"I'll put you down as a reference."

"Please do, please do."

Dr. Marlina Olivia-Yordan looked up at me over a copy of Material Engineering Quarterly. "Congratulations, Aristotle. Well done." Her hand was dry and raspy in mine.

"I want to ask you again to consider taking a post-graduate position here." She held up a hand. "I know how you feel about it. I feel the same way about academia myself sometimes. But perhaps, however sorrowful it may be, Dr. Rocque's death may change your mind."

"The man was merely a symptom, not a cause," I said. "Thank you for the offer, but no."

She nodded. "Well, I'm still quite taken with some of the materials you mentioned in Chapter 5 of your thesis. Your idea of using an aromatic collector as a plaster on walls or ceilings is quite ingenuous. Perhaps some eager new student will pick up where you left off."

"I hope not," I said, smiling as well as I could. I wanted to yell at her that I was suffocating in the sterile environment of the University. I was dying and would be as dead as Rocque if I stayed. I wanted out, and I wanted out now. I added, "Thank you again for the offer. I plan to get into the private sector perhaps."

"Yes, of course. They offer far more money than we ever can."

And far more air.

Dr. Mohammed Khomeli smiled nervously at me. "I am quite ruffled today, Aristotle. The police have been here already, and this matter of death in the building. Quite bothersome. And my productivity will be quite low today."

"The police questioned you already?"

"Yes. They checked the computer records and found everyone who was logged in at the time of the death. I was here on Sunday, but no one saw me but you." I had met with Khomeli briefly on Sunday to clarify a point in the thesis. That was before I had gone to see Rocque about the signature.

"I wanted to ask you about that pistol on your desk . . ."

"Do not make jokes, Aristotle! How atrocious a sense of humor you have." But I saw his lips quiver slightly. He came around his desk and shook hands warmly with me. "Good luck. Please contact me if there is anything I can do for you. Good luck."

"Thank you, sir. Thank you very much."

Sergeant Clarke was standing in the student lounge when I entered. She was interviewing a student, but stopped immediately when I walked in.

"Let's take a walk, Aristotle."

"Sure." I dropped the box on a chair and was about to follow her out the door, when she turned and picked up the original copy of my thesis.

The campus was quiet, like always a week after finals. A slight wind rustled the leaves of the trees lining the road. We walked for about a hundred feet down the curb before she spoke. Claudia said,

"How did you know that you had your doctorate Sunday night? You told a number of people in the Man Hole that you were done."

"I assumed it was done. All but the signatures."

"That was a big assumption. Faculty members have mentioned that Rocque was holding back. Hard enough to keep you here."

"Not that hard."

"Was this sitting on Rocque's desk?" She waved the thesis at me.

"No."

"You went to Thelma and picked it up. Slightly irregular."

"I wanted to make a few extra copies."

"You have an alibi."

"I was at the Man Hole."

"You have another alibi."

"Hmmm."

"Dr. Khomeli is quite certain you talked with him from just before four until 4:45pm. Two alibis, Stot, are better than one, even if one is a lie. So I know you didn't do it." Damn. I'd forgotten about Khomeli. Fernando had done me the favor of lying; but I hadn't needed it. I hadn't known that Rocque had been killed during the hour I'd spent with Khomeli.

"I'm glad you know that."

"You felt the need for an alibi, Stot. Why?"

"Fernando was obviously confused. Feebleminded."

"Was your thesis sitting on his desk?"

I stopped. "I answered that question already. More than anything else in the entire Universe, I want to get the fuck out of this hole. I want out! I didn't kill him and we both know that. And I don't know anything more than you do, so just let me go, okay?"

"I'll think about it."

"I'm leaving tonight, Claudia."

She paused, then said, "You are so fucking smug. Did you hate him so much?" She handed the thesis to me.

"No, just this place."

She smirked. "Welcome to the real world."

I was packed, my apartment empty except for cobwebs and dust bunnies. It had taken two trips to Goodwill, but I'd managed to get everything I owned in my car. Everything but the thesis sitting on the floor next to the telephone jack.

There was nothing holding me there, and I knew I should just get in my car and drive like I had meant to. But I kept looking back at my thesis.

It was the only witness to the death of my advisor. It was too bad that a book didn't reveal in its text what it saw.

I paused. What page had the book been opened to? I tried to recall. Chapter 4? No, Chapter 5, the chapter on alternative materials for aromatic collection. Dr. Olivia-Yordan had mentioned the plaster idea, but there were others, including a sample of filamented paper substance that worked rather well.

The sample. The thesis had been open to the sample collector. Rocque had known the murderer might take the eggs, but the murderer wouldn't have known about the filament. Perhaps Rocque had opened it, casually, desperately hoping that I would notice. Bastard. He was drawing me in again, just when I was almost away.

I flipped open the thesis, then shut it. I would have to hurry. It had been twenty-four hours already, and the paper had a definite time limit before the uncertainty was too great.

The lab was dark, and I fired up the mass spectrometer and the neutron activation system. While they warmed up, I cast a few micro-tubes from the sample. The eggs were filled with a micro-tubule structure that stored molecules from the air, larger than a certain size, in a temporal sequence. By excavating backwards, a researcher could determine the sequence of events around the egg. There were huge databases of odors maintained by the domestic and international agencies. Whenever a criminal was booked, fingerprinting was less common than an odor sample.

My paper sample worked the same way. The only difference was that the micro-structure was not ceramic, and so it required a more elaborate casting method. But, hey that's what Ph.D. dissertations are for: they take a simple idea and expound on it in more and more complicated ways until the original idea is buried beneath piles and piles of unrelated intellectual refuse.

The murder was easy to pinpoint. Blood has a unique signature. At that point, I needed only to identify the possible odor traces right before and right after the murder. It took me several castings to get a good enough sample of that time period. Luckily, there were several million samples in the paper collector.

Once I had my sample of molecules from the murder time, fifteen minutes on either side, I eliminated Rocque's signatures, then mine, then Thelma's, whose signature was all over the office. I was still left with a number of possibilities, since each person acts as a molecule collector. Whoever Rocque, Thelma, the murderer, and I were around on Sunday probably were in the sample in some small part. So I eliminated Rocque's wife, Thelma's poodle, and Khomeli. Then I opened my personal database, including samples from all my old lovers and all my aftershaves. It was amazing how a lover's odor can cling to you. I'd seen egg technicians fooled into thinking a husband had been there, when in fact it was the wife. There was a sort of melding of odor between lovers. I probably still smelled a little like Adrian.

I eliminated all that and I was left with nothing. I had eliminated Rocque's murderer. All that was left was inorganic or trace chemicals.

"Shit," I muttered. "Maybe I did do it and I don't remember."

Then I realized that it had to have been Thelma. Khomeli had an alibi, I had an alibi, and Rocque's wife probably had one or she'd have been arrested by now. "Thelma, you old dog. Twenty years of silence was too much for you, huh? Beware a lover scorned."

To be certain, I took another group of samples and eliminated Thelma's signature, then set about eliminating what was left completely. I got up to Rocque, his wife and me, then I was left with a couple trace odors, and one major one that my personal database had gotten rid of before. I figured the major one was Adrian — it had only been a week since we were living together — and the minor signatures were Khomeli and who knew who else.

To be certain, I queried my personal database, expecting Adrian's cologne to appear. I was surprised to see it was Russell's.

I let myself into Russell's apartment when he didn't answer my knock. All right, so I still had a key. I hated burning bridges. He was in the shower.

I rummaged around in the kitchen, then the living room. I had about given up when I noticed the line of seven eggs sitting on his mantel. Only Russel would store evidence of murder on his mantel.

Behind me, the shower turned off, and I heard Russell climb out of the shower. "Oh, hi, Aristotle. I was wondering if you were going to say good-bye before you left." He didn't bother to put on a towel before sitting across from me.

"Those eggs will put you away for a long time, Russell."

"Oh, those old things. I doubt it. I even have the gun around here somewhere." He looked under the magazines on the coffee table, then pulled out a small pistol. He put it squarely in my palm.

"You've just handed me your murder weapon. I could go to the police right now."

"No, you can't."

"Do you think I won't through some devotion to what we had? Do you think you still mean that much to me? Adrian doesn't mean that much to me."

"Oh, no, no. I have something stronger than Adrian does. You can't go to the police because I know the thesis wasn't signed."

A rush of blood filled my cheeks.

Russell added, "We are bound by more than lust or love, Aristotle. I had hoped to simply frame you for the murder. But then I realized that taking away your freedom would be so much better. You're not going anywhere, so you might as well have a seat."

"Russell . . ."

He stood and I stood too. "We're accomplices now. Maybe you should move in here with me. I know you really want to stay here with me."

"What have you done, Russell?" My stomach was churning. My mind was spinning. Had I forced him to this? The gun in my hand was heavy as I brought it to point at his chest.

Russell made a motion with his hand. "Shoot me, Aristotle? That will only incriminate you more. Face it, you're stuck here in this little piece of heaven. I've always thought you were a fool to want to leave."

I looked at the row of eggs. Each one would show that Russell had entered the Rocque's office, killed him, then left with the eggs. And when Russell was arrested, he would tell the police that the line for Rocque's signature had been empty. He would tell. Unless he was dead.

The gun wavered in my hand. "I can't let you do that," I said. I'd forged a signature, built an alibi, and lied to the police. It was the slippery slope to murder, just one more felony to be rid of this place forever.

"I can't let you do this," I said, but now I was unsure what I meant.

I put the gun on the table. No more. He looked at me with

unconcerned eyes.

I turned and left.

"I'll tell them, Aristotle," Russell yelled after me. "You'll have wasted six years."

What was six years in a lifetime? I thought as I pulled open the car door. Fishing in my pocket, I found Claudia's card.

I looked at it for a few moments, then I started my car.

WALLS OF THE UNIVERSE

The screen door slammed behind John Rayburn, rattling in its frame. He and his dad had been meaning to fix the hinges and paint it before winter, but just then he wanted to rip it off and fling it into the fields.

"Johnny?" his mother called after him, but by then he was in the dark shadow of the barn. He slipped around the far end and any more of his mother's calls were lost among the sliding of cricket legs. His breath blew from his mouth in clouds.

John came to the edge of the pumpkin patch, stood for a moment, then plunged into it. Through the pumpkin patch was east, toward Case Institute of Technology where he hoped to start as a freshman the next year. Not that it was likely. There was always the University of Toledo, his father had said. One or two years of work could pay for a year of tuition there.

He kicked a half-rotten pumpkin. Seeds and wispy strings of pumpkin guts spiraled through the air. The smell of dark earth and rotten pumpkin reminded him it was a week before Halloween and they hadn't had time to harvest the pumpkins: a waste and a thousand dollars lost to earthworms. He ignored how many credits that money would have bought.

The pumpkin field ended at the tree line, the eastern edge of the farm. The trees — old maples and elms — abutted Townline Road, beyond which was the abandoned quarry. He stood in the trees, just breathing, letting the anger seep away.

It wasn't his parents' fault. If anyone was to blame, it was he. He hadn't had to beat the crap out of Ted Carson. He hadn't had to tell Ted Carson's mom off. That had entirely been him. Though the look on Mrs. Carson's face had almost been worth it when he told her her son was an asshole. What a mess.

He spun at the sound of a stick cracking.

For a moment he thought that Ted Carson had chased him out of the farmhouse, that he and his mother were there in the woods. But the figure who stood there was just a boy, holding a broken branch in his hand.

"Johnny?" the boy said. The branch flagged in his grip, touching the ground.

John peered into the dark. He wasn't a boy; he was a teenager. John stepped closer. The teen was dressed in jeans and plaid shirt. Over the shirt he wore a sleeveless red coat that looked oddly out of date.

His eyes lingered on the stranger's face. No, not a stranger. The teen had *his* face.

"Hey, Johnny. It's me, Johnny."

The figure in the woods was him.

John looked at this other John, this John Subprime, and decided he would be the one. He was clearly a Johnny Farmboy, not one of the Johnny Rebels, not one of the Broken Johns, so he would be wide-eyed and gullible. He'd believe John's story, and then John could get on with his life.

"Who . . . who are you?" Johnny Farmboy asked. He was dressed in jeans and a shirt, no coat.

John forced his most honest smile. "I'm you, John."

"What?"

Johnny Farmboy could be so dense.

"Who do I look like?"

"You look like . . ."

"I look just like you, John. Because I am you." Johnny Farmboy took a step back, and John continued. "I know what you're thinking. Some trick. Someone is playing a trick on the farmboy. No. Let's get past that. Next you're going to think that you were twins and one of them was put up for adoption. Nope. It's much more interesting than that."

Johnny Farmboy crossed his arms. "Explain it, then."

"Listen, I'm really hungry; I could use some food and a place to sit down. I saw Dad go in the house. Maybe we can sit in the barn, and I can explain everything."

John waited for the wheels to turn.

"I don't think so," Johnny Farmboy finally said.

"Fine. I'll turn around and walk away. Then you'll never get to hear the story."

John watched the emotion play across Farmboy's face. Nominally skeptical, he was debating how full of crap this wraith in the night was, while desperately wanting to the know the answer to the riddle. Farmboy loved puzzles.

Finally his face relaxed. "Let's go to the barn," he said.

The man walked at his side, and John eased away from him. As they walked through the pumpkin patch, John noted that their strides matched. John pulled open the back door of the barn, and the young man entered ahead of him, tapping the light switch by the door.

"A little warmer," he said. He rubbed his hands together and turned to John.

The light hit his face squarely, and John was startled to see the uncanny match between them. The sandy hair was styled differently and was longer. The clothes were odd; John had never worn a coat like that. The young man was just a bit thinner as well. He wore a blue backpack, so fully stuffed that the zipper wouldn't close all the way. There was a cut above his eye. A bit of brown blood was crusted over his left brow, clotted but recent.

He could have passed as John's twin.

"So, who are you?"

"What about a bite of something to eat?"

John went to the horse stall and pulled an apple from a bag. He tossed it to the young man. He caught it and smiled at John.

"Tell the story, and I might get some dinner from the house."

"Did Dad teach you to be so mean to strangers? I bet if he found me in the woods, he'd invite me in to dinner."

"Tell," John said.

"Fine." The young man flung himself on a hay bale and munched the apple. "It's simple, really. I'm you. Or rather I'm you genetically, but I grew up on this same farm in another universe. And now I've come to visit myself."

"Bullshit. Who put you up to this?"

"Okay, okay. I didn't believe me either." A frown passed over his face. "But I can prove it. Hold on a second." He wiped his mouth with the back of his hand. "Here we go: That horse is named

Stan or Dan. You bought him from the McGregor's on Butte Road when you were ten. He's stubborn and willful and he hates being saddled. But he'll canter like a show horse if he knows you have an apple in your pocket." He turned to the stalls on his left. "That pig is called Rosey. That cow is Wilma. The chickens are called Ladies A through F. How am I doing so far?" He smiled an arrogant smile.

"You stole some of your uncle's cigarettes when you were twelve and smoked them all. You killed a big bullfrog with your bb gun when you were eight. You were so sickened by it you threw up and haven't used a gun since. Your first kiss was with Amy Walder when you were fourteen. She wanted to show you her underwear too, but you ran home to Mommy. I don't blame you. She's got cooties everywhere I go.

"Everyone calls you Johnny, but you prefer John. You have a stash of *Playboys* in the barn loft. And you burned a hole in the rug in your room once. No one knows because you rearranged your room so that the night stand is on top of it." He spread his arms like a gymnast who'd just stuck a landing.

"Well? How close did I come?" He smiled and tossed the apple core into Stan's stall.

"I never kissed Amy Walder." Amy had gotten pregnant when she was fifteen by Tyrone Biggens. She'd moved to Montana with her aunt and hadn't come back. John didn't mention that everything else he'd said was true.

"Well, was I right?"

John nodded. "Mostly."

"Mostly? I nailed it on the head with a hammer, because it all happened to me. Only it happened in another universe."

How did this guy know so much about him? Who had he talked to? His parents? "Okay. Answer this. What was my first cat's name?"

"Snowball."

"What is my favorite class?"

"Physics."

"What schools did I apply to?"

The man paused, frowned. "I don't know."

"Why not? You know everything else."

"I've been traveling, you know, for a while. I haven't applied to college yet, so I don't know. As soon as I used the device, I became someone different. Up till then, we were the same." He looked tired. "Listen. I'm you, but if I can't convince you, that's fine. Let me sleep in the loft tonight and then I'll leave."

John watched him grab the ladder, and he felt a twinge of guilt at treating him so shabbily. "Yeah, you can sleep in the loft. Let me get you some dinner. Stay here. Don't leave the barn, and hide if someone comes. You'd give my parents a heart attack."

"Thanks, John."

John watched Farmboy disappear through the door into the night, shuddering and then exhaling. He hadn't even come to the hard part yet.

It would have been so easy to kill Farmboy, a blow to the back of the head, and it was his. But John wouldn't do that. He hoped, not yet. He was desperate, but not willing to commit homicide. Or would it be suicide?

He chuckled grimly to himself. Dan the Man nickered in response.

John took an apple from the basket and reached out to the horse. Suddenly his eyes were filled with tears.

"Hold yourself together, man," he whispered as he let Dan gingerly chomp the apple from his hand. His own horse was dead, at his own hand.

He'd taken Dan riding and had tried for the fence beyond the back field. They had flown. But Dan's hind left hadn't cleared it. The bone had broken, and John ran sobbing to his farm.

His father met him halfway, a rifle in his hand, his face grim. He'd seen the whole thing.

"Dan's down!" John cried.

His father nodded and handed the rifle to him.

John took it blankly, then tried to hand it back to his father.

"No!"

"If the leg's broken, you must."

"Maybe . . ." But he stopped. Dan was whinnying shrilly; he could hear it from where they stood. The leg had been horribly twisted. There was no doubt.

"Couldn't Dr. Kimble look at him?"

"How will you pay for that?"

"Will you?"

His father snorted and walked away.

John watched him trod back to the house until Dan's cries became too much for him. He turned then, tears raining down his cheeks.

Dan's eyes were wide. He shook his head heavily at John, then he settled when John placed the barrel against his skull. Perhaps he knew. John fished an apple from his pocket and slipped it between Dan's teeth.

The horse held it there, not biting, waiting. He seemed to nod at John. Then John had pulled the trigger.

The horse had shuddered and fallen still. John sank to the ground and cried for Dan for an hour.

But here he was. Alive. He rubbed Dan's muzzle.

"Hello, Dan. Back from the dead," John said. "Just like me."

His mother and father stopped talking when the door slammed, so he knew they'd been talking about him.

"I'm gonna eat in the barn," he said. "I'm working on an electronics experiment."

He took a plate from the cabinet and began to dish out the lasagna. He filled the plate with enough to feed two of him.

His father caught his eye, then said, "Son, this business with the Carson boy . . ."

John slipped a second fork into his pocket. "Yeah?"

"I'm sure you did the right thing and all." John nodded at his father, saw his mother look away.

"He hates us because we're farmers and we dig in the dirt," John said. His mother lifted her apron strap over her neck, hung the apron on a chair, and slipped out of the kitchen.

"I know that, Johnny . . . John. But sometimes you gotta keep the peace."

John nodded. "Sometimes I have to throw a punch, Dad." He turned to go.

"John, you can eat in here with us."

"Not tonight, Dad."

Grabbing a quart of milk, he walked through the laundry room and left out the back door.

*

"Stan never lets anyone do that but me."

John turned from rubbing Dan's ears. "Just so," he said. He took the proffered paper towel full of lasagna, dug into it with the extra fork Farmboy had fetched.

"I always loved this lasagna. Thanks."

Farmboy frowned, and John recognized the stubbornness; he did the same thing when presented with the impossible. He decided to stay silent and stop goading him with the evidence. This John needed a softer touch.

John ate in silence while Farmboy watched, until finally he said, "Let's assume for a moment that you are me from another universe. How can you do it? And why you?"

Through a mouth of pasta, he said, "With my device, and I don't know."

"Elaborate," John said, angry.

"I was given a device that lets me pass from one universe to the next. It's right here under my shirt. I don't know why it was me. Or rather I don't know why it was us."

"Stop prancing around my questions!" Farmboy shouted. "Who gave you the device?"

"I did!" John grinned.

"One of us from another universe gave you the device."

"Yeah. Another John. Nice looking fellow." So far all he had said was the truth.

Farmboy was silent for a while, his lasagna half-eaten. Finally he said, "I need to feed the sheep." He poured a bag of corn into the trough. John lifted the end of it with him. "Thanks." They fed the cows and the horse afterwards, then finished their own dinner.

Farmboy said, "So if you are me, what do I call you?"

"Well, John won't work, will it? Well, it will if there's just the two of us, but as soon as you start adding the infinite number of Johns out there . . . How about John Prime?"

"Then who gave you the device?"

"John Superprime," John Prime said with a smile. "So do you believe me yet?"

Farmboy was still dubious. "Maybe."

"All right. Here's the last piece of evidence. No use denying this." He pulled up his pant leg to reveal a long white scar, devoid of hair. "Let's see yours," John said, pushing down his panic. The last time he'd tried this, it hadn't been there.

Farmboy looked at the scar, and then pulled his jeans up to the knee. The cold air of the barn drew goose bumps on his calf everywhere except the puckered flesh of his own identical scar.

When John Prime had been twelve, he and Bobby Walder had climbed the barbed wire fence of Old Mrs. Jones to swim in her pond. Mrs. Jones had set the dogs on them, and they'd had to run naked across the field, diving over the barbed wire fence. John hadn't quite cleared it.

Bobby had run off, and John had limped home. The cut on his leg had required three dozen stitches and a tetanus shot.

"Now do you believe?" John Prime asked.

John stared at the scar on his leg. "I believe. Hurt like hell, didn't it?"

"Yes," John Prime said with a grin. "Yes, it did, brother."

John sat in the fishbowl — the glass-enclosed room outside the principal's office — ignoring the eyes of his classmates and wondering what the hell John Prime was up to. He'd left his twin in the barn loft with half his lunch and an admonishment to stay out of sight.

"Don't worry," he'd said with a smirk. "Meet me at the library after school."

"Don't let anyone see you, all right?"

John Prime had smiled again.

"John?" Principal Gushman stuck his head out of his office. John's stomach dropped; he was never in trouble.

Mr. Gushman had a barrel chest, balding head, and perpetual frown. He motioned John to a chair and sat behind the desk, letting out his breath heavily as he sat. He'd been a major in the Army, people said. He liked to be strict. John had never talked with him in the year he'd been principal.

"John, we have a policy regarding violence and bullying."

John opened his mouth to speak.

"Hold on. Let me finish. The facts of the matter are these. You hit a classmate — a younger classmate — several times in the locker room. He required a trip to the emergency room and stitches." He opened a file on his desk.

"The rules are there for the protection of all students. There can be no violence in the school. There can be no exceptions. Do you understand?"

John stared, then said, "I understand the rule. But —"

"You're a straight-A student, varsity basketball and track. You're well-liked. Destined for a good college. This could be a blemish on your record."

John knew what the word "could" meant. Gushman was about to offer him a way out.

"A citation for violence, as stated in the student handbook, means a three-day suspension and the dropping of any sports activities. You'd be off the basketball and track teams."

John's throat tightened.

"Do you see the gravity of the situation?"

"Yes," John managed to say.

Gushman opened another folder on his desk. "But I recognize this as a special case. So if you write a letter of apology to Mrs. Carson, we'll drop the whole matter." Gushman looked at him, expecting an answer.

John felt cornered. Yes, he had hit Ted, because he was a prick. Ted needed hitting, if anyone did; he had dropped John's clothes in the urinal. He said, "Why does Mrs. Carson want the letter? I didn't hit her. I hit Ted."

"She feels that you showed her disrespect. She wants the letter to address that as well as the violence."

If he just wrote the letter, it would just all go away. But he'd always know that his mother and Mrs. Carson had squashed him. He hated that. He hated any form of defeat. He wanted to tell Gushman he'd take the suspension. He wanted to throw it all in the man's face.

Instead, he said, "I'd like to think about it over the weekend if that's okay."

Mr. Gushman's smile told John that he was sure he'd bent John to his will. John went along with it, smiling back. "Yes. You may. But I need a decision on Monday."

John left for his next class.

John walked past the librarian, his Toledo Meerkats cap low over his face. He didn't want to be recognized as John Rayburn. At least not yet. The reference section was where he expected it to be, which was a relief. If the little things were the same he had hope for the bigger things. He'd tried living in the weird places, but sooner or later something tripped him up and he had to run. He needed a place like what he remembered, and so far, this place seemed pretty close.

He reached for the almanac. Sure, an encyclopedia had more information, but he could be lost in the details for hours. All he needed was a gross comparison.

He ran his finger down the list of presidents, recognizing all of them. He already knew this wasn't a world where Washington served four terms and set a standard for a king-president serving for life. Turning the page, he found the next twenty presidents to be the same until the last four. Who the hell was Bill Clinton?

The deviation was small, even so. It had to be, he was so tired of running.

John found a quiet table, opened his backpack, and began re-searching.

The city library was just a couple of blocks from the school. John wandered through the stacks until he found John Prime at the center study desk in a row of three on the third floor. He had a dozen Findlay Heralds spread out, as well as a couple books. His backpack was open, and John saw that it was jammed with paper and folders.

To hide his features, John Prime wore a Toledo Meerkats base-ball hat and sunglasses. He pulled off his glasses when he saw John, and said, "You look like crap. What happened to you?"

"Nothing. Now what are you doing? I have to get back to the school by five. There's a game tonight."

"Yeah, yeah, yeah." John Prime picked up the history book. "In every universe I've been in, it's always something simple. Here George Bush raised taxes and he never got elected to a second term. Clinton beat him in '91." He opened the history book and pointed to the color panel of American Presidents. "In my world, Bush never backed down on the taxes thing, and the economy took off and he got elected to his second term. He was riding even higher when Hussein was assassinated in the middle of his second term. His son was elected in 1996."

John laughed, "That joker?"

John Prime scowled. "Dubya worked the national debt down to nothing. Unemployment was below three percent."

"It's low here too. Clinton did a good job."

John Prime pointed to a newspaper article he had copied. "Whitewater? Drug use? Vince Foster?" He handed the articles to John, then shook his head. "Never mind. It's all pretty much irrelevant anyway. At least we didn't grow up in a world where Nixon was never caught."

"What happened there?"

"The Second Depression usually. Russia and the US never coming to an arms agreement. Those are some totalitarian places." He took the articles back from John. "Are there Post-It notes in this world?"

"Yes. Of course."

John Prime shrugged. "Sometimes there aren't. It's worth a fortune. And so simple." He pulled out his notebook. "I have a hundred of them." He opened his notebook to a picture of the MTV astronaut. "MTV?"

"Yep."

"The World Wide Web?"

"I think so."

"Rubik's Cube?"

"Never heard of it."

John Prime checked the top of the figure with a multi-colored cube. "Ah ha. That's a big money maker."

"It is?"

He turned the page. "Dungeon and Dragons?"

"You mean that game where you pretend to be a wizard?"

"That's the one. How about Lozenos? You got that here?"

"Never heard of it. What is it?"

"Candy. South African diamond mines?"

They worked through a long list of things, about three-quarters of which John had heard of, fads, toys, or inventions.

"This is a good list to work from. Some good money makers on this."

"What are you going to do?" John asked. This was his world, and he didn't like what he suspected John Prime had in mind.

John Prime smiled. "There's money to be made in interdimensional trade."

"Interdimensional trade?"

"Not in actual goods. There's no way I can transport enough stuff to make a profit. Too complicated. But ideas are easy to transport, and what's in the public domain in the last universe is unheard of in the next. Rubik sold one hundred million Cubes. At ten dollars a cube, that's a billion dollars." He lifted up the notebook. "There are two dozen ideas in here that made hundreds of millions of dollars in other worlds."

"So what are you going to do?"

John Prime smiled his arrogant smile. "Not me. We. I need an agent in this world to work the deals. Who better than myself? The saying goes that you can't be in more than one place at a time. But I can."

"Uh huh."

"And we split it fifty-fifty."

"Uh huh."

"Listen. It's not stealing. These ideas have never been thought of here. The people who invented these things might not even be alive here."

"I never said it was stealing," John said. "I'm just not so sure I believe you still."

John Prime sighed. "So what's got you so down today?"

John said, "I may get suspended from school and kicked off the basketball and track teams."

"What? Why?" John Prime looked genuinely concerned.

"I beat up a kid, Ted Carson. His mother told my mother and the principal. They want me to apologize."

John Prime was angry. "You're not gonna, are you? I know Ted Carson. He's a little shit. In every universe."

"I don't have a choice."

"There's always a choice." John Prime pulled a notebook out of his bag. "Ted Carson, huh? I have something on him."

John looked over his shoulder at the notebook. Each page had a newspaper clipping, words highlighted and notes at the bottom referencing other pages. One title read, "Mayor and Council Members Indicted." The picture showed Mayor Thiessen yelling. Another article was a list of divorces granted. John Prime turned the page and pointed. "Here it is. Ted Carson picked up for torturing a neighbor's cat. Apparently the boy killed a dozen neighborhood animals before getting caught." He glanced at John.

"I've never heard anything about that."

"Then maybe he never got caught here."

"What are we going to do with that?" John asked. He read the article, shaking his head.

"Grease the gears, my brother." He handed John a newspaper listing of recent divorces. "Photocopy this."

"Why?"

"It's the best place to figure out who's sleeping with who. That usually doesn't change from one universe to the next. Speaking of which, how does Casey Nicholson look in this universe?"

"What?"

"Yeah. Is she a dog or a hottie? Half the time she's pregnant in her junior year and living in a trailer park."

"She's a cheerleader," John said.

John Prime glanced at him and smiled. "You like her, don't you? Are we dating her?"

"No!"

"Does she like us?"

"Me! Not us," John said. "And I think so. She smiles at me in class."

"What's not to love about us?" He glanced at his watch. "Time for you to head over to the school, isn't it?"

"Yeah."

"I'll meet you at home tonight. See ya."

"Don't talk to anyone," John said. "They'll think it was me. Don't get me in trouble."

"Don't worry. The last thing I want to do is screw up your life here."

Casey, Casey, Casey, John thought as he watched Johnny Farmboy depart. Casey Cheerleader was the best Casey of all. She smelled so clean. And it was all wasted on Johnny Farmboy.

He had planned on working until the library closed, but the idea of seeing Casey was overwhelming. He halfheartedly perused a few microfiched newspapers, then packed his things up and headed for the school.

Once again he was hit with nostalgia as he walked through the small Findlay downtown. He had spent his entire life in this little town — well, not *this* particular town. For a moment he wanted to run into Maude's Used Books and rummage through the old comic books. But the counter clerk would surely recognize him. *Not yet,* he thought.

The junior varsity team was playing when he reached the high school stadium. He found a seat at the top of the bleacher and made sure his ball cap covered his face. The sun was just dipping below the far end zone, casting long violent shadows as the JV teams — Findlay High was playing Gurion Valley — moved the ball haphazardly up and down the field. Watching the shadows was more interesting.

But then the game was over, and the stands were filling. He recognized faces, year old memories, but still vivid. He shrunk down on the bench, pulled up the collar on his ski coat. Then he laughed at himself. Always hiding, always running. Not this time.

The varsity cheerleaders came on the field. He spotted Casey immediately and he felt a spurt of hormones course through him. Across universes he'd come for her, he thought. How was that for a pickup line?

Goddamn, she was beautiful. He stood to get a better look.

"Hey, John!" someone shouted, two rows down.

John looked at him, shocked. He had no idea who he was. A wave of doubt shook him. He'd been gone a year; how much had he missed in that time?

"Hey."

"Shouldn't you be down with the team? I thought you were keeping stats."

"Yeah, I was just going."

John took the bleacher steps two at a time, nearly running. He had things to do before he could gawk at Casey.

After the game John left a copy of the stats with Coach Jessick and then met his father in the parking lot.

"Not a good game for the home team," his father said. He wore his overalls and a John Deere hat. John realized he'd sat in the stands like that, with manure on his shoes. Soft country and western whispered tinnily from the speakers. For a moment he was embarrassed, then he remembered why he'd had to fight Ted Carson.

"Thanks for picking me up, Dad."

"No problem." He dropped the truck into gear and pulled it out of the lot. "Odd thing. I thought I saw you in the stands."

John glanced at his father, forced himself to be calm. "I was down keeping stats."

"I know, I saw. Must be my old eyes, playing tricks."

Had John Prime not gone back to the barn? What was that bastard doing to him?

"Gushman called."

John nodded in the dark of the cab. "I figured."

"Said you were gonna write an apology."

"I don't want to," John said. "But . . ."

"I know. A stain on your permanent record and all." His father turned the radio off. "I was at the U in Toledo for a semester or two. Me and college didn't get along much. But you, Son. You can learn and do something interesting with it. Which is really what me and your mother want."

"Dad —"

"Hold on a second. I'm not saying what you did to the Carson boy was wrong, but you did get caught at it. And if you get caught at something, you usually have to pay for it. Writing a letter saying something isn't the same as believing it."

John nodded. "I think I'm gonna write the letter, Dad."

His father grunted, satisfied. "You helping with the apples tomorrow? We wait any longer and we won't get any good ones."

"Yeah, I'll help until lunch. Then I have basketball practice."

"Okay."

They sat in silence for the remainder of the trip. John was glad his father was so pragmatic.

As they drove up to the farmhouse, John considered what he was going to do about John Prime.

"Where are you?"

John paused in his scanning of the newspaper and gripped a shovel. It might have come to violence anyway; Johnny Farmboy looked pissed.

"Up here."

"You went to the football game," he accused as he climbed the ladder.

"Just for a bit."

"My dad saw you."

"But he didn't realize it was me, did he?"

Farmboy's anger faded a notch. "No, no. He thought he was seeing things."

"See? No one will believe it even if they see us together."
Farmboy shook his head. He grunted.

John added, "This Ted Carson thing is about to go away."

"What do you mean?"

"A bunch of cats have gone missing over there."

"You went out in public and talked to people?"

"Just kids. And it was dark. No one even saw my face. Three cats this month, by the way. Ted is an animal serial killer. We can pin this on him and his mom will have to back off."

"I'm writing the letter of apology," Farmboy said.

"What? No!"

"It's better this way. I don't want to screw up my future."

"Listen. It'll never get any better than this. The kid is a psychopath and we can shove it in his parents' faces!"

"No. And listen. You have got to lay low. I don't want you wandering around town messing up things," Farmboy said. "Going to the library today was too much."

John smiled. "Don't want me hitting on Casey Nicholson, huh?"

"Stop it!" He raised his hand. "That's it. Why don't you just move on? Hit the next town or the next universe or whatever. Just get out of my life!"

John frowned. It was time for the last shot. He lifted up his shirt. Under his gray sweatshirt was a shoulder harness with a thin disk the diameter of a softball attached at the center. It had a digital readout which said 7533, three blue buttons on the front, and dials and levers on the sides.

John began unstrapping the harness and said, "John, maybe it's time you saw for yourself."

John looked at the device. It was tiny for what it was supposed to do.

"How does it work?" he asked. John envisioned golden wires entwining black vortices of primal energy, x-ray claws tearing at the walls of the universe as if they were tissue.

"I don't know how it works," John Prime said, irritated. "I just know how to work it." He pointed to the digital readout. "This is your universe number."

"7533?"

"My universe is 7433." He pointed to the first blue button. "This increments the universe counter. See?" He pressed the button once and the number changed to 7534. "This one decrements the counter." He pressed the second blue button and the counter flipped back to 7533. He pointed to a metal lever on the side of the disk. "Once you've dialed in your universe, you pull the lever and — Pow! — you're in the next universe."

"It looks like a slot machine," John said.

John Prime pursed his lips. "It's the product of a powerful civilization."

"Does it hurt?" John asked.

"I don't feel a thing. Sometimes my ears pop because the weather's a little different. Sometimes I drop a few inches or my feet are stuck in the dirt."

"What's this other button for?"

John Prime shook his head. "I don't know. I've pressed it, but it doesn't seem to do anything. There's no owner's manual, you know?" He grinned. "Wanna try it out?"

More than anything, John wanted to try it. Not only would he know for sure if John Prime was full of crap, but he would get to see another universe. The idea was astounding. To travel, to be free of all this . . . detritus in his life. Ten more months in Findlay was a lifetime. Here in front of him was adventure.

"Show me."

John Prime frowned. "I can't. It takes twelve hours to recharge the device after it's used. If I left now, I'd be in some other universe for a day before I could come back."

"I don't want to be gone a day! I have chores. I have to write a letter."

"It's okay. I'll cover for you here."

"No way!"

"I can do it. No one would know. I've been you for as long as you have."

"No. There's no way I'm leaving for twelve hours with you in control of my life."

John Prime shook his head. "How about a test run? Tomorrow you're doing what?"

"Picking apples with my dad."

"I'll do it instead. If your dad doesn't notice a thing, then you take the trip, and I'll cover for you. If you leave tomorrow afternoon, you can be back on Sunday and not miss a day of school."

John Prime opened his backpack wider. "And to make the whole trip a lot more fun, here's some spending money." He pulled out a stack of twenty dollar bills.

"Where did you get that?" John had never seen so much money. His bank account had no more than 300 dollars in it.

John Prime handed him the stack of cash. The twenties were crisp, the paper smooth-sticky. "There's got to be two thousand dollars here."

"Yep."

"It's from another universe, isn't it? This is counterfeit."

"It's real money. And no one in this podunk town will be able to tell me that it's not." John Prime pulled a twenty out of his own pocket. "This is from your universe. See any differences?"

John took the first twenty off the stack and compared it to the crumpled bill. They looked identical to him.

"How'd you get it?"

"Investments." John Prime's smile was ambiguous.

"Did you steal it?"

John Prime shook his head. "Even if I did steal it, the police looking for it are in another universe."

John felt a twinge of apprehension. John Prime had his fingerprints, his looks, his voice. He knew everything there was to know about him. He could rob a bank, kill someone, and then escape to another universe, leaving John holding the bag. All the evidence of such a crime would point to him, and there was no way he could prove that it wasn't him.

Would he do such a thing? John Prime had called John his brother. In a sense they were identical brothers. And John Prime was letting John use his device, in effect stranding him in this universe. That took trust.

"Twenty-four hours," John Prime said. "Think of it as a vacation. A break from all this shit with Ted Carson."

The lure of seeing another universe was too strong. "You pick apples with my father tomorrow. If he doesn't suspect anything, then maybe I'll take the trip."

"You won't regret it, John."

"But you have got to promise not to mess anything up!"

John Prime nodded. "That's the last thing I'd want to do, John."

"Damn, it's early," John said, rubbing the straw from his hair.

"Don't let my dad hear you cursing," Johnny Farmboy said.

"Right, no cursing." John stood, stretching. "Apple picking? I haven't done that . . . in a while." It had been a lot longer than a year. His own father hadn't bothered with the orchard in years.

John peered out a small window. Farmboy's father was already out there with the tractor.

"What's up between you and your dad? Anything heavy?" John asked. Johnny Farmboy took off his coat and handed it to John, taking John's in return.

John shook his head. "We talked last night about the Carson thing. He wanted me to write the letter."

"So that's it. What about your mother?"

"She was pissed with me before. She still may be. We haven't talked since Thursday."

"Anything happening this afternoon?" John Prime took a pencil out and started jotting things down.

"Nothing until tomorrow. Church, then chores. Muck the stalls. Homework. But I'll do that."

"What's due for Monday?"

"Reading for Physics. Essay for English on Gerard Manley Hopkins. Problem set in Calculus. That's it."

"What's your class schedule like?"

Farmboy began to tell him, but then said, "Why do you need to know that? I'll be back."

"In case someone asks."

"No one's gonna ask." As Farmboy pulled John's ski jacket on, he looked through his binoculars. "I'll watch from here. If anything goes wrong, you pretend to be sick and come back to the barn. You'll brief me and then we switch back."

John Prime smiled. "Nothing's gonna happen. Relax." He pulled on gloves and climbed down the ladder. "See ya at lunch."

With more trepidation than he felt, John walked out to the orchard. He cast one glance over his shoulder and saw Farmboy watching him through binoculars. This was a test in more ways than one. He could still run. He could still find another bolthole.

His father barely glanced at him. "How 'bout we start this end?"

"Okay," John said, his throat dry. His father stood tall, and when he walked past he smelled of dirt, not booze. He walked up to a tree and turned to look at him.

"Well? Come on."

John gripped a branch and pulled himself into the tree. The rough bark cut his hands through the gloves. His foot missed a hold, and he slipped.

"Careful there."

"I'm getting too big for this," John said.

"Next year, I'll have to hire someone to help me."

John paused, words of banter on his lips. He smiled. "I bet Mom could do it."

His father laughed. "Now there's a thought."

John felt a twinge of jealousy as he watched his father laugh at John Prime's joke. He wondered what John Prime had said to make his father laugh. Then he realized that if his father was laughing at John Prime's jokes, there was no danger of being found out.

The precarious nature of his situation bothered him. Effectively, John Prime was him. And he was . . . nobody. Would it be that hard for someone to slip into his life? He realized that it wouldn't. He had a few immediate relationships, interactions that had happened within the last few weeks that were unique to him, but in a month, those would all be absorbed into the past. He had no girlfriend. No real friends, except for Erik, and that stopped at the edge of the court. The hardest part would be for someone to pick up his studies, but even that wouldn't be too hard. All his classes were a breeze, except for Advanced Physics, and they were starting a new module on Monday. It was a clear breaking point.

John wondered what he would find in another universe. Would there be different advances in science? Could he photocopy a scientific journal and bring it back? Maybe someone had discovered a unified theory in the other universe. Or a simple solution to Fermat's Last Theorem. Or . . . But what could he really do with someone else's ideas? Publish them under his own name? Was that any different than John Prime's scheme to get rich with Rubik's Square, whatever that was? He laughed and picked up his physics book. He needed to stay caught up in this universe. They were starting Quantum Mechanics on Monday after all.

*

John brought Johnny Farmboy a sandwich.

"Your mom didn't notice either."

He took the sandwich, pausing to look John in the eye. "You look happy."

John started. His clothes were covered in sap. His hands were cut and raw. His shoulders ached. He had always loathed farm work. Yet . . .

"It felt good. I haven't done that in a while."

Around a bite of sandwich, Farmboy said, "You've been gone a long time."

"Yeah," John said. "You don't know what you have here. Why do you even want to go to college?"

Farmboy laughed. "It's great for the first fifteen years, then it really begins to drag."

"I hear you."

Farmboy handed John his ski jacket. "What will I see in the next universe?"

John heart caught. "So you're gonna take me up on the offer?" he said casually.

"Yeah, I think so. Tell me what I'll see."

"It's pretty much like this one, you know. I don't know the exact differences."

"So we're in the next universe?"

"Yeah. I wouldn't try to meet him or anything. He doesn't know about us."

"Why'd you pick me to talk to? Why not some other me? Or why not all of us?"

"This is the most like home," John said. "This feels like I remember."

"In 100 universes this is the one that is most like yours? How different are we from one to the next? It can't be too different."

"Do you really want to hear this?"

Farmboy nodded.

"Well, there are a couple types of us. There's the farm boy us, like you and me. Then there's the dirt bag us."

"Dirt bag?"

"Yeah. We smoke and hang out under the bleachers."

"What the hell happened there?"

"And sometimes we've knocked up Casey Nicholson and we

live in the low income houses on Stuart. Then there's the places
where we've died."

"Died?"

"Yeah. Car accidents. Tractor accidents. Gun accidents. We're
pretty lucky to be here, really."

Farmboy looked away, and John knew what he was thinking. It
was the time he and his father had been tossing hay bales and the
pitchfork had fallen. Or it was the time he had walked out on Old
Mrs. Jones' frozen pond, and the ice had cracked, and he'd kept
going. Or the time the quarry truck had run him off the road. It was
a fluke really that either of them was alive.

Finally Farmboy said, "I think I'm ready. What's the plan?"

John Prime lifted up his shirt and began unbuckling the harness.
"You leave from the pumpkin field. Select the universe one forward.
Press the toggle. Spend the day exploring. Go to the library. Figure
out what's different. If you want, write down any money-making
ideas you come across." When he saw Farmboy's face, John added,
"Fine. Then don't. Tomorrow, flip the counter back to this universe
and pull the lever. You'll be back for school on Monday."

"Sounds easy enough."

"Don't lose the device! Don't get busted by the police! Don't
do anything to draw attention to yourself."

"Right."

"Don't flash your money either. If anyone recognizes you, go
with it and then duck out. You don't want to make it hot for our guy
over there."

"Right."

"Johnny, you look a little nervous. Calm down. I'll keep you
covered on this end." John slapped him on the back, then handed
him the harness.

Farmboy pulled off his shirt and shivered. He passed the two
bands of the harness over his shoulders, then connected the center
belt behind his back. The disk was cold against his belly. The straps
looked like a synthetic material.

"It fits."

"It should," John said. "I copied some of my materials for you
in case you need them." John Prime pulled a binder from his own
bag, opened it to show him pages of clippings and notes. "You never
know. You might need something. And here's a backpack to hold it
all in."

John felt a twinge pass through him. He was powerless. The device was out of his control.

"What's wrong?" Farmboy asked.

"I haven't been away from the device in a long time. It's my talisman, my escape. I feel naked without it. You gotta' be careful with it."

"Hey," John said. "I'm leaving my life in your hands. How about a little two-way trust?"

John smiled grimly. "Okay. Are you ready? I've got 12:30 on my watch. Which means you can return half an hour past midnight. Okay?"

John checked his watch. "Okay."

"Toggle the universe."

John lifted the shirt and switched the number forward to 7534. "Check."

"Okay. I'll watch from the loft." John climbed the ladder, then turned. "Make sure no one sees you."

His heart was racing. This was it. It was almost his. He looked down from barn window, waved.

Farmboy waved back, then he lifted up his shirt. Sunlight caught the brushed metal of the device.

Farmboy hesitated.

"Go!" John whispered. "Do it."

Farmboy smiled, pulled the switch, and disappeared.

John's ears popped and his feet caught in the dirt. He stumbled and fell forward, catching himself on his gloved hands. He wasn't in a pumpkin patch anymore. Noting the smell of manure, he realized he was in a cow pasture.

He worked his feet free. His shoes were embedded an inch into the earth. He wondered if there was dirt lodged in his feet now. It looked like the dirt in the current universe was an inch higher here than in the old one. Where did that extra inch of dirt go? He shook his feet and the dirt fell free.

It worked! He felt a thrill. He'd doubted to the last second, but here he was, in a new universe.

He paused. John Prime had said there was a John in this universe. He spun around. Cows grazed contentedly a few hundred yards away, but otherwise the fields were empty, the trees gone. There was no farmhouse.

McMaster Road was there and so was Gurney Road. John walked from the field, hopped the fence, and stood at the corner of the roads. Looking to the north toward town, he saw nothing but a farmhouse maybe a mile up the road. To the east, where the stacks of the GE plant should have been, he saw nothing but forest. To the south, more fields.

John Prime had said there was a John Rayburn in this universe. He'd said that the farm was here. He'd told John he'd been to this universe.

John pawed up his jacket and shirt and tried to read the number on the device. He cupped his hand to shield the sun and read 7534. He was where he expected to be, according to the device. There was nothing here.

The panic settled into his gut. Something was wrong. Something had gone wrong. He wasn't where he was supposed to be. But that's okay, he thought, calming himself. It's okay. He walked to the edge of road and sat on the small berm there.

Maybe John Prime had it wrong; there were a lot of universes and if all of them were different that was a lot of facts to keep straight.

He stood, determined to assume the best. He'd spend the next twelve hours working according to the plan. Then he'd go back home. He set off for town, a black mood nipping at his heels.

John watched his other self disappear from the pumpkin field and felt his body relax. Now he wouldn't have to kill him. This way was so much better. A body could always be found, unless it was in some other universe. He didn't have the device, of course, but then he'd never need it again. In fact he was glad to be rid of it. John had something more important than the device; he had his life back.

It had taken him three days of arguing and cajoling, but finally Johnny Farmboy had taken the bait. Good riddance and good bye. He had been that naive once. He'd once had that wide-eyed gullibility, ready to explore new worlds. There was nothing out there but pain. He was alive again. He had parents again. He had money — $125,000. And he had his notebook. That was the most important part. The notebook was worth a billion dollars right there.

John looked around the loft. This would be a good place for

some of his money. If he remembered right, there was a small cubbyhole in the rafters on the south side of the loft. He found it and pulled out the bubble gum cards and slingshot that was hidden there.

"Damn farmboy."

He placed about a third of his money in the hiding place. Another third he'd hide in his room. The last third, he'd bury. He wouldn't deposit it like he'd done in 7489. Or had that been 7490? The cops had been on his ass so fast. So Franklin had been looking the wrong way on all those bills. He'd lost $80,000.

No, he'd be careful this time. He'd show legitimate sources for all his cash. He'd be the talk of Findlay, Ohio as his inventions started panning out. No one would suspect the young physics genius. They'd be jealous, sure, but everybody knew Johnny Rayburn was a brain. The Rubik's Cube — no, the Rayburn's Cube — would be his road to fame and riches.

John reached the outskirts of town in an hour, passing a green sign that said "Findlay, Ohio. Population 6232." His Findlay had a population in the twenty thousand range. As he stood there, he heard a high-pitched whine grow behind him. He stepped off the berm as a truck flew by him, at about forty-five miles per hour. It was in fact two trucks in tandem pulling a large trailer filled with gravel. The fronts of the trucks were flat, probably to aid in stacking several together for larger loads, like a train with more than one locomotive. The trailer was smaller than a typical dump truck in his universe. A driver sat in each truck. Expecting to be enveloped in a cloud of exhaust, John found nothing fouler than moist air.

Flywheel? he wondered. *Steam?*

Despite his predicament, John was intrigued by the engineering of the trucks. Ten more minutes of walking, past two motels and a diner, he came to the city square, the Civil War monument displayed as proudly as ever, cannon pointed toward the South. A few people were strolling the square, but no one noticed him.

Across the square was the courthouse. Beside it stood the library, identical to what he remembered, a three-story building, its entrance framed by granite lions reclining on brick pedestals. There was the place to start figuring this universe out.

The library was identical in layout to the one he knew. John walked to the card catalog — there were no computer terminals —

and looked up the numbers for American history. On the shelf he found a volume by Albert Trey called *US History and Heritage: Major Events that Shaped a Nation*. He sat in a low chair and paged through it. He found the divergence in moments.

The American Revolution, War of 1812, and Civil War all had the expected results. The presidents were the same through Woodrow Wilson. World War I was a minor war, listed as the Greco-Turkish War. World War II was listed as the Great War and was England and the US against Germany, Russia, and Japan. A truce was called in 1956 after years of no resolution to the fighting. Hostilities had flared for years until the 80s when peace was declared and disarmament accomplished in France, which was split up and given to Germany and Spain.

But all of those things happened after Alexander Graham Bell developed an effective battery for the automobile. Instead of an internal combustion engine, cars and trucks in this universe used electric engines. That explained the trucks: electric engines.

But even as he read about the use of zeppelins for transport, the relatively peaceful twentieth century, his anger began to grow. This universe was nothing like his own. John Prime had lied. Finally, he stood and found the local telephone book. He paged through it, looking for Rayburns. As he expected, there were none.

He checked his watch; in eight hours he was going back home and kicking the crap out of John Prime.

His mother called him to dinner, and for a moment he froze with fear. *They'll know,* he thought. *They'll know I'm not their son.*

Breathing slowly, he hid the money back under his comic book collection in the closet.

"Coming!" he called.

During dinner he kept quiet, focusing on what his parents mentioned, filing key facts away for later use. There was too much he didn't know. He couldn't volunteer anything until he had all his facts right.

Cousin Paul was still in jail. They were staying after church tomorrow for a spaghetti lunch. His mother would be canning and making vinegar that week. His father was buying a turkey from Sam Riley, who had a flock of twenty or so. The dinner finished with homemade apple pie that made the cuts on his hands and the soreness in his back worth it.

After dinner he excused himself. In his room he rooted through Johnny Farmboy's bookbag. He'd missed a year of school; he had a lot of make-up to do. And, crap, an essay on Gerard Manley Hopkins, whoever the heck that was.

By the time the library closed, John's head was full of facts and details about the new universe. There were a thousand things he'd like to research, but there was no time. He stopped at a newspaper shop and picked an almanac off the shelf. After a moment's hesitation, he offered to buy the three dollar book with one of the twenties John Prime had given him. The counter man barely glanced at the bill and handed John sixteen dollars and change. The bills were identical to those in his own world. The coins bore other faces.

He ate a late dinner at Eckart's cafe, listening to rockabilly music. None of it was familiar music, but it was music that was playable on the country stations at home. Even at ten in the evening, there was a sizeable crowd, drinking coffee and hard liquor. There was no beer to be had.

It was a tame crowd for a Saturday night. He read the almanac and listened in to the conversations around him. Most of it was about cars, girls, and guys, just like in his universe.

By midnight, the crowd had thinned. At half-past midnight, John walked into the square and stood behind the Civil War statue. He lifted his shirt and toggled the number back to 7533.

He paused, checked his watch and saw it was a quarter till one. Close enough, he figured.

He pressed the button.

Nothing happened.

He managed to get through church without falling asleep. Luckily the communion ritual was the same. If there was one thing that didn't change from one universe to the next, it was church.

He expected the spaghetti lunch afterwards to be just as boring, but across the gymnasium, John saw Casey Nicholson sitting with her family. That was one person he knew where Johnny Farmboy stood with. She liked him, it was clear, but Johnny Farmboy had been too clean-cut to make a move. Not so for him. John excused himself and walked over to her.

"Hi, Casey," he said.

She blushed at him, perhaps because her parents were there.

Her father said, "Oh, hello, John. How's the basketball team going to do this year?"

John wanted to yell at him that he didn't give a rat's ass. But instead he smiled and said, "We'll go all the way if Casey is there to cheer for us."

Casey looked away, her face flush again. She was dressed in a white Sunday dress that covered her breasts, waist, and hips with enough material to hide the fact that she had any of those features. But he knew what was there. He'd seduced Casey Nicholson in a dozen universes at least.

"I'm only cheering fall sports, John," she said softly. "I play field hockey in the spring."

John looked at her mother and asked, "Can I walk with Casey around the church grounds, Mrs. Nicholson?"

She smiled at him, glanced at her husband, and said, "I don't see why not."

"That's a great idea," Mr. Nicholson said.

Casey stood up quickly, and John had to race after her. She stopped after she had gotten out of sight of the gymnasium, hidden in the alcove where the rest rooms were. When John caught up to her, she said, "My parents are so embarrassing."

"No shit," John said.

Her eyes went wide at his cursing, then she smiled.

"I'm glad you're finally talking to me," she said.

John smiled and said, "Let's walk." He slipped his arm around her waist, and she didn't protest.

There was no sensation of shifting, no pressure change. The electric car in the parking lot was still there. The device hadn't worked.

He checked the number: 7533. His finger was on the right switch. He tried it again. Nothing.

It had been twelve hours. Twelve hours and forty-five minutes. But maybe John Prime had been estimating. Maybe it took thirteen hours to recharge. He leaned against the base of the statue and slid to the ground.

He couldn't shake the feeling that something was wrong. John Prime had lied to him about what was in Universe 7534. Maybe he had lied about the recharge time. Maybe it took days or months to recharge the device. And when he got back, he'd find that John Prime was entrenched in his life.

He sat there, trying the switch every fifteen minutes until three in the morning. He was cold, but finally he fell asleep on the grass, leaning against the Civil War Memorial.

He awoke at dawn, the sun in his eyes as it streamed down Washington Avenue. He stood and jumped up and down to revive his body. His back ached, but the kinks receded after he did some stretches.

At a donut shop off the square, he bought a glazed and an orange juice with the change he had left over from the almanac. A dozen people filed in over the course of an hour to buy donuts and coffee before church or work. On the surface, this world was a lot like his.

John couldn't stand the waiting. He walked across the square and climbed the library steps and yanked at the door. They were locked, and he saw the sign showing the library's hours. It was closed until noon.

John looked around. There was an alcove behind the lions with a bench. No one would easily see him from the street. He sat there and tried the device. Nothing.

He continued to try the lever every ten or fifteen minutes. As he sat on the steps of the library, his apprehension grew. He was going to miss school. He was going to miss more than twenty-four hours. He was going to miss the rest of his life. Why wouldn't the device work like it was supposed to?

He realized then that everything John Prime had told him was probably a lie. He had to assume that he was the victim of John Prime's scheming, trapped in another universe. The question was how he would return to his life.

He had the device. It had worked once, to bring him from Universe 7533 to Universe 7534. It would not allow him to return because it wasn't recharged yet. It took longer than — he checked his watch — twenty hours to recharge the device apparently.

He stopped. He was basing that logic on information he had gotten from John Prime. Nothing that John Prime had said could be used as valid information. Only things that John had seen or gotten from a valid source were true. And John Prime was not a valid source.

The twelve hour recharge time was false. He had assumed that it meant the length of time was what was false in John Prime's statement. What if there was no recharge time at all?

There were two possibilities that John could see. First, there was no recharge time and he was being prevented from returning to his universe for some other reason. Second, the device no longer worked. Perhaps he had used the last of its energy source.

For some reason he still wanted to believe John Prime. If it was simply a mechanical issue, then he could use intelligence to solve the problem. Maybe John Prime was truthful, and something happened to the device that he didn't know about. Maybe John Prime would be surprised when John never returned with the device, effectively trapping John Prime in John's life. John Prime might even think that John had stolen his device.

But mechanical failure seemed unlikely. John Prime said he had used the device 100 times. His home universe was around 7433. If he'd used it exactly 100 times, that was the distance in universes between John's and John Prime's. Did that mean he only used the device to move forward one universe at a time? Or did he hop around? No, the numbers were too similar. John Prime probably moved from one universe to the next systematically.

John decided that he was just too ignorant to ignore all of John Prime's information. Some of it had to be taken at face value.

The 100 number indicated that John only incremented the universe counter upward. Why? Did the device only allow travel in one direction?

He played with the theory, fitting the pieces together. The device was defective or designed in such a way that only travel upward was allowed. John Prime mentioned the recharge time to eliminate any possibility of a demonstration. There was perhaps no recharge time. The device was of no value to John Prime, since he planned to stay. That explained the personal questions John Prime had asked; he wanted to ease into John's life. Some things he knew, but other things he had to learn from John.

The fury built in John.

"Bastard!" he said softly. John Prime had screwed him. He'd tempted him with universes, and John had fallen for it. And now he was in another universe, where he didn't exist. He had to get back.

There was nothing to do, he realized, but test the theory.

He pulled his backpack onto his shoulders and checked around the bench for his things. Then, with a quick check to see if anyone was looking, he toggled the device to 7535 and pulled the lever.

He fell.

Monday morning at school went no worse than expected. John barely made it to homeroom and ended up sitting with the stoners by accident. He had no idea what the word "Buckle" meant in the Hopkins poem. And Mr. Wallace had to flag him down for physics class.

"Forget which room it is?" he asked.

"Er."

There was no Mr. Wallace in John's home universe, and he had to dodge in-jokes and history between him and Johnny Farmboy; the class was independent study! John realized he'd have to drop it. He was grateful when a kid knocked on the door.

"Mr. Gushman needs to see John Rayburn."

Mr. Wallace took the slip of paper from the acne-ridden freshman. "Again? Read the assignment for tomorrow, John. We have a lot to cover." The man was disappointed in him, but John couldn't find the emotion to care. He hardly knew him.

John nodded, then grabbed his stuff. He nudged the freshman hall monitor as they walked down the hall. "Where's Mr. Gushman at?"

The freshman's eye widened like marbles. "He's in the front office. He's the principal."

"No shit, douche bag," John said.

John entered the fish bowl and gave his name to the receptionist. After just a few minutes, Mr. Gushman called him in.

John didn't have anything on Gushman. He'd come to Findlay High School in the time John had been away. The old principal had fucked a student at his old school and that had come out in one of the universes that John had visited. That bit of dirt would be no good in this universe.

"Have you got the letter of apology for Mrs. Carson?" he asked.

John suddenly realized what the meeting was about. He'd not written the letter.

"No, sir. I've decided not to write the letter."

Mr. Gushman raised his eyebrows, then frowned. "You realize that this will have grave consequences for your future."

"No, I don't think so. In fact, I've contacted a lawyer. I'll be suing Ted Carson." John hadn't thought of doing that until that moment, but now that he'd said it, he decided it was a good idea. "I'm an honor student, Gushman. I'm a varsity player in two sports. There will be fallout because of this. Big fallout."

"It's Mr. Gushman, please. I'll have your respect." His knuckles were white, and John realized that Gushman had expected him to cave. Well, maybe Johnny Farmboy would have caved, but not him. He had dirt on the education board members. He had dirt on the mayor. This would be a slam dunk for him.

"Respect is earned," John said.

"I see. Shall I have your mother called or do you have transportation home?"

"Home? Why?" John said.

"Your three day suspension starts right now." John had forgotten about that. He shrugged. Johnny Farmboy would have shit a brick at being expelled. To John, it didn't really matter.

"I can take care of myself."

"You are not allowed on school property until Thursday at noon. I'll be sending a letter home to your parents. I'll also inform Coach Jessick that you are off the roster for basketball and track."

"Whatever."

Mr. Gushman stood, leaning heavily on the desk. His voice was strained as he said, "I expected better of you, John. Everything I know about you says that you're a good boy. Everything I've seen since you walked in this door has made me reevaluate my opinions."

John shrugged again. "Whatever." He stood, ignoring Gushman's anger. "We done here?"

"Yes. You are dismissed."

At least he didn't have to worry about learning basketball. And three days was enough time to get started on his plans. He smiled as he passed the receptionist, smiled at the dirt bags waiting in the office. This was actually working out better than he expected.

John's arms flailed and his left foot hit the ground, catching his weight. He groaned as his leg collapsed under him. He rolled across the grass.

Grass? he thought as the pain erupted in his knee. He sat up, rocking as he held his knee to his chest. He'd been on the steps of the library and now he was on a plain. The wind blew the smell of outside: dirt, pollen, clover.

He tried to stretch his leg, but the pain was too much. He leaned back, pulling off his backpack with one hand, and looked up at the sky, breathing deeply. It hurt like hell.

The device had worked. He had changed universes again. Only this universe had no library, no Findlay, Ohio. This universe didn't seem to have anything but grass. He fell because the steps he'd been standing on weren't in the universe he was in now.

He checked the readout on the device. He was in 7535. He'd gone forward one universe.

John looked around him, but didn't see anything through the green-yellow grass. It rustled in the wind, making sounds like sandpaper rubbing on wood.

John stood gingerly on his other leg. He was on a broad plain, stretching for a good distance in every direction. There were small groves of trees to the north and east. To the west and south, the grass stretched as far as he could see.

There was no library to use to figure out what was different in this universe. No humans at all, maybe. A Mayan empire? If he wanted to find the differences, he'd have to do some field research.

He sat back down. No, he thought. He had to get back to his life. John Prime had some answers to give and a price to pay. It was Sunday afternoon. He still had half a day to figure out how to get back to his universe.

His knee was swelling, so he took off his coat and shirt. He ripped his t-shirt into long strips and used that to wrap his knee as tightly as possible. It wasn't broken, but he may have sprained it.

He took the sandwich that he had packed on Saturday from his backpack and unwrapped it. He finished it in several bites and rinsed it down with some of the water in his water bottle. The taste of the sandwich made him angry. John Prime was eating his food and sleeping in his bed. John wondered how he would feel punching someone who looked like him in the face. He decided that he could do it.

John spent the afternoon nursing his knee and considering what he knew, what he thought he knew, and what John Prime had told him. The latter category he considered biased or false. What he knew, however, was growing.

Universe 7535 was the second one he'd visited. The device clearly still worked. His going from 7534 to 7535 proved that.

It was also support for his theory that the device only allowed travel to universes higher in number than the one a traveller currently resided in. But not proof. Hypotheses required repeatable experimental proof. He'd used the device to move forward through two universes. He'd have to do it a couple more times before he was certain that that was the way the device worked.

He took a blade of grass and chewed on it. This was an unspoiled universe, he thought. Which gave him another piece of data. Universes sequentially next to each other could have little in common. John couldn't even begin to guess what had happened for a universe to not have North America settled by the Europeans.

There'd been no library steps here, so he had fallen ten feet to the ground. More data: There was no guarantee that a man-made object in one universe would exist in the next. Nor even natural objects. Hills were removed or added by machines. Rivers were dammed and moved. Lakes were created. What would happen if he jumped to the next universe and the steps were there? Would he be trapped in the cement that formed the steps? Would he die of asphyxiation, unable to press the lever because he was encased in the library steps?

The thought of being entombed, blind and without air, horrified him. It was no way to die.

He would have to be careful when he changed universes. He'd have to be as certain as possible that there was nothing solid where he was going. But how?

Movement caught his eye and he looked up to see a large beast walking in the distance. It was so tall he saw it from his seat in the grass. A cross between a rhinoceros and a giraffe, it munched at the leaves of a tree. It was gray with legs like tree limbs, a face like a horse. Leaves and branches gave way quickly to its gobbling teeth.

No animal like that existed in his universe.

John watched, amazed. He wished he had a camera. A picture of this beast would be a nice addition to his scrap book. Would it be worth cash? he wondered.

Ponderously it moved to the next tree in the grove.

John looked around him with more interest. This was no longer a desolate North America. There were animals here that no longer existed in his timeline. This universe was more radically different than he could have imagined.

The wave of the grass to the west caught his attention. The grass bobbed against the wind, and he was suddenly alert. Something was in the grass not twenty yards from him. He realized that large herbivores meant large carnivores. Bears, mountain lions, and wolves could be roaming these plains. And he had no weapons. Worse still he had a bum knee.

He looked around him for a stick or a rock, but there was nothing. Quickly he gathered the notebook into the backpack. He pulled his coat on.

Was the thing closer? he wondered. He glanced at the grass around him. Why hadn't he thought of that earlier?

John felt beneath his shirt for the device. He glanced down and toggled the universe counter up one to 7536. But he dared not pull the lever. He could be under the library right now.

He looked around him, tried to orient himself. The library entrance faced east, toward the Civil War Memorial. If he traveled east two hundred feet, he'd be in the middle of the park and it was unlikely that anything would be in his way. It was the safest place he could think of to do the transfer.

Suppressing a groan he moved off in an easterly direction, counting his steps.

At fifty-two steps he heard a sound behind him. A dog-like creature stood ten yards away from him in his wake in the grass. It had a dog's snout and ears, but its eyes were slit and its back was arched more like a cat's. It had no tail. Its fur was tan with black spots the size of quarters along its flank.

John froze, considering. It was small, the size of a border collie. He was big prey and it may just have been curious about him.

"Boo-yah!" he cried, waved his arms. It didn't move, just stared at him with its slit eyes. Then two more appeared behind it.

It was a pack animal. Pack animals could easily bring down an animal larger than a pack member. He saw three of them, but there could be a dozen hidden in the grass. John turned and ran.

The things took him from behind, nipping his legs, flinging themselves onto his back. He fell, his leg screaming. He felt weight on his back, so he let the straps of his back pack slide off. He crawled forward another yard. Hoping he'd come far enough, he pulled the lever on the device.

John took the two o'clock Silver Mongoose to Toledo, right after he stood in line at the Department of Motor Vehicles trying to convince the clerk to file the paperwork for his lost license.

"I am positive that it won't turn up," John said.

"So many people say that, and then there it is in the last place you look."

"Really. It won't."

"All righty, then. I'll take that form from you."

He was tempted to rent a car, but that would have raised as many eyebrows as hiring a patent lawyer in Findlay. John had to go to Toledo to get his business done. Three days off school was just about perfect.

As the northern Ohio farmland rolled by, he wondered how hurt he'd be if he had to transfer out right now. He was always considering his escape routes, always sleeping on the ground floor, always in structures that were as old as he could find. His chest itched where the device should have been. It was Johnny Farmboy's problem now. He was free of it. No one would come looking for him here. He blended right in. No police would come barging in at three AM. No FBI agents wanting his device.

What an innocent he'd been. What a piece of work. How many times had he almost died? How many times had he screwed up within inches of the end?

For a moment, he had a twinge of guilt for the displaced John. He hoped that he figured out a few things quickly, before things went to hell. Maybe he could find a place to settle down just like he had. *Maybe I should have written him a note,* he thought.

Then he laughed to himself. Too late for that. Johnny Farmboy was on his own. Just like he had been.

A car horn screeched and a massive shape bore down on him. John tried to scramble away, but his hand was stuck. As his wrist flexed the wrong way, pain shot up his arm.

He looked up, over his shoulder, into the grill of a car. John hadn't made it into the park. He was still in the street, the sidewalk a few feet in front of him.

John got to his knees. His hand was embedded in the asphalt. He planted his feet and pulled. Nothing happened except pain.

"Buddy, you okay?" The driver was standing with his door open. John's eyes were just over the hood of the man's car.

John didn't reply. Instead he pulled again and his hand tore lose with a spray of tar and stones. The impression of his palm was cast in the asphalt.

The man came around his car and took John's arm. "You better sit down. I'm really sorry about this. You came outta nowhere." The man led him to the curb, then looked back and said, "Jesus. Is that your dog?"

John looked and saw the head and shoulders of one of the cat-dogs. The transfer had caught only half the beast. Its jaws were open, revealing yellowed teeth. Its milky eyes were glazed over. Blood from its severed torso flowed across the street. A strand of intestine had unraveled onto the pavement.

"Oh, man. I killed your dog," the motorist cried.

John said between breaths, "Not . . . my . . . dog . . . Chasing me."

The man looked around. "There's Harvey," he said, pointing to a police officer sitting in the donut shop that John had eaten in that morning. Well, not the same one, John thought. This wasn't the same universe, since this car was gas powered.

"Hey, Harvey," he yelled, waving his arms. Someone nudged the police officer and he turned, looking at the blood spreading across the street.

Harvey was a big man, but he moved quickly. He dropped his donut and coffee in a trash can at the door of the shop. As he approached he brushed his hands on his pants.

"What happened, Roger?" he said. He glanced at John, who was too winded and too sore to move. He looked at the cat-dog on the street. "What the hell is that?"

He kicked it with his boot.

"This young man was being chased, I think. I nearly clipped him and I definitely got that thing. What is it? A badger."

"Whatever it is, you knocked the crap out of it." He turned to John. "Son, you okay?"

"No," John said. "I twisted my knee and my wrist. I think that thing was rabid. It chased me from around the library."

"Well, I'll be," said the officer. He squatted next to John. "Looks like it got a piece of your leg." He lifted up John's pant leg, pointed to the line of bite marks. "Son, you bought yourself some rabies shots."

The officer called Animal Control for the carcass and an ambulance for John. The white-uniformed Animal Control man spent some time looking for the other half of the cat-dog. To Harvey's questions about what it was, he shrugged. "Never seen nothing like it." When he lifted up the torso, John saw the severed arm straps of his backpack on the ground. He groaned. His backpack, with 1700 dollars in cash, was in the last universe under the other half of the cat-dog.

A paramedic cleaned John's calf, looked at his wrist and his knee. She touched his forehead gingerly. "What's this?"

"Ow," he said, wincing.

"You may have a concussion. Chased by a rabid dog into a moving car. Quite a day you've had."

"It's been a less than banner day," John said.

"'Banner day,'" she repeated. "I haven't heard that term in a long time. I think my grandmother said that."

"Mine too."

They loaded him into the ambulance on a stretcher. By the time the door had shut on the ambulance, quite a few people had gathered. John kept expecting someone to shout his name in recognition, but no one did. Maybe he didn't exist in this universe.

They took him to Roth Hospital, and it looked just like it did in his universe, an institutional building from the 50s. He sat for fifteen minutes on an examining table off of the emergency room. Finally, an older doctor came in and checked him thoroughly.

"Lacerations on the palm. The wrist has a slight sprain. Minor. The hand is fine." Looking at John's knee, he added, "Sprain of the right knee. We'll wrap that. You'll probably need crutches for a couple days."

A few minutes later, a woman showed up with a clipboard. "We'll need to fill these forms out," she said. "Are you over eighteen?"

John shook his head, thinking fast. "My parents are on the way."

"Did you call them?"

"Yes."

"We'll need their insurance information," she said as she left.

John stood wincing and peered out the door until she disappeared. Then he limped the other way until he found an emergency exit door. He pushed it open and hobbled off into the parking lot, the bleating of the siren behind him.

The first lawyer John visited listened to him for fifteen minutes until she said she wasn't taking any new clients. John almost screamed at her, "Then why did you let me blather on for so long?"

The second took thirty seconds to say no. But the third listened dubiously to his idea for the Rayburn Cube. He didn't even blink at the cash retainer John handed over for the three patents he wanted him to research and acquire.

He called Casey from his cheap hotel.

"Hey, Casey. It's John!"

"John! I heard you were expelled for a month."

"News of my expulsion has been greatly exaggerated."

"What happened?"

"Just more of the Ted Carson saga. I told Gushman I wasn't going to apologize, so he kicked me out of school. You should have seen the colors on his face."

"You told Gushman no?" she asked. "Wow. He used to be a colonel in the army."

"He used to molest small children too," John.

"Don't say that."

"Why? He sucks."

"But it's not true."

"It could be true, probably is in some other universe."

"But we don't know for sure."

John switched subjects. "Listen, I called to see if you wanted to go out on Saturday."

"Yeah, sure," she said quickly. "Yeah."

"Movie?"

"Sounds good. What's playing?"

"Does it matter?"

She giggled. "No." After a moment, she added, "Didn't your parents ground you?"

"Oh, shit!"

"What?"

"They don't know yet," John said. He looked at the cheap clock radio next to the bed: six-thirty. "Shit."

"Do you think we can still go out?"

"One way or another, Casey, I'll see you on Saturday."

"I'm looking forward to it."

He hung up.

His parents. He'd forgotten to call his parents. They were going to be pissed. Damn. He'd been without them for so long, he'd forgotten how they worked.

He dialed his home number.

"Mom?"

"Oh, my God!" she yelled. Then to his father, she said, "Bill, it's John. It's John."

"Where is he? Is he all right?"

"Mom, I'm okay." He waited. He knew how Johnny Subprime would play this. Sure, he'd never have gone to Toledo, but John could play the suspension for all it was worth. "Did you hear from Gushman?"

"John, yes, and it's okay. We understand. You can come home. We aren't angry with you."

"Then, Mom, you know how I feel. I did the right thing, Mom, and they took everything away from me." It was what Farmboy would have said.

"I know, dear. I know."

"It's not fair."

"I know, Johnny. Now where are you? You've got to come home." His mother sounded pitiful.

"I won't be home tonight, Mom. I've got things to do."

"He's not coming home, Bill!"

"Give me the phone, Janet." Into the phone, his father said, "John, I want you home tonight. We understand that you're upset, but you need to be home, and we'll handle this here, under our roof."

"Dad, I'll be home tomorrow."

"John —"

"Dad, I'll be home tomorrow." He hung up the phone and almost chortled.

Then he turned on Home Theatre Office and watched bad movies until midnight.

*

John shivered in the morning cold. His knee was the size of a melon, throbbing from the night spent on the library steps. The bell tower struck eight; John Prime would be on his way to school right now. He'd be heading for English class. John hoped the bastard had done the essay on Gerard Manley Hopkins.

He'd slept little, his knee throbbing, his heart aching. He'd lost the 1700 dollars John Prime had given, save eighty dollars in his wallet. He'd lost his backpack. His clothes were ripped and tattered. He'd skipped out on his doctor's bill. He was as far from home as he'd ever been.

He needed help.

He couldn't stay here; the hospital probably called the police on his unpaid bill. He needed a fresh universe to work in.

Limping, he walked across to the Ben Franklin, buying new dungarees and a backpack.

Then he stood in the center of the town square and waited for a moment when no one was around. He toggled the universe counter upward and pressed the lever.

"It turns *this* way, *this* way, and *this* way!" John made the motions with his hands for the fourth time, wishing again that he'd bought the keychain Cube when he'd had the chance.

"Why?" Joe Patadorn was the foreman for an industrial design shop. A pad of paper on his drafting board was covered in pencil sketches of cubes. "Rotate against what? It's a cube."

"Against itself! Against itself! Each column and each row rotates."

"Seems like it could get caught up with itself."

"Yes! If it's not a cube when you try to turn it, it'll not turn."

"And this is a toy people will want to play with?"

"I'll handle that part."

Joe shrugged. "Fine. It's your money."

"Yes, it is."

"We'll have a prototype in two weeks."

They shook on it.

His errands were finally done in Toledo. His lawyer was doing the patent searches and Patadorn was building the prototype. If he was lucky, he could have the first batch of Cubes ready to ship by Christmas, perfect timing.

From the bus stop, he hiked the three miles to the farm and stashed his contracts in the loft with the money there. When he was climbing down, he saw his dad standing next to the stalls.

"Hey. Am I in time for dinner?" John asked.

His father didn't reply, and then he realized that he was in trouble.

His father's face was red, his cheeks puffed out. He stood in overalls, his fists at his hips.

"In the house." The words were soft, punctuated.

"Dad —"

"In the house, now." His father lifted an arm, pointing.

John went, and as he entered the house, he was angry too. How dare he order him around?

His mother was waiting at the kitchen table, her fingers folded in a clenched, white mound.

"Where were you?" his father demanded.

"None of your business," John said.

"While you're in my house, you'll answer my questions!" his father roared.

"I'll get my things and go," John said.

"Bill . . ." his mother said. "We've discussed this."

His father looked away, then said, "He pranced into the barn like he'd done nothing wrong."

His mother turned to him. "Where were you, John?"

He opened his mouth to rail, but instead he said, "Toledo. I had to . . . cool off."

His mother nodded. "That's important."

"Yeah."

"Are you feeling better now?"

"Yes . . . no." Suddenly he was sick to his stomach. Suddenly he was more angry with himself than with his father.

"It's okay," she said. "It's okay what you did, and we're glad you're back. Bill?"

His father grunted, then said, "Son, we're glad you're back." And then he took John in his big farmer arms and squeezed him.

John sobbed before he could fight it down, and then he was bawling like he hadn't since he was ten.

"I'm sorry, Dad." The words were muffled in his shoulder. His throat was tight.

"It's okay. It's okay."

His mother joined them and they held onto him for a long time.

John found he didn't want to let go. He hadn't hugged his parents in a long time.

John climbed the steps to the library. This universe looked just like his own. He didn't really care how it was different. All he wanted was to figure out how to get home. He'd tried the device a dozen times in the square, but the device would not allow him to go backwards, not even to universes before his own.

He needed help; he needed professional help. He needed to understand about parallel universes.

Browsing the card catalog, it soon became apparent the Findlay library was not the place to do a scientific search on advanced physics. All he could find were a dozen science fiction novels which were no help at all.

He was going to have to go to Toledo. U of T was his second choice after Case. It was a state school and close. Half his friends would be going there. It had a decent if not stellar physics department.

He took the bus to Toledo, dozing along the way. A local brought him to the campus.

The Physics Library was a single room with three tables. Stacks lined all the walls and extended into the middle of the room, making it seem cramped and tiny. It smelled of dust, just like the Findlay Public Library.

"Student ID?"

John turned to the bespectacled student sitting at the front desk. For a moment, he froze, then patted his front pockets. "I left it at the dorm."

The student looked peeved then said, "Well, bring it next time, frosh." He waved him in.

"I will."

John brought the catalog up on a terminal and searched for "Parallel Universe." There wasn't much. In fact there was nothing at all in the Physics Library. He was searching for the wrong subject. Physicists didn't call them parallel universes of course. TV and movies called them parallel universes.

He couldn't think what else to search for. Perhaps there was a more formal term for what he was looking for, but he had no idea what it was. He'd have to ask his dumb questions directly of a professor.

He left the library and walked down the second floor hall, looking at name plates above doors. Billboards lined the walls, stapled and tacked with colloquia notices, assistantship postings, apartments to share. A lot of the offices were empty. At the end of the hall was the small office of Dr. Frank Wilson, Associate Professor of Physics, lit and occupied.

John knew associate professors were low on the totem pole, which was probably why he was the only one in his office. And maybe a younger professor would be more willing to listen to what he had to say.

He knocked on the door.

"Come on in."

He entered the office, found it cluttered on all sides with bookshelves stacked to bursting with papers and tomes, but neat at the center, where a man sat at an empty desk reading a journal.

"You're the first person to show for office hours today," he said. Professor Wilson was in his late twenties, with black glasses, sandy beard, and hair that seemed in need of a cut. He wore a gray jacket over a blue oxford.

"Yeah," John said. "I have some questions, and I don't know how to ask them."

"On the homework set?"

"No. On another topic." John was suddenly uncertain. "Parallel universes."

Professor Wilson nodded. "Hmmm." He took a drink of his coffee, then said, "Are you one of my students? Freshman Physics?"

"No," John said.

"Then what's your interest in this? Are you from the creative writing department?"

"No, I . . ."

"Your question, while it seems simple to you, is extremely complex. Have you taken calculus?"

"Just half a semester . . ."

"Then you'll never understand the math behind it. The authorities here are Hawking, Wheeler, Everett." He ticked them off on his fingers. "You're talking about quantum cosmology. Graduate level stuff."

John said quickly before he could cut him off again. "But my question is more practical. Not theoretical."

"Practical parallel worlds? Nonsense. Quantum cosmology states that there may be multiple universes out there, but the most likely one is ours, via the weak anthropic principle. Which means since we're here, we can take it as a given that we exist. Well, it's more complex than that."

"But what about other universes, other people just like us."

The man laughed. "Highly unlikely. Occam's razor divests us of that idea."

"How would I travel between universes?" John said, grasping at straws against the man's brisk manner.

"You can't, you won't, not even remotely possible."

"But what if I said it was. What if I knew for sure it was possible."

"I'd say your observations were manipulated or you saw something that you interpreted incorrectly."

John touched the wound in his calf where the cat-dog had bitten him. No, he'd seen what he'd seen. He'd felt what he'd felt. There was no doubt about that.

"I know what I saw."

Wilson waved his hands. "I won't debate your observations. It's a waste of my time. Tell me what you think you saw."

John paused not sure where to start and what to tell, and Professor Wilson jumped in. "See? You aren't sure what you saw, are you?" He leaned forward. "A physicist must have a discerning eye. It must be nurtured, tested, used to separate the chaff from the wheat." He leaned back again, glanced out his window onto the quad below. "My guess is that you've seen too many Schwarzenegger movies or read too many books. You may have seen something peculiar, but before you start applying complex physical theories to explain it, you should eliminate the obvious. Now, I have another student of mine waiting, one I know is in my class, so I think you should run along and think about what you really saw."

John turned and saw a female student standing behind him, waiting. His rage surged inside him. The man was patronizing him, making assumptions based on his questions and demeanor. Wilson was dismissing him.

"I can prove it," he said, his jaw clenched.

The professor just looked at him, then beckoned the student into his office.

John turned and stalked down the hall. He was asking for help, and he'd been laughed at.

"I'll show him," John said. He took the steps two at a time and flung open the door to the quadrangle that McCormick faced.

"Watch it, dude," a student said, almost hit by the swinging door. John brushed past him.

He grabbed a handful of stones and, standing at the edge of the quadrangle, began flinging them at the window that he thought was Wilson's. He threw a dozen and started to draw a crowd of students, until Wilson looked out the window, opened it and shouted, "Campus security will be along in a moment."

John yelled back, "Watch this, you stupid bastard!" He toggled the device forward one universe and pulled the lever.

John awoke in the night, gripped by the same nightmare, trapped in darkness, no air, his body held rigid. He sat up and flung the covers away from him, unable to have anything touching him. He ripped off his pajamas as well and stood naked in the bedroom, just breathing. It was too hot; he opened the window and stood before it.

His breathing slowed, as the heavy air of the October night brought the smells of the farm to him: manure and dirt. He leaned against the edge of the window, and his flesh rose in goose pimples.

It was a dream he'd had before, and he knew where it came from. He'd transferred near Lake Erie, on a small, deserted beach not far from Port Clinton and ended up buried in a sand dune. He'd choked on the sand and would have died there if a fisherman hadn't seen his arm flailing. He could have died. It was pure luck that the guy had been there to dig his head out. He'd never transferred near a body of water or a river again.

That hadn't been the only time either. In Columbus, Ohio, he'd transferred into a concrete step, his chest and lower body stuck. He'd been unable to reach the toggle button on the device and had to wait until someone wandered by and called the fire department. They'd used a jackhammer to free him. When they'd turned to him, demanding how he'd been trapped, he'd feigned unconsciousness and transferred out from the ambulance.

After that, each time he touched the trigger he did so with the fear that he'd end up in something solid, unable to transfer out again, unable to breath, unable to move. He was nauseated, his stomach kicking, his armpits soaked, before the jumps.

It was the cruelest of jokes. He had the most powerful device in the world and it was broken.

"No more," he said to himself. "No more of that." He had a family now, in ways he hadn't expected.

The confrontation with his parents had been angry, then sad, and ended with all of them crying and hugging. He'd meant to be tough; he'd meant to tell his parents that he was an adult now, and could take care of himself, but his resolve had melted in the face of their genuine care for him. He'd cried, goddamn it all.

He'd promised to reconsider the letter. He'd promised to talk with Gushman again. He'd promised to be more considerate to his parents. Was he turning into Johnny Farmboy?

He'd gone to bed empty, spent, his mind placid. But his subconscious had pulled the dream out. Smothering, suffocating, his body held inflexible as his lungs screamed. He shivered, then shut the window. His body had expelled all its heat.

He slipped back into bed and closed his eyes.

"I'm becoming Johnny Farmboy," he whispered. "Screw it all."

McCormick Hall looked identical. In fact the same student guarded the door of the Physics Library, asked him the same question.

"Student ID?"

"I left it in my dorm room," John replied without hesitation.

"Well, bring it next time, frosh."

John smiled at him. "Don't call me frosh again, geek."

The student blinked at him, dismayed.

His visit with Professor Wilson had not been a total loss. Wilson had mentioned the subject that he should have searched for instead of parallel universe. He had said that the field of study was called quantum cosmology.

Cosmology, John knew, was the study of the origin of the universe. Quantum theory, however, was applied to individual particles, such as atoms and electrons. It was a statistical way to model those particles. Quantum cosmology, John figured, was a statistical way to model the universe. Not just one universe, either, John hoped, but all universes.

He sat down at a terminal. This time there were thirty hits. He printed the list and began combing the stacks.

Half of the books were summaries of colloquia or workshops. The papers were riddled with equations, and all of them assumed an advanced understanding of the subject matter. John had no basis to understand any of the math.

In the front matter of one of the books was a quote from a physicist regarding a theory called the Many-Worlds Theory. "When a quantum transition occurs, an irreversible one, which is happening in our universe at nearly an infinite rate, a new universe branches off from that transition in which the transition did not occur. Our universe is just a single one of a myriad copies, each slightly different than the others."

John felt an affinity for the quote immediately. He had seen other universes in which small changes had resulted in totally different futures, such as Alexander Graham Bell's invention of the electric motor. It almost made sense then, that every universe he visited was one of billions in which some quantum event or decision occurred differently.

He shut the book. He thought he had enough to ask his questions of Wilson now.

The second floor hallway seemed identical, right down to the empty offices and cluttered billboards. Professor Wilson's office was again at the end of the hall, and he was there, reading a journal. John wondered if it was the same one.

"Come on in," he said at John's knock.

"I have a couple questions."

"About the homework set?"

"No, this is unrelated. It's about quantum cosmology."

Wilson put his paper down and nodded. "A complex subject. What's your question?"

"Do you agree with the Many-Worlds Theory?" John asked.

"No."

John waited, unsure what to make of the single syllable answer. Then he said, "Uh, no?"

"No. It's hogwash in my opinion. What's your interest in it? Are you one of my students?" Wilson sported the same gray jacket over the same blue oxford.

"You don't believe in multiple universes as an explanation . . . for . . ." John was at a loss again. He didn't know as much as he thought he knew. He still couldn't ask the right questions.

"For quantum theory?" asked Wilson. "No. It's not necessary. Do you know Occam's Theory?"

John nodded.

"Which is simpler? One universe that moves under statistical laws at the quantum level or an infinite number of universes each stemming from every random event? How many universes have you seen?"

John began to answer the rhetoric question.

"One," said Wilson before John could open his mouth. Wilson looked John up and down. "Are you a student here?"

"Uh, no. I'm in high school," John admitted.

"I see. This is really pretty advanced stuff, young man. Graduate level stuff. Have you had calculus?"

"Just half a semester."

"Let me try to explain it another way." He picked up a paperweight off his desk, a rock with eyes and mouth painted on it. "I am going to make a decision to drop this rock between now and ten seconds from now." He paused, then dropped the rock after perhaps seven seconds. "A random process. In ten other universes, assuming for simplicity that I could only drop the rock at integer seconds and not fractional seconds, I dropped the rock at each of the seconds from one to ten. I made ten universes by generating a random event. By the Many-Worlds Theory, they all exist. The question is, where did all the matter and energy come from to build ten new universes just like that?" He snapped his fingers. "Now extrapolate to the nearly infinite number of quantum transitions happening on the earth this second. How much energy is required to build all those universes? Where does it come from? Clearly the Many-Worlds Theory is absurd."

John shook his head, trying to get his arms around the idea. He couldn't refute Wilson's argument. He realized how little he really knew. He said, "But what if multiple worlds did exist? Could you travel between the worlds?"

"You can't, you won't, not even remotely possible."

"But —"

"It can't happen, even if the theory were true."

"Then the theory is wrong," John said to himself.

"I told you it was wrong. There are no parallel universes."

John felt the frustration growing in him. "But I know there are. I've seen them."

"I'd say your observations were manipulated or you saw something that you interpreted incorrectly."

"Don't condescend to me again!" John shouted.

Wilson looked at him calmly, then stood.

"Get out of this office, and I suggest you get off this campus right now. I recommend that you seek medical attention immediately," Wilson said coldly.

John's frustration turned to rage. Wilson was no different here than in the last universe. He assumed John was wrong because he acted like a hick, a farm boy. He was certain John knew nothing that he didn't already know.

John flung himself at the man. Wilson's papers scattered across his chest and onto the floor. John grabbed at his jacket from across the desk and yelled into his face, "I'll prove it to you, goddamnit! I'll prove it."

"Get off me," Wilson yelled and pushed John away. Wilson lost his balance when John's grip on his jacket slipped and he fell on the floor against his chair. "You maniac!"

John stood across from the desk from him, his breathing coming hard. He needed proof. His eyes saw the diploma on the wall of Wilson's office. He grabbed it and ran out of the office. If he couldn't convince this Wilson, he'd convince the next. He found an alcove beside the building and transferred out.

John stood clutching Wilson's diploma to his chest, his heart still thumping from the confrontation. Suddenly he felt silly. He'd attacked the man and stolen his diploma to prove to another version of him that he wasn't a wacko.

He looked across the quad. He watched a boy catch a frisbee, and then saw juxtaposed the images of him tripping and not catching it, just missing it to the left, to the right, a million permutations. Everything in the quad was suddenly a blur.

He shook his head, then lifted the diploma so that he could read it. He'd try again, and this time he'd try the direct approach.

John climbed the steps to Wilson's office and knocked.

"Come on in."

"I have a problem."

Wilson nodded and asked, "How can I help?"

"I've visited you three times. Twice before you wouldn't believe me," John said.

"I don't think I've ever seen you before," he said. "You're not one of my students, are you?"

"No, I'm not. We've never met, but I've met versions of you."

"Really."

John yelled, "Don't patronize me! You do that every fucking time, and I've had enough." His arms were shaking. "I don't belong in this universe. I belong in another. Do you understand?"

Wilson's face was emotionless, still. "No, please explain."

"I was tricked into using a device. I was tricked by another version of myself because he wanted my life. He told me I could get back, but the device either doesn't work right or only goes in one direction. I want to get back to my universe, and I need help."

Wilson nodded. "Why don't you sit down?"

John nodded, tears welling in his eyes. He'd finally gotten through to Wilson.

"So you've tried talking with me — other versions of me — in other universes, and I won't help. Why not?"

"We start by discussing parallel universes or quantum cosmology or Multi-Worlds Theory, and you end up shooting it all down with Occam's Razor."

"Sounds like something I'd say," Wilson said nodding. "So you have a device."

"Yeah. It's here." John pointed to his chest, then unbuttoned his shirt.

Wilson looked at the device gravely. "What's that in your hand?"

John glanced down at the diploma. "It's . . . your diploma from the last universe. I sorta took it for proof."

Wilson held out his hand, and John handed it over. There was an identical one on the wall. The professor glanced from one to the other. "Uh huh," he said, then after a moment, "I see."

He put the diploma down and said, "My middle name is Lawrence."

John saw that the script of the diploma he'd stolen said "Frank B. Wilson" while the one on the wall said "Frank L. Wilson."

"I guess it's just a difference–"

"Who put you up to this? Was it Greene? This is just the sort of thing he'd put together."

Anguish washed over John. "No! This is all real."

"That device strapped to your chest. Now that's classic. And the diploma. Nice touch."

"Really. This is no hoax."

"Enough already. I'm on to you. Is Greene in the hall?" Wilson

Paul Melko

called through the door. "You can come out now, Charles. I'm on to you."

"There is no Charles. There is no Greene," John said quietly.

"And you must be from the drama department, because you are good. Two more copies of me! As if the universe can handle one."

John stood up and walked out of the office, his body suddenly too heavy.

"Don't forget the shingle," Wilson called, holding up the diploma. John shrugged and continued walking down the hall.

He sat on a bench next to the quad for a long time. The sun set and the warm summer day vanished along with the kids playing frisbee with their shirts tied around their waists.

Finally he stood and walked toward the Student Union. He needed food. He'd skipped lunch at some point; his stomach was growling at him. He didn't feel hungry but his body was demanding food. He just felt tired.

There was a pizza franchise in the Student Union called Papa Bob's. He ordered a small pizza and a Coke, ate it mechanically. It tasted like cardboard, chewy cardboard.

The Union was desolate as well, all the students driving home or heading to the dorms for studying and TV. John spotted a pay phone as he sat pondering what he would do next, whether he should confront Wilson again. John realized that he should have taken a picture of the man or demanded he write himself a note. But he would have told John that it was computer generated or forged.

He walked over to the phone and dialed his number. The phone demanded 75 cents. He inserted the coins and the phone began to ring.

"Hello?" his mother answered.

"Hello," he replied.

"Johnny?" she asked, surprised.

"No, could I talk to John please?"

She laughed. "You sound just like him. Gave me a fright, hearing that, but he's standing right here. Here he is."

"Hello?" It was his voice.

"Hi, this is Karl Smith from your English class," John said making up a name and a class.

"Yeah?"

"I missed class today, and I was wondering if we had an assignment."

"Yeah we did. We had an essay on the poem we read, Tennyson's 'Maud.' Identify the poetic components, like the last one."

"Oh, yeah," John said. The poem was in the same unit as the Hopkins one. He remembered seeing it. "Thanks." He hung up the phone.

This universe seemed just like his own. He could fit right in here. The thought startled him, and then he asked himself what was stopping him.

He walked to the bus station and bought a ticket back to Findlay.

John helped his father around the farm the next day. He took it as penance for upsetting his parents. They still thought he was Johnny Farmboy, and so he had to act the part, at least until his projects started churning.

As they replaced some of the older wood in the fence, John said, "Dad, I'm going to need to borrow the truck on Saturday night."

His father paused, a big smile on his face. "Got a big date, do you?" He said it in such a way that John realized he didn't think his son really had a date.

"Yes. I'm taking Casey Nicholson out."

"Casey?" His father held the plank as John hammered a nail into it. "Nice girl."

"Yeah, I'm taking her to a movie at the Bijou."

"The Bijou?"

"I mean the Strand," John said, silently yelling at himself for sharing details that could catch him up. The movie theatre was always called the Palace, Bijou, or Strand.

"Uh-huh."

John took the shovel and began shoring up the next post.

"What movie you gonna see?"

Before he could stop himself, he answered, "Does it matter?"

His father paused, then laughed heartily. "Not if you're in the balcony, it doesn't." John was surprised, then he laughed too.

"Don't tell your mother I told you, but we used to go to the Strand all the time. I don't think we watched a single movie."

"Dad!" John said. "You guys were . . . make-out artists?"

"Only place we could go to do it," he said with a grin. "Couldn't use this place; your grampa would have beat the tar out of me. Couldn't use her place; your other grampa would have shot me." He eyed John and nodded. "You're lucky we live in more liberal times."

John laughed, recalling the universe where the free love expressions of the 60s had never ended, where AIDS had killed a quarter of the population and syphilis and gonorrhea had been contracted by 90 percent of the population by 1980. There, dating involved elaborate chaperone systems and blood tests.

"I know I'm lucky."

In the early hours of the morning, John slipped across Gurney, through the Walder's field and found a place to watch the farm from the copse of maple trees. He knelt on the soft ground, wondering if this was where John Prime had waited for him.

John's arms tingled as he anticipated his course of action. He was owed a life, he figured. His had been stolen and he was owed another. He'd wanted his own back, and he'd tried to get it. He'd researched and questioned and figured, but he couldn't see any way back.

So he was ready to settle for second best.

He'd trick the John Rayburn here, just like he'd been tricked. Tease him with the possibilities. Tickle his curiosity. And if he wasn't interested, he'd forced him. Knock him out and strap the device on his chest and send him on.

Let him figure it out like John had. Let him find another universe to be a part of. John deserved his life back. He'd played by the rules all his life. He'd been a good kid; he'd loved his parents. He'd gone to church every Sunday.

He'd been pushed around for too long. John Prime had pushed him around, Professor Wilson, the cat-dogs. He'd been running and running and with no purpose. And enough of that. It was time to take back what had been stolen from him.

Dawn cast a slow red upon the woods. His mother opened the back door and stepped out into the yard with a basket. He watched her open the hen house and collect eggs. She was far away, but he recognized her as his mother instantly. Logically, he knew she wasn't his mother, but to his eyes, she was. That was all that mattered.

His father pecked her lightly on the cheek as he headed for the barn. He wore heavy boots, thick ones, coveralls, and a John Deere cap. He entered the barn, started the tractor and drove toward the fields. He'd be back for breakfast in an hour, John knew. Bacon, eggs, toast, and, of course, coffee.

They were his parents. It was his farm. Everything was as he remembered it. And that was enough for him.

The light in John's room turned on. John Rayburn was awake. He'd be coming out soon to do his chores. John waited until this John went into the barn, then he dashed across the empty pumpkin field for the barn's rear door. The rear door was locked, but if you jiggled it, John knew, it came loose.

John grabbed the handle, listening for sounds from within the barn, then shook it once for a few seconds. The door held. He paused, then shook it again and it came open suddenly, loudly. He slipped into the barn and hid between two rows of stacked bales.

"Hey, Stan-Man. How are you this morning?"

The voice came from near the stalls. This John — he started thinking of him as John Subprime — was feeding his horse.

"Here's an apple. How about some oats?"

John crept along the row of bales, then stopped when he could see the side of John Subprime's face from across the barn. John was safe in the shadows, but he needed to get closer to him.

Stan nickered and nuzzled John Subprime's head, drawing his tongue across his forehead.

"Stop that," he said, with a smile.

John Subprime turned his attention to the sheep, and when he did so, John slipped around the bales and behind the corn picker.

He realized something as he sat in the woods, and his plan had changed accordingly. John wasn't a liar. He wasn't a smooth talker. He couldn't do what John Prime had done to him, that is, talk him into using the device. John would have to do it some other way. And the only way he could think to do it was the hard way.

John lifted a shovel off a pole next to the corn picker. It was a short shovel with a flat blade. He figured one blow to the head and John Subprime would be out cold. Then he'd strap the device to his chest, toggle the universe counter up one, and then hit the lever with the end of the shovel. It'd take half the shovel with him, but that was okay. Then John would finish feeding the animals and go in for break-fast. No one would ever know.

John ignored the queasy feeling in his stomach. Gripping the shovel in two hands, he advanced on John Subprime.

John's faint shadow must have alerted him.

"Dad?" John Subprime said, then turned. "My God!" He shrank away from the raised shovel, his eyes passing from it to John's face. His expression changed from shock to fear.

John's body strained, the shovel raised above his head.

John Subprime leaned against the sheep pen, one arm raised, the other . . .

He had only one arm.

Nausea washed through John's body and he dropped the shovel. It clattered on the wood floor of the barn, settled at John Subprime's feet.

"What am I doing?" he cried. His stomach heaved, but nothing came up but a yellow bile that he spat on the floor. He heaved again at the smell of it.

He was no better than John Prime. He didn't deserve a life.

John staggered to the back door of the barn.

"Wait!"

He ran across the field. Something grabbed at his feet and he fell. He pulled his foot free and ran into the woods.

"Wait! Don't run!"

John turned to see John Subprime running after him, just one arm, the right, pumping. He slowed twenty feet in front of John, then stopped, his hand extended.

"You're me," he said. "Only you have both arms."

John nodded, his breath too ragged, his stomach too tense to speak. Tears were welling in his eyes as he looked at the man he had contemplated clubbing.

"How can that be?"

John found his voice. "I'm a version of you."

John Subprime nodded vigorously. "Only you never lost your arm!"

"No, I never lost it." John nodded his head. "How did it happen?"

John Subprime grimaced. "Pitchfork. I was helping dad in the barn loft. I lost my balance, fell. The pitchfork caught my bicep, sliced it . . ."

"I remember." In John's universe, he'd been twelve, and he had fallen from the loft while he and his father loaded it with hay.

He had thought he could carry the bale, but he hadn't been strong enough and he'd fallen to the farm yard, knocking the wind out of himself, bumping the pitchfork over as he fell. The pitchfork had landed next to him, nicking his shoulder. His father had looked on in horror and then anger. The scolding from his mother had been worse than the nick. "I just got a cut on my shoulder."

John Subprime laughed. "In one world, I lose my arm, and in another I get a scratch. Don't that beat all." Why was he laughing? Didn't he realize that John had meant to steal his life?

"Yeah."

"Why don't you come inside and have some breakfast?"

John looked at him, unsure of how he could ask that. He yelled, "I was going to steal your life!"

John Subprime nodded. "Is that why you had the shovel? Then you saw my arm. No way you could steal my life. You've got two arms." He laughed.

"It wasn't just that," John said. "I couldn't bring myself to hurt . . ."

"Yeah, I know."

"How could you possibly?" John yelled. "I've lost everything!" He reached into his shirt and toggled the universe counter. "I'm sorry, but I have to leave."

"No. Wait!" John Subprime yelled.

John backed away and pulled the lever.

The world blurred and John Subprime blinked away.

There was the barn and the farmhouse, and off in the distance his father on the tractor. Another universe where he didn't belong. He toggled the device and pulled the lever. Again the farmhouse. He didn't belong here either. Again he moved forward through the universes. The farmhouse was gone. And again. Then it was there, but green instead of red. He toggled it again and again, wanting to get as far away from his contemplated crime as possible.

The clouds flew around in chaotic fast motion. The trees he stood in were sometimes there, sometimes not. The farmhouse bounced left and right a foot, a half foot. The barn more, sometimes behind the house, sometimes to the east of it. The land was the one constant, a gently sloping field. Once he found himself facing the aluminum siding of a house. And then it was gone as he transferred out.

A hundred times, he must have transferred through universe after universe where he didn't belong until finally he stopped and collapsed to the ground, sobbing.

He'd lost his life. He'd lost it all, and he'd never get it back.

He rested his head against the trunk of a maple and closed his eyes. After the tears were gone, after his breathing had slowed, he slept, exhausted.

"Hey there, fella. Time to get up."

Someone poked him. John looked up into his father's face. "Dad?"

"Not unless my wife's been hiding something from me." He offered a hand, and John pulled himself up. John was in the copse of maples, his father from this universe standing beside him, holding a walking stick. He didn't recognize John.

"Sorry for sleeping here in your woods. Got tired."

"Yeah. It'll happen." He pointed toward Gurney with his stick. "Better be heading along. The town's that way." He pointed north. "About two miles."

"Yes, sir." John began walking. Then he stopped. His father hadn't recognized him. Which meant what? John wasn't sure. He turned back to him. "Sir, I could use some lunch. If you have extra. I could work it off."

Bill Rayburn — John forced himself to use the name in his head. This man was not his father — checked his watch, then nodded. "Lunch in a few minutes, my watch and my stomach tell me. Cold cuts. As to working it off, no need."

"That's fine."

"What's your name?"

"John . . . John Wilson." He took Professor Wilson's last name spontaneously.

John turned and followed Bill across the pumpkin field toward the house. The pumpkins were still on the vine, unpicked and just a week until Halloween. Some of them were already going bad. He passed a large one with its top caved in, a swarm of gnats boiling out of it.

He remembered the joke his father had told him a week ago.

"How do you fix a broken jack-o-lantern?" he asked.

Bill turned and glanced at him as if he were a darn fool.

"I don't know."

"With a pumpkin patch," John replied, his face straight.

Bill stopped, looked at him for a moment, then a small smile crept across his lips. "I'll have to remember that one."

The barn was behind the house, smaller than he remembered and in need of paint. There was a hole in the roof that should have been patched. In fact the farm seemed just a bit more decrepit than he remembered. Had hard times fallen on his parents here?

"Janet, another one for lunch," Bill called as he opened the back door. "Leave your shoes."

John took his shoes off, left them where he always did. He hung his bag on a hook. It was a different hook, brass and molded, where he remembered a row of dowels that he and his father had glued into the sideboard.

John could tell Janet wasn't keen on a stranger for lunch, but she didn't say anything, and she wouldn't until she and Bill were alone. John smiled at her, thanked her for letting him have lunch.

She wore the same apron he remembered. No, he realized. She'd worn this one, with a red check pattern and deep pockets in front, when he was younger.

She served John a turkey sandwich, with a slice of cheese on it. He thanked her again as she did, and ate the sandwich slowly. Janet had not recognized him either.

Bill said to Janet, "Got some good apples for cider, I think, a few bushels."

John raised his eyebrows at that. He and his father could get a couple bushels per tree. Maybe the orchard was smaller here. Or maybe it had been hit with blight. He glanced at Bill and saw the shake in his hand. He'd never realized how old his father was, or maybe he had aged more quickly in this universe for reasons unknown. Maybe a few bushels was all he could gather.

"I should work on the drainage in the far field tomorrow. I've got a lake there now and it's going to rot my seed next season." The far field had always been a problem, the middle lower than the edges, a pond in the making.

"You need to pick those pumpkins too, before they go bad," John said suddenly.

Bill looked at him.

"What do you know of farming?"

John swallowed his bite of sandwich, angry at himself for drawing the man's resentment. John knew better than to pretend farm another farmer's fields.

"Uh, I grew up on a farm like this. We grew pumpkins, sold them before Halloween and got a good price for them. You'll have to throw half your crop away if you wait until Sunday, and then who'll buy that late?"

Janet said to Bill, "You've been meaning to pick those pumpkins."

"Practically too late now," Bill said. "The young man's right. Half the crop's bad."

"I could help you pick them this afternoon." John said it because he wanted to spend more time there. It was the first chance he'd had in a long time to relax. They weren't his parents; he knew that. But they were good people.

Bill eyed him again appraisingly.

"You worked a farm like this, you say. What else you know how to do?"

"I can pick apples. I can lay wood shingles for that hole in your barn."

"You been meaning to do that too, Bill," Janet said. She was warming to him.

"It's hard getting that high up, and I have a few other priorities," he said. He looked back at John. "We'll try you out for the day, for lunch and dinner and three dollars an hour. If it isn't working out, you hit the road at sundown, no complaining."

John said, "Deal."

"Janet, call McHenry and ask him if he needs another load of pumpkins and if he wants me to drop 'em off tonight."

John waited outside the County Clerk's window, his rage mounting. How damn long did it take to hand over a marriage certificate? Casey was waiting for him outside the judge's chamber, nine-months pregnant. If the man behind the glass wall took any longer, the kid was going to be born a bastard. And Casey's and his parents had been adamant about that. No bastard. He'd said he'd take care of the kid and he meant it, but they wanted it official.

Finally the clerk handed over the license and the two notarized blood tests and John snatched them from his hand.

"Thanks," he said, turning and heading for the court building.

After the wedding he and Casey were driving up to Toledo to honeymoon on the last of his cash. In a week he was scheduled to start his GE job. He was going to work one of the assembly lines, but that was just until the book he was writing — *The Shining* — took off.

The trip to Toledo served the purpose of the honeymoon, as well as the fact that he had meetings regarding the screwed-up Rubik's Cube. It still irked him. The patent search had turned up nothing and they had built a design, one that finally worked, and they'd sunk $95,000 into a production run. Then they'd gotten a call from the lawyer in Belgium. Apparently there was a patent filed in Hungary by that bastard Rubik. The company Rubik had hired in New York to market the things had gone under and he'd never bothered to try again. Someone had gotten wind of their product and now they wanted a piece of the deal.

The lawyer had wanted to drop him like a hot potato, but he'd convinced him that there was still cash to be made from it. Some cash at least. He'd have to pay a licensing fee probably. Kiss some ass. But there was money to be made. He'd stick it out with John, though the retainer was just about gone.

Casey waved as he rounded the corner on the third floor in front of the judge's office. Casey sat on a bench, her belly seeming to rest on her knees. Her face was puffy and pink, as if someone had pumped her with saline.

"Hi, Johnny," she said. "Did you get the paper?"

He hated being called Johnny and he'd told her that, but she still did it. Everybody used to call Johnny Farmboy Johnny so he was stuck with it. Some things just couldn't be changed.

He put on a smile and waved the certificate. "Yeah," he said. "Everything's ready." He kissed Casey on the cheek. "Darling, you look radiant." He'd be glad once the baby was out of her body; then she could start dressing the way he liked again. He hoped her cheerleading uniform still fit.

The ceremony was quick, though Casey had to dab her eyes. John wasn't surprised that none of Casey's friends were there. Getting pregnant had put a lot of stress on her relationships. Field hockey had been right out.

The judge signed the certificate and it was done. John was glad Casey's and his parents hadn't come. They'd wanted to, but John had axed that request. They had settled for a reception after the baby was born.

He knew his parents were disappointed in what had happened, and John hadn't wanted to face them during the ceremony. They'd wanted him to go to college, to better himself. But those were the dreams they had for Johnny Farmboy. He was a completely different thing.

They'd understand once the money started rolling in. They'd not be disappointed in their son any more.

John slowly lowered Casey into the bucket seat of the Trans-Am, a splurge with the last of his cash. He had to have decent wheels. The Trans Am pulled away and he headed for Route 16. "Glad that's over with," he said.

"Really?" Casey asked.

"Well, I'm glad it's over with and we're married now," he said quickly.

"Yeah, I know what you mean."

John nodded. He had to be careful what he said with Casey, what he shared. About the time she'd started showing and they'd had to tell their parents, John had wished he had the device, wished he could jump to the next universe and start over. John realized he should have killed Johnny Farmboy, hid the body, and kept the device. Now the Cube had to work right. With his money almost gone, he might not have another chance, no matter how good an idea the AbCruncher was. He'd wanted to come clean and tell Casey all about his past, but he didn't dare. How could she believe him?

He was stuck here and he had to make it work. There were no other choices now. This was the life he'd chosen. He patted Casey's leg and smiled at her. He'd make some money, enough to set her and the kid up, and then he'd have his freedom to do what he wanted with his money. It would take a little longer now; there were some bumps in the road, but he'd succeed. He was Johnny Prime.

Spring had arrived, but without the sun on his shoulders, John was chilly. He'd started working on the car in the morning and the sun had been on him, and now, after lunch, it was downright cold. He considered getting the tractor out and hauling the beat-up Trans Am into the sun. He finally decided it was too much trouble. It was late and there was no way he'd get the carburetor back together before dinner.

He'd bought the car for fifty dollars, but the car had yet to start. He'd need it soon. He started a second shift job at the GE plant in May. And then in the fall he was taking classes at the University of Toledo.

He'd applied to the University of Toledo's continuing education program. He couldn't enroll as a traditional freshman, which was all right with him, because of the fact that he'd taken the GED instead of graduating from high school. He wouldn't get into the stuff he wanted to learn until his senior year: quantum field theory, cosmology, general relativity. That was all right. He was okay where he was for the time being. If he didn't think about home, he could keep going.

With the plant job, washing machine assembly line work from four until midnight, he'd have enough for tuition for the year. Plus Bill and Janet were still paying him three an hour for chores he was helping out with. In his own universe he wouldn't have been paid a dime. In September he'd get another job for pocket money and rent near the university.

He set the carburetor on the front seat and rolled the car back into the barn. This was a good universe, John had decided, but he wasn't staying. No, he was happy with Bill and Janet taking him in. They were kind and generous, just like his own parents in nearly every respect, but he couldn't stay here. Not for the long term.

The universe was a mansion with a million rooms. People didn't know they were in just one room. They didn't know there was a way through the walls to other rooms.

But John did. He knew there were walls. And he knew something else too. He knew walls came down. There were holes between worlds.

John had listed his major as physics, and he'd laughed when the manila envelope from the department had arrived, welcoming him and listing his faculty advisor as Dr. Frank Wilson. Professor Wilson's world was going to shatter one day, and John was going to do it for him.

John knew something that no other physicist in this world knew. A human could pass through the walls of the universe. Just knowing that it was possible, just knowing, without a bit of doubt — he needed only to pull up his pant leg and look at the scars from the cat-dog bite — that there were a million universes out there, was all it would take for John to figure the science of it out.

That was his goal. He had the device and he had his knowledge. He'd reverse engineer it, take it apart, ask the questions of the masters in the field, he would himself become one of those masters, to find out how it was done.

And then, once the secrets of the universe lay open to him, he would go back and he would kick the shit out of John Prime.

He smiled as he shut the barn door.

SNAIL
STONES

W ho's that wagger?" Edeo asked. He was so distracted by the cloaked figure he missed the ball Haron had bounced off the wall of the abandoned building, and it rolled across the sewer grate, bumbling like a pachinko ball before disappearing into the foulness below.

"That's great, Edeo! That was our only ball."

But Edeo's attention was on the gray-coated man who couldn't have looked more conspicuous, head darting left and right, arms clutching a bundle of sack cloth.

Haron scooted on his belly by the grate, finger brushing slimy water, trying to find the ball.

"Who cares who he is?" Haron said. "Unless he has some more balls."

Edeo, oblivious to Haron's effort to extract the ball, edged between the two warehouses to get a better look at the figure. He climbed a pile of rubble.

"It's Fruge, the jeweler," he said. "My new dad bought my mom a ring from him. Then he hocked it for ringseed ale."

"It's Fruge, so what?" Haron said, certain that Edeo should be the one fishing for the ball. His fingers touched something furry. He pulled his hand out with a squeal.

Fruge, some hundred meters away, turned, searching the broken buildings for the sound. Edeo dropped down among the rubble pieces. "Shush, now. He'll see us, you breather."

"So? He ain't the muni?"

Haron, angry that he had screamed like a little kid, stuck his hand back in, now searching for the rodent and the ball. Either would be fun to play with.

Fruge stared at the derelict buildings. He was clearly doing something nefarious, Edeo thought. He fumbled in his pocket with one hand while the other clutched the cloth to his chest.

"Holy Captain. He's got a gun."

Haron turned his head, hand still in the grate. "A gun?"

"He's coming this way."

Something brushed Haron's hand and he squeezed. "Hey, I got the ball!" He tried to pull his hand out, but his fist was too thick to fit between the bars of the grate. Something chittered in the darkness.

Haron watched Fruge advance on them. He was still a long way off, and he had no doubt that they could outrun the pudgy man in the ruins near the spaceport. He and Edeo were small and knew a lot of good hiding places they shouldn't have, given that their moms had forbidden them to come to the old abandoned firstfall zone.

Edeo was mesmerized by Fruge's gun. He'd never seen one; they were illegal. Why was Fruge carrying one? It was obvious after a moment; Fruge was a jeweler. He had to carry a gun for protection.

Haron, having banged his fist against the bars a dozen times, was convinced he couldn't bring the ball through the grate while holding it. He peered down into the sewer. Stupid ball. Edeo had picked the biggest one on the ball tree, of course.

"Who's there?" Fruge cried. "I have a gun." He waved it. "Don't come near me."

"What's he squawking on about?" Haron asked.

"He's afraid," Edeo replied. "We'd better go. He might mistake us for robbers."

"Not without my ball."

"We'll get another one."

"Not until tonight!" The ball tree was in Mr. Hebway's garden. Any balls that fell, he burned in his incinerator instead of giving them to the kids. No way he'd let them have one, even if they asked. They'd have to climb the fence and tree in the dark.

"Come on," Edeo said. He scrambled down the rubble pile.

"No way!"

Haron reached in with his other hand, cupping the ball. He let go and then pushed it through the grate. "I got it."

Edeo peered around the rubble. Fruge was running at them.

"Come on!"

The sound of thunder erupted above, and radiant heat basked them in warmth. The cargo ship sprayed orange flame as it drove into the sky. The boys paused, watching the rocket climb. They'd come to watch it anyway, but then been distracted.

"Wow," Edeo said, forgetting Fruge for the moment. It was off to Highpoint, where the bigger spline ships docked. Edeo couldn't imagine that the spline ships were hundreds of times bigger than the simple rockets that launched from the spaceport.

When the rocket had finally become just a blur of red, they remembered Fruge. But when they turned, he was gone, perhaps scared by the sound of the rocket.

"What's that?" Edeo asked. Where Fruge had been standing, something twinkled in the sunlight.

Haron and Edeo ran for it, Haron edging Edeo out by a hair. He scooped the glittering thing up, then dropped it as if it were a snake.

Edeo skidded to a stop, his hand frozen. The shape and size made it obvious, but he'd never seen one so big. The boys looked at each other. Then Edeo reached down to pick it up.

"Snail stone."

Haron was at Edeo's door five minutes after dinner.

"You got it?" he whispered.

Edeo's mom was busy on the vid with her friends, all six faces on the screen showing a similar head covered with a checked cloth. His step-father was collapsed on the couch sipping a ringseed. That left just his older brother Gremon to arch a brow and say, "Got what?"

"Nothing," Edeo and Haron said in unison.

"I bet," Gremon said, standing up from the table to block Edeo's way out of the kitchen. Edeo had the snail stone in his back pocket, and he knew Gremon well enough to know he'd search him until he found the artifact in question.

He sighed, as if in resignation, then tipped Gremon's plate of food out of his hand. While Gremon juggled the plate, Edeo slid under the table. Edeo and Haron were almost to the stairwell firedoor when gravity finally won the battle and Gremon's plate clattered to the floor, breaking in pieces.

They shared a quick grin, though Edeo knew he'd pay later. It was worth it.

"You got it?" Haron asked again.

"Yeah," Edeo said.

Instead of heading out into the courtyard, they kept going down, sliding between boxes in the space under the last flight of stairs. Haron switched on his flashlight as Edeo pulled out the snail stone.

It felt like a rock in Edeo's hand, cold and heavy, but it didn't look like a rock. It shimmered with orange light, cutting the flashlight's beam into prisms. Edeo turned his hand, and the prisms danced on the wall.

"You sleep with it under your bed and your willy gets longer," Haron said.

"Does not!" Edeo replied, though truth be told, he wasn't sure. People said the snail stones did all sorts of things, that they powered rockets, caused cold fusion, cured colds. Why else did the government decide they owned them all?

"How much you think it's worth?"

"We can't ask Fruge, that's for sure," Edeo said.

"Lotta jewelers," Haron said.

Footsteps on the stair, and Haron snapped off the flashlight. The steps stopped, as if the soft click had been enough to alert the stepper.

With extra-fraternal senses, Edeo knew it was Gremon. He held his breath, willed Haron to do the same. Haron sensed his friend's fear and remained silent, waiting.

Finally, the steps continued and the courtyard door swung open and closed.

They waited. It wasn't above Gremon to fool them from their hiding places with a fake door opening. Then a chatting couple came in, and that was enough for the two. They slipped up the steps and, with an eye for Gremon, headed for the Guild district.

Most of the shops were closed, the gemologists and dealers off to their homes. Fruge's shop was closed tight. None of the shops displayed any snail stones in their barred windows.

"Tomorrow?" Edeo asked. He was thinking he'd slip the stone under his mattress for safe keeping.

"Nah," Haron said. "Here."

The place was a pawn shop. A few rings lined the front display windows. A neon sign flickered, revealed that the shop was open twenty-two hours.

They pushed through the revolving door into the cluttered shop. Junk lined the walls; space suits hung next to stringless violins. Two rows of trikes sat covered in dust, one of them a Keebler Three-X.

"We'll be able to buy two of those with this," Haron whispered.

"You think?"

"I ain't buying anymore trikes!"

A head had popped up through a glass partition at the back of the store.

"We don't got no trikes," Haron said.

"Well, you don't look like you can buy one, either of you. What you want?"

Edeo nudged Haron forward in front of him. They stepped to within two meters of the pawnbroker. He was old enough to be second generation. Wispy white hair medusaed around his head.

"Snail stones," Haron said. "How much one of those go for?"

The man's eyes narrowed. "You trying to trick old Kort? You working with the munis, seeing if I'm on the up and up?" His voice rose as if he were addressing someone beyond the room, listening in. "I don't traffic in restricted items, no sir."

Haron was annoyed. "Yeah, but how much would it be worth if you did?"

The pawnbroker peered down at Haron. His eyes had a devious look to them, as if he'd just made a decision to do a bad thing for his own good. "What you find in your granddame's attic? Something that should have been turned in years ago? Something forgotten?"

Edeo backed away, hand deep in his pocket, cupping the snail stone.

"We didn't find nothing!" Haron said, standing fast.

The booth the pawnbroker sat in flew up to the ceiling with a whoosh, leaving the old man standing in front of Haron. He reached out with a fist and took hold of Haron's shirt, dragging him forward with one hand while the other dug into Haron's pants pocket.

"What you got there, pinter? What'd you find?"

Edeo ran, abandoning Haron for the gem's safety. But when he slammed into the revolving door, it held fast.

"Maybe *you've* got the stone," the man cried.

"We don't have nothing," Edeo screamed. "It was all Gremon's idea. He sent us in to ask!"

The old man's strength seemed to flag, and Haron's feet touched the ground. He pulled away and huddled with Edeo in the pie-shaped slot of the revolving door.

"A trick? You playing a trick on old Kort?"

The old man spat at them, then kicked a lever with his feet. The reluctant door whipped them around and spat them onto the street. They ran, then, ducking between two women window shopping in the dusk.

Edeo ran only as far as the first turn, then he sagged against a solar shield booth, rusted and left over from before the atmosphere was thick enough. The thing was covered in graffiti, but the seats were relatively clean, so they sat there under the lead shielding and took deep breaths.

"They're on the munis restricted lists," Haron finally said.

"Yeah."

"We staying out?" Haron asked after awhile.

"Ain't going home," Edeo replied. Gremon was sure to beat the crap out of him when he got there, unless he planned it right.

They sat there until the sun was long gone.

"Look there," Haron said. "Fruge."

Indeed the jeweler had stepped out of his dark shop and was glancing left and right as he locked his door.

"Looking mighty suspish, ain't he?" Edeo said.

"Mighty."

Without a word, they left the confines of the solar shield, ambling with precise nonchalance in the same direction as Fruge, but on the other side of the street.

"He's going back to the spaceport," Edeo said, when he took a sudden turn.

"Sell his jewels off planet. Only place he can, I bet, if they're on the restricted lists," Haron said.

Edeo glanced at his friend. Sometimes he made a lot of sense.

Fruge kept throwing glances over his shoulder, and finally Edeo pulled Haron aside into a dark side street, certain Fruge'd see the duo soon.

"We know where he's going," Edeo said. "Come on." They ran through the side streets for the spaceport, trying to reach the corner where they had seen Fruge earlier in the day.

Panting, they found a crumbled doorway that gave them a view of two streets.

"There he is," Haron said.

In the dark, he was little more than a bumbling shadow, but clearly it was him, edging down the street, looking over his shoulder.

"Probably has his gun," Edeo said.

Fruge stopped before he reached the intersection, slipping into a doorway. They heard the jiggle of keys, then the scrape of a door opening.

"I thought all these warehouses were abandoned," Edeo said. When the new spaceport terminal went in on the far side of the landing fields, there'd been no need to keep up these old buildings. Old Firstfall had crumbled into decay.

"Not," said Haron.

Light flickered from within the building, barely visible through blinded windows in the basement. Edeo and Haron shared a quick grin in the darkness and slipped from their hiding place.

Fruge had gone to some trouble to cover the windows, using tape to wedge a curtain across all of the glass. But at some point, the tape had dried up, and a corner of the curtain had drooped to reveal the inside of the building.

Haron was there first, kneeling and pushing his eye into the space. Edeo danced around him, tried the other two windows to no avail.

"Watcha see?"

"Shhh," Haron said, not because he was afraid Fruge would hear them but rather because he had nothing to report. All he saw was an empty, cement-block-lined basement.

Then Fruge appeared, coming down steps on the far side of the basement. He carried a bag. He laid it on the ground and drew from it a crowbar. Then he pulled open a door and thrust the crowbar into the small dark space beyond. He wiggled it, urging something forth. He reached in and grabbed a rope and pulled.

Something moved forward in a huddle, sliding across the floor. When Haron saw what it was, he jumped back, which was enough for Edeo to take his place at the window.

Edeo gasped. He turned to his friend and said, "He has a snail."

It was just stuff everybody knew, stuff from school, stuff from parents, stuff from older brothers. The colony ship arrived with eminent domain. There was no way the ship was going back! That would have been outrageous.

And the snails weren't even that intelligent. No tools, no language, no cities. Not really molluscs, but they looked enough like their namesake, if two meters tall instead of two millimeters. How can a snail be sentient?

And when humans figured out you could pry the pretty gems off their carapaces and they'd grow back, well. That was just another resource to be used. The fact that the crystals had different composition depending on what you fed the snails, that was just grease for the herding and round-up of twenty million slugs.

By the time Edeo and Haron were born, there wasn't a snail on the northern continent, and only a handful on the southern. But Fruge had one in the basement of that abandoned building, and he was prying the gems loose to sell. And now Edeo and Haron knew.

They shared a horrified glance, and then they ran. They ran home as fast as they could in the face of this unfathomable perversion, all the way home.

They skidded to a halt outside Edeo's building, their chests heaving, their legs leaden.

"We should tell . . ." Haron started, then stopped.

Edeo shook his head, then they swore each other to silence and promised to meet the next day. Haron asked for the stone, but Edeo swore it would be safe with him. He snuck it upstairs to the room he shared with Gremon without seeing his brother and slipped it under his mattress. Perhaps Gremon would forget all about the indignity Edeo had foisted upon him. But probably not.

Haron, sworn to secrecy about their snail, was not so sworn on snails in general.

"Mom, any snails around here?" he asked.

"Snails all gone, sweetie," she replied, her head mounted unmoving in front of the vid.

"Yeah, any still around?"

"In the zoo, maybe. Maybe on the south continent. Shush now. My favorite part."

Haron shrugged and went off to bed, sleeping fitfully on his mattress that protected no stone. Edeo slept just as poorly, but they both met ready the next morning.

"What happened to you?"

Edeo touched his tender eye. "Gremon."

"Yeah. Got it?"

"Got it."

"We should go to the zoo. See if there's any snails there," Haron said.

Edeo shook his head. "Naw. Zoo's three buses away. Take all day."

"What then?"

"Where's Fruge right now?"

"In his store."

"He's there all day, right?" Edeo said. "He's not with the snail."

"What are you saying?"

Edeo said, "Let's go look at the snail right here."

Haron shook his head, but he already knew he'd be going with Edeo. They walked back to the spaceport ruins, hiding in their doorway, waiting until they were sure the building was empty, then they sauntered across the road and tried the door.

"Locked," Haron said.

Edeo knelt down and jiggled the window they'd looked through the night before.

"Locked too," Haron said.

Edeo surveyed the street; he walked along the length of the building. The building to the left was in much worse a state of decay than Fruge's. Its door hung off its hinges and it looked liked squatters had camped there not too long ago. Both buildings were the same height.

"Roof," Edeo said. They pushed their way through the door, blinking in the darkness. Right there, steps led up. Edeo took them first, testing each one with his weight. On the first landing, rats scurried away into dark shadows.

"Cool," Haron said.

They found a ladder on the top floor that opened onto the roof. From there they had a fabulous view of the spaceport. A dozen rockets stood beside gangways, ready to ride fire into the sky. They paused to write the numbers on their fins in Haron's book.

Though the two buildings had looked the same height, Fruge's in fact was a meter lower. Edeo jumped down, rolling on the gravel-tar. Haron shook his head and dropped down after hanging by his arms first.

The roof door was locked, but the lock was so rusted that it gave when Edeo pulled on it. Down they walked, eyes alert for snails in dark corners.

"Whoa!" Haron said. He had nearly stepped into darkness. The entire first floor was demolished, leaving a view into the basement from the second floor. All that was left was a narrow path to the basement stairs.

They fell to their stomachs and looked over the edge. The door behind which the snail was caged was invisible in the darkness.

"No way down," Haron said.

"Rope," Edeo said.

"No way, man," Haron said. "It's just a snail."

"Fruge is *using* it," Edeo said. "Don't you see? We have to help it."

"This isn't about getting more jewels?"

"No!"

"Quiet!"

The door of the building opened, and Fruge entered. Light filled the basement as he hit the switch. He carried a bundle.

Fruge took the steps carefully, then threw his bundle on the ground. It clattered and clanked, revealing that it was metal parts: junk.

He opened the door and used the rope to pull the snail out. In the dim bulbs of the basement, the snail's carapace glittered with rainbow iridescence. There were no jewels, though Fruge hunted for any that might have formed. He shined a flashlight around the edges of the snail, which tried to slide away from him, but appeared to have no purchase on the floor.

"Nothing!" Fruge muttered. "Nothing growing on you today."

He crossed to the bundle and pulled out what looked like a handful of steel ball bearings.

"See what this will do, eh? I lost one, so I need another fast."

The snail's head disappeared under its shell as Fruge approached, but he reached right in and grasped it by the swirling antennae of which the snail had three. The head popped out, and Fruge wedged its mouth open with a knee. He dropped the ball bearings in, and then held the mouth closed.

"I've been trying to find cobalt, but who carries that? It costs more to feed you than I can make in gems off your back. Can't get but a tenth what they're worth due to the munis."

The snail tossed its head, trying to dislodge its food, tossing its head and grunting. Fruge took a handful of nuts and bolts, pulled opened the snail's mouth again, and forced them in.

It slurped and burbled, choking, but the snail was unable to dislodge what was forced into its mouth, unable to vomit. It grunted and twisted, but Fruge held it steady with a grip on its tender antennae.

Edeo and Haron watched as Fruge again filled the snail's gullet with bits of metal, even some glass and rocks, all sorts of junk, waiting until the material disappeared from its mouth. When the bag was empty, he pushed the snail back into its cave and left.

Edeo said to Haron, "See? We have to help."

Haron nodded slowly.

The rope they stole from Edeo's house. For a time, his father had held a job as a painter, until he'd started showing up too drunk to climb a ladder. But he still had a neat coil of rope that Edeo snuck from his "workshop" one night while he was passed out on the couch. They gathered lillweed seeds and scattered them all over the street outside the building. As every child knew, a lillweed seed had a bit of compressed air inside that it used to blow itself far from its parent; but, before autumn came, the seeds made excellent noise toys, or, in this case, early warning systems. The third thing they gathered was native plants.

This proved rather difficult. The colony ship had brought fine strains of plants that ousted the local varieties with little effort. There didn't seem to be a tree in Old Firstfall that wasn't an oak, maple, or elm.

Finally Edeo said, "Ball trees didn't come from Earth."

"No?"

"No way." They looked over the fence at Mr. Hebway's garden.

"Look at that," Haron said. In addition to the ball tree, Hebway had lillweed plants, rotordendrends, rozes, and blue-eyed susies. Instead of stealing balls, that night they took handfuls of the native plants, ripping them up by the root or breaking their stems.

The next day, after they were certain Fruge was well ensconced in his store, they scattered the lillweed seed up and down the street. Then they climbed the building, knotted the rope every foot, and lowered it down to the basement level.

Edeo glanced at Haron, and Haron shrugged his shoulders. They did stones with their fingers and Edeo lost. He reached for the rope and descended hand-over-hand into the basement, some six meters down.

"Toss it down," he whispered, then louder, "Toss it down."

Haron dropped the bundle of native plants, and they fell with a thwack on the basement floor.

"Come on."

Haron descended, and they turned to face the snail's door.

"Maybe we can just toss it through the door," Haron said.

Edeo shook his head. The door was wooden, painted gray, and peeling. It shut with a simple latch. He took a step toward it, then another, and finally reached forward to undo the latch before backpeddling away. The door squeaked, then slowly tilted open thirty degrees before scraping on the concrete floor. Darkness lay within.

Edeo peered into the space. The snail peered back with its floppy antennae. It emitted a chuff, its mucous membrane rattling above its maw. A whiff of iron, blood-like, washed over him.

"Phew."

"Maybe it's saying 'Hi,'" Haron said.

"Or 'Where's Fruge?'"

Edeo took the bundles of native flora in his hands, reached toward the snail with it. The snail twisted its three antennae, craned them in three directions as if to get a trinocular view of the proffered vegetable matter. Then it jumped forward with more speed than Edeo had thought possible, slurping the material into its gullet.

Edeo fumbled backward, surprised by the speed. Its face was gray and eyeless. The antennae swarmed and danced, taking in the boys and their food. Its mouth, shaped into a perpetual underbite, was twenty-five centimeters wide and opened into its flabby, sack-like gullet.

Haron said, "We certainly didn't have to force feed the thing like Fruge."

"No," Edeo said, mesmerized by the massive snail. It was taller than he was by twenty centimeters and he was taller than Haron.

The snail chuffed again, then burbled. It advanced, then stopped with a jingle. Haron realized that the snail's shell was chained to the wall of its cave.

"That wagger welded him to the wall!"

Edeo picked up the rest of the bundle and fed it piece by piece to the snail. When the last of the material had disappeared, the snail sent an antenna slithering around Edeo's palm, leaving a trail of mucous.

"Ick," he said.

Haron laughed, then jumped as another antenna entered his pocket faster than he could back away.

"Hey!"

But then the feeler had withdrawn, holding the ball that he'd picked from Mr. Hebway's ball tree. The snail ate it.

"That was our last ball."

"Yeah," said Edeo. "We're going to need a whole bunch more."

They couldn't keep raiding Mr. Hebway's garden; he'd have noticed pretty quickly at the rate the snail consumed plants. But with the flora in the garden as a guide, the two managed to find small sanctuaries of native plants within a few kilometers of the building. In fact, the fields around the spaceport housed a dozen prairie fields of gila grass, bleet weed, and curdleberries. Of these, the snail showed a distinct bias toward the gila grass, eating this first before anything else.

They visited the snail every day, determining Mr. Fruge's schedule quickly. He came every other day with a load of metal to feed the snail. At the same time, he scoured its shell for any new jewels that were forming, and if they were large enough, he pried them off with a crowbar, causing the snail to erupt in mucousy, blubbery moans.

Watching Fruge feed the snail nauseated Edeo. Finally, after one such feeding, Edeo immediately descended when Fruge left, stuck his hand down the snail's throat, and retrieved as much of the metal as he could.

"What are you doing?" Haron shrilled.

"Getting this crap out of our snail!"

"Our snail?"

Edeo dumped a pile of nails on the floor. His arm up to his shoulder was covered in slime.

"Yeah. We treat him way better than Fruge," Edeo said.

The snail sat obediently as Edeo emptied its gullet, then it slid forward and rooted through the pile of junk. It took several blue-colored ball bearings in its tendrils and scooped them back into its mouth.

"It wants those, apparently," Haron said. The rest of the junk it left on the floor.

Edeo's head whipped around at the sound of popping on the street.

"Fruge!" he cried. "He's coming back!"

Haron jumped for the rope, scurrying up onto the second floor. "Come on!"

Edeo looked around the floor at the piles of slimy junk. Fruge would know for sure that someone had found his snail. Edeo grabbed a handful of the metal and threw it behind some barrels.

The popping sound grew louder.

"Come on, Edeo!" Haron said. "Leave it."

"No! Pull up the rope."

He took another handful, tossing the junk atop the rest with a clatter. He pushed the snail back into its cave and grabbed the last of the metal, hiding himself with the junk behind the barrels.

A key rattled in the lock of the door.

He searched the floor for some sign of them, then made sure Haron had pulled up the rope. Nothing in sight.

Then he saw the half-ajar door!

Cursing issued from the front door, as Fruge searched for the right key. Edeo bounded forward, slammed the door shut, slid the bolt, and dashed back to his spot just as the light flashed on.

Edeo listened and Haron watched from above as Fruge creaked down the steps. His bag jingled with scrap. Edeo crouched lower as he saw his shadow pass on the floor not far from him. Fruge opened the gate and dragged the snail out.

"You need more junk, I think, if I'm going to get more jewels," Fruge said.

Edeo listened, his anger growing, as Fruge stuffed their snail with heavy metal. After he had left and the last sounds of the lillweed seed popping under his feet had faded away, Haron descended again.

Edeo turned to him. "We have to get our snail out of here."

They tried a hacksaw that Haron had swiped from a trike repair shop while Edeo distracted the owner, but the blade didn't even scratch the chain that held the snail in its cave. The far end was embedded in the rock wall, not into plaster, but into granite with spikes that must have been twenty centimeters long. The only thing that had any effect on the chain was a rasp file that Edeo stole from his step-dad's workshop, but it was soon clear it would take days of muscle-numbing work to get through the metal.

"This is useless," Haron said.

Edeo was bent over the back of the snail, rasping. The snail was sniffing at Haron's pocket for the ball he had hidden there. He giggled as the tendril plunged in and pulled it out. The snail was far better than a dog.

"Is not."

"Snail won't eat anything but curdleberries today. We'll have to go get some more."

Edeo looked up. "Not even the lillweed roots. He loved those before."

"Naw. Balls and curdleberries is all he's eating." Haron looked around. "And a kilo of copper wiring."

"Sheesh."

Haron's head tilted. "What was that?"

They pushed the snail back into its cave.

"It's way early for Fruge." After a week they had his comings and goings down: every other day to feed the snail and check for new jewels. And sometimes he brought a second load of metal, so they had to be careful.

Just as Haron was going for the rope, it jerked up into the air. Someone laughed above them.

"Gremon," Edeo whispered fiercely.

"What you little boys doing in the basement all alone? Comparing sizes?" His head appeared over the edge.

"None of your business," Edeo said.

"Yeah? You think?" He slid down the rope, one hand out raised. "Let's see what you're doing down here."

Edeo moved to stand in front of the gate, casually with one hand on the wall. Gremon looked around the basement, smiled once at Edeo. "What's behind the door?"

He pushed Edeo out of the way, pulled the door open.

"Marbles? Dirty pictures? Rock co —" His voice shriveled inside him, as he backed away. He pushed Edeo in front of him. "What!" He tripped over his own feet as the snail slid forward waving its antennae. A weird trilling sound came from the snail, one that Haron and Edeo had never heard before.

Gremon ran up the steps, his face white, his pants wet. He slammed against the locked door, turned the lock with fumbling hands, and disappeared into the street.

The snail's trilling turned to a heavy chuff.

"I think he's laughing," Haron said, rubbing under the snail's mouth.

Edeo watched the door swing shut. "Huh," he said.

"You know what you got there?" Gremon was hanging over the top bunkbed, his head dark against the gray ceiling.

"No."

"Hell! It's a snail, Edeo. A snail! You know what that means?"

"No. What?"

"Snails grow gems on their backs if you feed it the right crap. You hear me? Gems."

"I know."

"You feed it iron, it grows emerald. You feed it copper, it grows diamonds. You feed it–"

"They're not really diamonds and emeralds," he replied. What the snails grew weren't found naturally.

"We could be rich."

"We?"

"Yeah, we, little boy."

Edeo stared up at his brother. "You breathe a word, little boy," he said softly, "and Nelli Ione learns you pissed your pants."

Gremon was silent. This was all Edeo had over him. He hoped it would work.

A dark shape dropped from the top bunk. Pain shot up Edeo's arm, and he stifled a gasp.

"This isn't yours to keep, stupid. It's to use."

Then Gremon climbed back up into his bunk.

The next day, the snail thrashed around in its cave when they came to see it.

"Is it sick?" Haron asked.

"I dunno," Edeo said. He was still concerned about what Gremon would do. Perhaps he'd try to take the snail for himself.

The snail slammed its carapace against the stone walls of the alcove, again and again.

"What's wrong with it?" They dared not go near the thing. It weighed twice as much as they did together, and its shell was hard. They'd be smashed.

Finally it stopped and something tinkled inside its grotto.

"What was that?" Edeo asked.

The snail slid forward and Edeo leaned into the darkness. Something sparkled on the floor. He reached for it, but jerked his hand back.

He stuck his bleeding finger in his mouth.

Haron shined the flashlight. "It's a gem."

This was the first gem they'd seen the snail grow since they'd started feeding it a week earlier.

"It's sharp."

Edeo reached for it again, carefully. It was metallic, not a gem stone at all. It was heavy, like lead. One edge was rounded and had indentations in it. The other edge was sharp. It looked like a clamming knife the divers at the ocean used to open crustaceans.

The snail shook itself and its chain jingled.

Edeo and Haron shared a look. Edeo then bent down and started sawing at the chain with the stone. In the light of Haron's flashlight, they saw the stone had chipped the metal. The stone was cutting the chain.

"It grew a saw!" Haron said.

Edeo worked until his arm was too sore to continue, then Haron took a turn. By noon they were halfway through the link, and so engrossed in the process they failed to hear Fruge's arrival until he flung open the door.

"What do you think you're doing?"

Edeo and Haron backed away from the snail. Haron eyed the rope, then the gun in Fruge's hand. No way he'd make it.

Fruge took the steps, his eyes riveted on the two kids.

"This explains what happened to my supply of gems. You two have been feeding my snail the wrong stuff." He kicked at the pile of curdleberry leaves. "Do you know what you've cost me?"

"You can't do this to a snail," Edeo said, his voice cracking halfway through.

"Just shut up," Fruge said. "I can do whatever I want with my snail. And that includes feeding you to it."

The snail charged at Fruge, coming up just short on the end of the chain.

"Look what you did!" Fruge yelled. "You made it crazy!"

The snail lurched again, pulling the chain tight.

"If I have to get a new snail because of you," Fruge said, "I'm going to chain you both to the wall and feed you iron scrap."

The snail backed up into its cave.

"That's right. Back in your cave."

But the snail wasn't submitting, it was getting some distance.
It charged.

For a moment, Edeo was certain the chain would hold, but the weakened link gave way with a snap and the snail was on top of Fruge.

"He's going to eat him," Haron said, with some amount of relish.

Fruge screamed and the gun flew from his hand as he tried to fight off the snail. The snail rolled right over him, covering his head, then backed up so it could roll over him again with its giant foot.

"He's not going to eat him," Edeo said. "That's not his mouth down there; it's his foot."

"He's sliming him," Haron said, which was better.

The snail rolled off Fruge, found his gun and stowed it in his gullet with a slurp.

Fruge stood, his body dripping snail slime in huge dollops. He coughed.

"I'm going to kill you with my bare hands."

The snail lunged at him then, and Fruge backed up. Fruge tried to move around him, but the snail was far faster than he. Fruge backed into the cave.

Edeo slammed the door shut and Haron threw the bolt.

"That'll never hold him."

But the snail had apparently realized that and was pushing barrels in front of it, as well as crates and other bits of junk that lined the walls of the basement.

Surveying Fruge's cage, Edeo said, "Let's get out of here."

Haron looked at the snail. "What about him?"

Edeo looked up at the rope, wondering if they could haul the snail out, but he need not have worried. The snail slithered up the steps, its flexible foot molding itself to the stairs. It was up to the landing in seconds, pushing open the door.

It hesitated there, its antennae waving around.

"It's probably never been outside," Haron said.

"It's scared."

Edeo and Haron walked around it and stood out in the middle of the street, waving it on.

Finally the snail scooted out of the building and into the open.

Edeo grinned. "We'll take it to my house. It can live in my room. Then Gremon can't bully me anymore. It can make me gems whenever I want. We'll be rich . . . ."

Haron looked at Edeo, his eyebrows raised.

Edeo caught his friend's look.

"I mean —"

"We'd be no better than that wagger," Haron said with a nod

toward the building. Edeo paused, sipping at his dream one last time.

"No," Edeo said. "I guess not. Then where?"

"He likes curdleberries." He pointed to the spaceport, where the tarmacs were surrounded with native flora. "Of course, we could take the long way."

By the time they reached their street, they had quite a parade: dozens of children, the mailman, shop clerks, a team of street cleaners, even Gremon followed.

The snail slid happily along, unperturbed by it all, as if it was expecting a parade.

A magistrate caught up to them on Jury Street.

"What is this? Where did this snail come from?"

Edeo was brave enough to answer.

"Fruge had him chained in a vacant building by the spaceport." He showed the magistrate the soldered end of the chain. "We're taking him to the spaceport so he can eat."

"Fruge," the magistrate said with undisguised venom. He sent a muni to the vacant building, then accompanied the parade to the spaceport where he had one of the bumbling maintenance men open the gate so that the snail could crawl into the fields of lillweed and curdleberry bushes. In the distance, on the far side of the spaceport, a rocket roared into the sky. The snail cocked one antenna at it as it munched contentedly on a tuff of vegetation.

It chuffed once at Edeo and Haron, then ambled off into the prairie.

STORY
NOTES

"Ten Sigmas" is one of three parallel universe stories in this collection — yes, I'm a bit infatuated with the idea — but this one is the one with the most interesting core idea. It first appeared in *Talebones* and later was published in Dozois' *Year's Best Science Fiction*, the first story from *Talebones* to make it into that long-running series. My pride in this story is enough that I chose it for this collection's title.

I can not recommend Jared Diamond's *Guns, Germs, and Steel: The Fates of Human Societies* enough. It speculates on why societies rise and fall and boils it down to the practical aspect of domesticable plants and animals. His ideas led me to wonder how scientists could actually test them. It's easy now to see how mankind developed in the Crescent Valley, but what if we could test those theories with real universes? "The Teosinte War" tries to answer that "what-if."

It's not easy being a normal person, with family and work commitments. Having a superhero's job only makes it tougher. "Doctor Mighty and the Case of Ennui" is my take on superheros — and supervillains — who just aren't in the right line of work. I put as many superhero jokes and puns in as I could and threw half of them out.

Stories I write end up being set in the cities I live in at the time. When I wrote "Alien Fantasies" I lived in Pittsburgh. I was also watching a lot of Late Night. I actually did write the entire top-ten list.

It's not easy being a teen, and if there's seven of you, you end up with seven times the pimples. "Summer of the Seven" is about growing up, jealousy, friendship, responsibility, all those things a teenager needs to learn, but also with a theme of scientific responsibility. "Summer of the Seven" is set in the same universe as my first novel *Singularity's Ring*. (Tor Books, February 2008.) In the editing process, I realized the chapter didn't add to the over plot arc, and so here it sits, cut from the final novel.

The novel begins with the novelette "Strength Alone" instead. This story made the preliminary Nebula ballot, but not the final one. Strom's story still is moving when I read it.

"Singletons in Love" is the first story in the Ring universe that I wrote. It was a stand-alone novelette for Lou Anders' *Live Without a Net* anthology. His theme for the anthology was one where the Internet was not the central technological gadget it seems to be for our world today. I posited a universe in which humans used biological means to create high-density human computers called pods. This story was reprinted in Gardner Dozois' *The Year's Best Science Fiction*, a first for me.

"Dysfunctional Family Cat" is my wife Stacey's fault. She's allergic to cats. That, combined with the fact that many seem to hold felines sacred, caused me to make cats the clueless villains of this piece. The earlobe-based drug dispenser is still one of my favorite bits of technological extrapolation.

I grew up in a trailer park very similar to the one in "Fallow Earth." We never did come across an alien as shown here, though the people aren't too far from the truth.

You seldom understand what a bastion university life is until you leave it. "Death of the Egg King" draws on my emotional state during my time in graduate school at the University of Michigan.

"Walls of the Universe" takes the nurture versus nature argument and uses parallel selves to see what happens when the selves are stressed to the limit. The people you end up hurting the most are those closest to yourself, and, of course, yourself. "Walls of the Universe" made the short lists for the Nebulas, Sturgeon, and Hugo Awards in 2007. It won the Asimov's Readers Award for Best Novella.

In writing "Snail Stones" I borrowed a bit of Haldeman's *All My Sins Remembered* and Tiptree's *Brightness Falls From the Air*, but with none of their drama. My protagonists are kids who find something wrong and do what they can to fix it. These are my favorite types of characters; these are my favorite types of drama.

ACKNOWLEDGEMENTS

There are just too many people who are a part of these stories. Where do I start? First I note my debt to my writers workshops: Mary Soon Lee's Pittsburgh Worldwrights where I learned to put nouns and verbs together in an interesting way, the Semi-Omniscents who saw most of these stories first, Writeshop where I started *thinking* about craft, the Million Monkeys who polished all the rough edges, and Blue Heaven where I came to trust my instincts. Every one of those groups seemed to happen at the right time for me, and every one of them is filled with fine writers with whom I have been lucky to work.

Many thanks to Patrick, not just for making this collection happen, but for giving me a chance when I was starting out. And thanks to the other editors who published my work: Jed Hartman (and the rest of the *Strange Horizon* crew), Gardner Dozois, Sheila Williams, Lou Anders, Richard Blair, and Jan Berrien Berends.

ABOUT THE AUTHOR

Paul Melko lives in Ohio with his beautiful wife and four fairly wonderful children. He is an active member of the Science Fiction Writers of America, where he sits on the board of directors as the South-Central Regional Director and is chair of the Grievance Committee.

Paul's fiction has appeared in *Asimov's Science Fiction, Realms of Fantasy, Spider Magazine, The Year's Best Science Fiction, Talebones*, and other magazines and anthologies. His work has been translated into Spanish, Hungarian, Czech, and Russian, and it has been nominated for the Sturgeon, Nebula, and Hugo Awards. *Ten Sigmas & Other Unlikelihoods* is his first collection of stories.

LaVergne, TN USA
14 July 2010
189439LV00006B/6/P